Shanghai Sui

by

Kathleen McKee

DORRANCE PUBLISHING CO., INC.
PITTSBURGH, PENNSYLVANIA 15222

ISBN # 0-8059-5754-5
Printed in the United States of America

First Printing

For information or to order additional books, please write:
Dorrance Publishing Co., Inc.
643 Smithfield Street
Pittsburgh, Pennsylvania 15222
U.S.A.
1-800-788-7654
Or visit our web site and on-line catalog at *www.dorrancepublishing.com*

Soon after beginning this book I realized how greatly I had underestimated the amount of hours that would be necessary to complete it. But writing *Shanghai Sui* became much more than just an extra activity. Since then, I seem to force myself to concentrate on anything else. The generous encouragement of my husband has been awesome and I would especially like to thank Doug and my dad for their support and suggestions.

Chapter 1

Icy wind caught Drew full in the face. Strong blasts whipped his clothes. Driving rain jabbed at his eyes. He fell back a step and moved forward quickly, away from the ship's edge. Wild ocean currents played havoc with *Marybeth's* rudder. The helm twisted out of his hands.

Bone-chilling rain flooded the shore and everything within a fifty mile radius of San Pedro, California. Fifty miles encompassed his present location, seemingly ten degrees north-south of nowhere.

Drew positioned himself beneath the ship's awning. His thin oilskin parka offered little protection against such a turgid storm. Cold water streamed beneath his jacket. He secured it more tightly, then fingered the edge of his daguerreotype of Suiteiko held securely on a chain next to his heart.

Unwavering steel gray eyes penetrated the liquid sky. Swollen waves battered the hull, groaning with each breaker crashing into the weight of *Marybeth's* cargo. Solid shoulders bulged against the wrenching drag of the great helm. The ship's frame tugged to the right, then jerked to the left. Muscle-hardened legs arched mechanically, adapting to the thrust of each jarring swell.

For hours the gale gathered speed. Suddenly it made a staggering lunge, throwing the ship farther off course. Drew ducked his head. A cold blast landed on his shoulders and he didn't feel as much. The next gust caught him in the chest. It tried to pull him down. His fists closed tightly over the wheel. A wave gushed forth. It caught him from behind. He tried to straighten, but was already off balance. Drew felt himself falling. The ship's faltering motion turned him over and over across the deck. His hand extended. His fingers stretched wide.

He struggled to safety. Reeling about unrestrained, he couldn't identify the hatch in front of him, or behind. In a moment of stormy calm, he looked up and saw the gate open.

1

The ship took another plunge. His face connected with the hard wooden frame. His right hand pressed against a throbbing cheek. His left hand reached for the barrier. He heard the sound of voices and turned. Light through the hatch showed his crew willing to endanger their own lives for his.

"Go below!" he ordered loudly. He feared his words would be lost in the stormy gale. But their voices quieted. Good. He'd seen men tossed overboard in storms much like this one. He refused to risk their lives unnecessarily.

March of 1851 was later described as the coldest day in the history of San Pedro.

Wind from the Pacific Ocean rushed non-stop, threatening more destruction. A chilling blast rushed in and pulled him away. An instant before he would have plunged into the ocean he heard the hatch slam shut. Unexpectedly, his outstretched hand caught hold of the lip bordering the main deck. Cold and rain made it impossible to grasp. Drew lost his grip.

He felt himself going and struggled to grab anything stationary. When the next enormous wave reached up to meet him, Drew was certain it was nearly over. He prayed. Oh, how he prayed. And suddenly the wind changed direction, hurling him away from the edge. He slid swiftly across the slippery deck, straight into the mast. It caught him in the stomach, and he moaned.

It was an awful moment before he struggled to his feet, another long moment before he suspected the storm was beginning to relent. Drew stood there, nearly frozen. He held the wooden wheel tightly as he turned to inspect the deck for damages. Everything bolted to the floor seemed to be in one piece. The rest was gone forever.

Numb fingers steadied the wheel. Through churning water of driving rain, he repositioned and steadied the vessel's course for Shanghai. Drew felt in his pocket for a pair of dry gloves, then tugged his hood over rich, auburn hair.

Rich eastern commerce drove him on. That, and the memory of Suiteiko Wong. The thought of her warmed something from deep within. He tried not to admit how much she came to mean during this stay in ancient Shanghai. Sui visited his thoughts daily.

Drew made a rapid calculation. Two months. When he entered Shanghai's port, deals were made. But above all the trading abided his love for people. His casual way put others at ease, allowing him to share his faith in God unobtrusively.

While the ship plunged into a weakening wave, and then tipped uncertainly with another, Drew allowed his mind to wander. The storm reminded him of the night he and Sui got caught in a downpour near the water's edge, along the Yangtze River. Her nearly straight hair dampened into a halo of soft curls. He suspected she took great pains to straighten those curls in order to blend into the general population.

Twice he wrote to her and twice he decided against sending the letters. Time and again he forced her from his thoughts, her response to his witty remarks, her dark sparkling eyes that hid a sensitive nature. Instead of seeking her out, Drew satisfied himself with ongoing prayers for her salvation and safety. But no longer. Nearly a year of separation convinced him he owed her an explanation. He would introduce his God. The rest, he left up to her.

He was about to embark on the most important challenge of his life. For some reason the thought didn't calm his nerves. He felt at cross-purposes with himself where Sui was concerned. He needed her desperately and wondered what would have been gained had he been less cautious.

Drew turned his head and his heart nearly stopped. An enormous wave came from out of the ocean with tremendous force. It appeared immense and more savage than the rest. And it was moving straight for him. With no time to reach safety below, Drew reacted automatically. Within seconds his wrist became strapped in place with the strength of a leather belt. He secured his left ankle to a flange with the rope he carried in his pocket. The wave hastened toward him. Nothing could stop it. He counted seconds.

The wave came closer!

It was almost on top of him. He gripped the solid post, took a deep breath and held it. The surge lunged forward without mercy, cutting off his supply of oxygen. *Marybeth* plunged sideways. Intense pressure battered him again and again. When he could withstand no more, the wave dissolved.

He stood there for a long time, shaking water off, sucking in air, and driving a hand through the river flowing off his hair. Sinking back on his heels, Drew prepared himself for a lesser wave that advanced and poured off the wooden deck. A deep-voiced shout startled him from his preoccupation.

"Care for a break?" Noah yelled above the roar of waves.

Drew turned his attention to the man on his right. Noah's pale blue eyes narrowed against streams of rain coursing down weather-reddened cheeks. Silver-streaked, blond hair escaped his brown hood, plastering it to a high forehead.

Drew was only too glad to release the wheel. He needed a chance to catch his breath.

"Charming weather, isn't it?" For Noah McKeen, life couldn't get much better. Despite the ravaging storm, the ship remained afloat. Within an hour they would be out of the storm's path. Why, the waves already looked calmer. He hadn't seen that last one, but he sure felt the effects.

Squinting against gust and rain, Noah's unfeigned momentum swung with the next swell, out of long practice. He greeted the succeeding wave with ease, whistling the tune to "Camptown Races."

"A truly outstanding vacation, this."

Drew wasn't sure how to answer. The throbbing in his head, stomach, entire body, seemed to be competing for intensity. "You're right. Some vacation it turned out to be."

3

"Listen, you'd better get inside."

"Yeah, I'd better get inside."

Neither of them moved.

"You shouldn't be out here by yourself," Noah said. "You know that, don't you?"

"You're absolutely right."

"Then why did you order us below?"

"Because some of us have brains in our head."

"And some of us have no brains at all. For a while there, I feared you planned to take a permanent vacation beneath the sea."

Drew started laughing behind the sleeve of his parka. "I thought that last wave would knock us all off our feet when it struck."

"The guys sure spooked when they realized it was headed straight for us."

"There's really nothing to worry about."

"Sure, now that it's nearly over."

"Most everything seems to be intact." Drew looked about the *Marybeth* with a practiced eye, never more aware of her beauty. A builder's dream, *Marybeth* showed off rich, gleaming wood from stem to stern. She stood alone for speed and strength. He'd installed extra reinforcements during her construction. The extra supports had paid off.

"It's a good thing this freighter is riding low. Her weight kept us from rolling."

"She's loaded to the rafters."

"With what?"

Drew began to tell him when a breaker curled toward them with a roar. "Hang on!"

"You don't have to tell me twice!"

There was a breathless moment after the shock wave before the mast caved in, just enough time to hurl themselves beneath protection of the bolted table top. Quick reflexes alone saved them from being crushed.

Water continued to pour down around them. They unwound themselves and stood up. Except for the broken mast, remarkably little appeared damaged.

Noah looked down at the broken upright, considered the time it would take to repair, and gave Drew a crooked smile. "Are we on a schedule?"

"Strictly temporary, of course." Drew tensed inside. He considered time needed to replace the damaged mast. It would delay their arrival in Shanghai. The thought left him feeling strangely empty.

"Got anything perishable below?"

"No. Cotton should keep just fine."

Noah sniffed and made a curious chuckle. "There's more than balls riding on these waves. Cotton can't counterbalance this tug enough to keep it from rolling over, not with swells the size we encountered."

"Cotton is a staple, like medical equipment. We're moving a load of chloroform, ether, and ophthalmoscopes."

"What else?"

"Thought I'd see what sort of response we get with two hundred sewing machines. They're selling well in the states."

"Don't count on sewing machines to pay bills."

"These are new. They're a modern lock-stitch type."

Noah whistled through his teeth. "First I've heard of them. Guess I've been out of circulation for a while. Did you bring along any of those machine-made watches I've been hearing about?"

"You bet. Finally, watches are affordable."

"I might just get one for myself."

"Remind me. I'll give you first choice."

"Whoa! This wave looks to be competing with Mount McKinley for size." Noah leaned into the wheel, smoothly directing their course. "The men certainly didn't enjoy the wild ride. Want to go look below?"

"Yeah, sure. I will."

"Their stomachs didn't take it nearly as well as ours. They may be embarrassed."

"Well, give them time to clean up. I won't mention it."

"This life has lonely moments and troublesome spots, but there's nothing like it." Noah peered up at the young captain through one eye. Drew appeared tireless, even with the swelling purple knot on his cheek and forehead. His reputation preceded him as a hard taskmaster who refused to tolerate insubordination. Perceived as honest, dependable, and fair, Drew could be frighteningly cool with those who opposed his code of ethics. He earned his share of enemies. Not every man loved Drew's standards.

"Not everyone believes that," Drew said. So many enjoyed the idea of his life. Not so many asked to join him, especially men otherwise committed. "You married?"

"I was. Carla passed away last year." For twenty-one years, Noah had lived with a wife who understood and encouraged him in his travels. It became his decision to sell out in order to spend more time together. Since Carla's death he dreaded coming home to a silent house. It made him sad to watch crowds, buggies lining the streets, people leaving work and rushing home in the early evening, folks going out to dinner.

"I'm sorry," Drew said sincerely.

Noah sort of smiled. "A man should die a bachelor. It makes more sense." He chuckled softly, but the way he said it hinted at what he and Carla shared.

"Any children?"

"One. Shanna." White teeth flashed in the shadowed haze of his features. "She got married and moved on. Wanted me to go live with them. I couldn't bring myself to leave the ocean front. Besides, she doesn't need her old dad interfering in her life."

Drew grinned and stuffed rough hands into his pockets. Silently he observed Noah's careful ministrations, noting how the ship rode waves effortlessly under his expert skill.

"You're not new at this."

"Sailed years ago. Missed it too," Noah hollered into the wind. At length he spoke as if debating with himself. "It wasn't easy, you know, losing a wife. You always think about things you will do together when your only child grows up, how they'll be there for you in your old age. Then you realize you're thinking selfishly, and how you can't depend on others to make you happy. It's sure hard letting go."

Noah pulled down on the wheel. The ship steadied. After the rampart slapped the water, he continued talking. "Family's gone. I'm back."

"Who did you work for?" Drew studied the reflection of lamp lights in Noah's eyes. A stirring in the back of his mind made him curious.

Noah's aging face looked almost sad as he considered the bank, his own private prison. Something passed through him that squeezed at his heart. He recalled that old clock on the back wall that ticked interminably. Every day for twelve years he'd stared out the window overlooking the park. From where he'd stood, he could view the ocean far beyond. Late afternoon, just as the sun slowly fell, he joined the rushing throngs of people outside. Carla's beguiling smile and Shanna's squeal of delight as he stepped through the front door made life tolerable.

"A bank. I worked for a bank," Noah finally answered.

"Before the bank, I mean. Who did you sail for?"

"Myself. I owned a fleet of ships."

Drew hesitated as reality sunk in. Then he chuckled. "You are the Noah McKeen?"

Noah nodded, smiling slowly. "The same. How do you know me?"

"How does anyone know you? You were the talk aboard every ship I ever sailed on. I listened and learned." Drew cleared his throat. "Bought a couple of your ships recently."

"Right. *The Sea Wind* and *Ocean Skiff*."

"You knew?"

"At one time they were all the family I had." His fleet of eight ships had been divided and sold twelve years ago. He failed to mention he knew who took possession of every ship he'd ever owned. When the *Night Star* sunk in the Atlantic Ocean four years ago, his grief became almost as great as losing a child. A week ago he had become a hired hand. And that was good, he told himself. He didn't have the headaches that came with running a company.

"My purchasing agent did a fair amount of business in Shanghai."

"Makes sense. Shanghai is responsible for its own prosperity. You don't feel strapped to some complicated order of authority. India, China, and some of the others charge absolutely exorbitant duties and require a multitude of obligations."

"All a waste of time and energy. I still hold names and addresses if you're interested."

"Sure." The reminder of Shanghai dropped between them like an invisible shield. Drew stood for a while without speaking, considering how his thoughts always seemed to roll around to Sui.

Noah laughed silently. Only two things gave a man that distracted look, and he believed Drew wasn't overly concerned with finances. "You got yourself a woman, don't you?"

Drew's startled eyes filled with pain.

"Well, that's how life goes. It's funny, isn't it, how they can test your patience, then make your heart zing with the smallest thing."

Ignoring Noah would be rude, but Drew thought about doing just that.

"Let me guess. You left her in San Pedro." Noah eased up on the helm, allowing his gaze to study the Captain. Drew offered no smile, simply the impression that he battled emotions he wasn't comfortable with.

"Ah, so you didn't leave her behind. The little woman waits for you in the East as we speak." He turned his attention back to the job at hand and chuckled knowingly.

"Shanghai. Suiteiko lives in Shanghai," Drew admitted, surprised by Noah's insight.

"Does your Sui have a last name?"

"Her name is pronounced S-u-e. Sui Wong. Suiteiko Itsi Wong."

"Wong?" Concentrating on the dark body of water, Noah prayed what he suspected would prove to be an absurd mistake. If not, Drew could be in for a heap of trouble. He paused, not knowing how to broach the subject. But he did, of course.

Noah spelled out the name, "W-o-n-g?"

"Wong is not an unusual name in Shanghai."

"No, it's not. Wong ranks right up there with Chin and Chan."

"What are you getting at?" Night began to set in. Drew felt exhausted. His feet hurt, his legs ached, his stomach hammered, he felt a nasty bruise on his head. He'd been pushed, pulled, and flung against every hard surface imaginable. Standing in the wind, his wet clothes clung coldly. They felt like torture. And now Noah seemed intent to add to his discomfort by pointing out reasons he should avoid Sui.

Drew threw his oilskin parka across the table and plunked down to remove his soggy boots, too tired to notice the calming storm. He yawned and stared absently at the downed mast, with clumps of green seaweed scattering the deck. He hadn't slept for thirty-two hours, he smelled like dead fish, and he felt too tired to care. A shower could wait until morning.

"I heard about a Wong in Shanghai. His pockets are full of rocks. I wouldn't take a coin to be in his shoes though. Corrupt fellow, trouble."

"I don't suppose that ever stopped you." Drew thought he saw Noah frown beneath his deep hood.

"I wonder, that's all, if there's a connection between your Sui and the Wong I knew."

"I hate to bring this up, Noah, but it makes no difference if there is a connection."

"You're right. Don't give it another thought. Besides, how many Xhiang Wongs can there be?" Noah was in no way prepared for what came next.

"Only one I know of-Sui's father."

"Sui's father?" Noah drew a deep breath and let it out slowly. When he'd emptied his lungs, he tried to put to rest a sinking feeling. Drew may be in for a heap of trouble. "I'm sorry. You know about him then?"

Drew nodded. "I think so. Not everything probably. Enough."

"And you believe courting his daughter is a good thing?"

Drew grinned tiredly. "Obviously, you've never met Sui."

"No, I suppose I haven't." But he had met her father. Several years ago an entire shipment of revolvers disappeared while Noah's craft, the *Night Star*, docked in Shanghai's port. He'd done a lot of explaining to the Department of Law Enforcement.

Noah had traced the guns back to Xhiang's facility. Rather than having Xhiang arrested, Noah hired an established and completely discreet surveillance team to follow Xhiang. They were to report directly to him.

Their account included Xhiang's association with criminal activities, along with corrupt political involvement. Noah left Shanghai quietly. In his heart of hearts, the sixty-four year old Xhiang did nothing to assuage Noah's concern for Shanghai's future, or that of Drew.

"My interest lies in Sui, not especially in her father."

If Drew meant it as a joke, Noah wasn't laughing. He knew too much. Releasing a long-held breath, his eyes forged down the narrow hall, settling on the solid door as it clanged shut behind the captain's retreating figure. He could only pray Drew wasn't biting off more than he could chew.

Chapter 2

Sui Wong didn't care if she'd only slept two hours. She must escape Xhiang's suffocating sick room. His wife's shrewd eyes ignited a hot spark in her soul. Father's house overflowed with extremely expensive objects of art the way he preferred, showy and pretentious. Her eyes scanned the beautiful prison with beautiful things, but a prison nevertheless.

Sui slipped out of her extravagantly embellished room during the wee hours of morning, leaving behind the lavish interior of Xhiang's house, for fresh air at dusk in the elegant courtyard. She hastened around the fountain and passed silently through wrought iron rails. Massive stone lions guarded each side of the drive.

The boldly lettered slate sign squeaked, swinging from an iron arm, boasting XHIANG'S ESTATE. Sui flinched. She swallowed hard, attempting to keep a handle on her nerves. Although accustomed to solitary trekking, her normal calm deserted her for the moment. Call it careless, foolish, or whatever, more than anything she simply needed to get out of the house. Land stretched for miles in either direction.

Dry leaves swept along the empty path. A disquieting sensation filled her as she searched the area with a cautious glance, tossing about in her mind how exposure might cost the daughter of a wealthy landowner.

Sui forged ahead at double time until the Yangtze River bank gave a misty view of the dark outline of Shanghai in the early morning haze. Falling silent, Sui glanced ahead, then behind. Unfounded apprehension sparked an amused glow in Sui's dark eyes.

Xhiang's shadowy house clung to a tome of rock some twenty feet above the cemetery. Sui stopped beneath a tall Banyan Tree. Her father meant the entire family to be buried here beside Mother.

After a year, the tall polished Georgia Marble headstone was beginning to fade. Sui wiped away bird droppings from the numbers. A local craftsman had designed the inscription of Chinese characters to include her mother's date of birth and death, still so fresh in her mind.

As a Buddhist, Xhiang had reluctantly made the funeral arrangements. He grudgingly sought out a Christian minister to perform a foreign-style mass, believing some sort of rite should be performed. His comrades would expect it. If Elizabeth thought Christian service best, then fine, Christian it would be.

Sui couldn't forget sitting at the funeral, not knowing what to expect. Halfway through the service she frowned not accustomed to Xhiang's obvious unease. He sat upright in the hard pew with his hands clasped together and a stillness which conveyed uncertainty.

Reverend Elliott People's natural, easygoing spirit reached out to the congregation as he explained death and rebirth made possible through salvation's plan. While Sui liked the suggestion of rebirth, she knew Xhiang expected something very different of her. Buddhist faith became part of nearly every Shanghainese and Chinese.

Sui placed a dozen English roses on the damp grass at her feet, reading Mother's name aloud. "ELIZABETH SUZANNE WONG" MARCH 2, 1808-MAY 14, 1850."

"Imagine, that simple engraved hyphen represents your entire life, Mother," she whispered softly. "Happy times, sad times, accomplishments, failures.

"We talked this through, remember: I know you're not really here, but it doesn't hurt to talk the way we used to."

Sui busied herself removing dead leaves and dried, brittle stems. Elizabeth's small plot was clear when she stood back on her heels.

Sui chewed her lip. "We Chinese are a die-hard people. We won't call it a day today until every man and woman leaves food at grave sides. Except me, of course. I would feel better if I could do something in your remembrance." Rubbing her arms lightly to offset a prickly sensation, a hesitant smile replaced tension. "You made it very clear that you consider Chinese All Saints' Day a waste of good food. You even made that holiday fun."

If anyone witnessed her bending over the grave, Sui would have looked strangely out of place. She remained flawlessly groomed, her waist-length dark brown hair knotted neatly at the nape of a slender neck, smooth and creamy complexion, slender figure, and perfectly done nails.

For twenty-one years she had been the perfect daughter, with impressive musical ability, total integrity, and high morals. With such rare beauty, Sui could easily become vain. But unlike the local women whose eyes arched softly, her soft, brown, almond-shaped eyes caused her embarrassment. Dressed in apparel only the wealthiest could afford, everything about her hinted perfection. Father demanded excellence of all his employees.

Perhaps it's not surprising she became acquainted with Reverend Elliott Pepple and his wife Effie. Without the support of a mother, Sui felt drawn to Effie's caring nature and genuine interest.

Focusing on the roses at her mother's headstone, she allowed her mind to wander to the one particular day she had accepted the way of Christ. A dark shadow lifted itself that day. A very troubled world looked cleaner and brighter.

Now her gaze followed the path up a gentle rise, past a field of ginseng, and beyond individual attendant quarters. Armed guards moved silently about her father's estate.

Xhiang remained one of the most influential men in Shanghai. That could all change if he didn't recover soon. Her own relationship as his daughter stood between a tottering empire and sustaining power. Sui alone knew how perfect everything must be kept, how everything must look and be just right. Xhiang demanded high standards, a smoothly run household, and impressive management skills both at home and in business. For a moment she reflected on how different life would be if Xhiang lived the sober, decent life he portrayed to the rest of the world.

Birds called to one another in the early morning calm of the Yangtze Valley as the sun rose steadily over the horizon. Golden honey rotated to a lavender glow, the sky bursting into an artist's palate of vibrant color, giving a false impression of peace.

Running a lip lightly against her teeth, Sui bowed her head and spoke naturally from her heart when she took her needs before God's throne.

"Dear Lord, there's such a small thread between the living and death. Oh please, Lord, keep Xhiang from passing on through from life to death. I fear he's at death's door as I speak.

"If Xhiang were to be taken away now, before he gets one more chance to accept You, all the hope in this life would dry up in me. Nothing would be left but the reminder of him burning in the eternal lake of fire."

After a long moment she managed to go on.

"And you, Mama," Sui swallowed back tears. "I miss you so much." She touched her own cheek, recalling her mother's soft hands. It tore at her heart as she recollected a few sweet memories of childhood. Then she thought of Xhiang, willing her mind to remember a special moment in their lives together, and she couldn't.

"Put a word in his favor."

Her voice whispered softly. "You're free now, Mama."

Using both hands, she wiped the corners of her eyes. "It bothers me that I didn't listen more attentively to every word you ever said. What I wouldn't give for one more encouraging smile, one more hug."

Sui stopped battling the well of tears and began to cry earnestly. "Now that you dwell in the shelter of the Most High, maybe you can find it in your heart to forgive me. I can only imagine what may have happened if we'd prayed for Xhiang together.

"I told God how sorry I am for wasting all those years running from Him. A word from you wouldn't hurt. And please, Mama, please whisper a word in Xhiang's favor. In spite of everything, he is all I have left."

Sui gazed unseeingly at a withered, dry leaf hanging uncertainly from the hedge, no longer denying the loneliness welling up within her. Now she concentrated on its source. A year without Drew hadn't eased the pain of loneliness. In her solitude she kept breathing, working, talking, singing, but deep within something kept hurting.

Pulling a handkerchief from her pocket, a sheet of paper fell to the ground. Sui reached over, knowing what she would find even before she touched it. With no one to confide in, she'd made a habit of writing down her thoughts. Later she read them back. Opening the paper, she smoothed out the wrinkles.

> Since the day you took my heart,
> I haven't been the same.
> Where love and joy once did abide,
> Now there's only pain.
>
> I'm staring at the ceiling,
> My head rests on arms crossed.
> I see your eyes, I hear your voice,
> And consider all we lost.
>
> Now I'm sitting down to lunch,
> Food doesn't taste the same,
> Are you listening real careful?
> Did you hear me call your name?
>
> Now you're gone, but who knows where?
> My heart sure aches, I cry,
> My thoughts, they stop, except of you,
> So slow the time goes by.
>
> If and when you find it,
> In your heart to love again,
> I hope it's me you long for,
> As your life, your love, your friend.

Clenching her fists, the paper crumpled into a useless ball.

"Father God, I know You love Drew, maybe even more than I do. Wherever he might be, please watch and protect him. I don't know why he left a year ago, he never said. If it wouldn't disturb Your scheme of things, give us another chance. And if it's not-Your will, I mean-then please, drive him from my heart and mind forever. Thank you."

Sui stood quietly for a long time and wondered what would happen if she simply pretended to be someone else and vanish. But that wouldn't be wise.

The administrators handling Xhiang's government dealings would pull contracts her father worked so hard to acquire.

Memories of her first corporate meeting brought a tired smile. She'd carried a very official-looking briefcase into a regal room where deals were made and things happened.

When Chu-the, a powerful corporate lawyer, showed her to the door, it wasn't unusual or even unexpected. Everyone knew a woman didn't possess qualifications capable of conducting business.

Then Xhiang entered through his private door. His exuding presence demanded esteem. Portentous and foreboding with snapping black eyes, most people followed his orders with a single glance. But this time, when he spelled our why their best interest lay in doing exactly what he requisitioned, the room became a madhouse, an appalling uproar. Xhiang allowed them a full minute and a half. Without raising his voice, he took control.

Xhiang possessed one weakness, abuse of Sake, a Japanese alcoholic drink. Opium never become a personal habit, though he did deal the drug. When Xhiang became progressively ill, Sui began to take over his responsibilities. If the corporate world discovered she managed their accounts almost single-handedly, it would snatch its business away.

This morning a mountain of files waited on her desk, along with priceless items to be displayed, orders to be taken, inventory to be checked, and ledgers to balance.

If only Xhiang recovers soon, she thought, never knowing answered prayer was being set in motion, and that changes already began.

Chapter 3

Breeze off the East China Sea held familiar salty fish smells. Drew dropped anchor alongside the warehouse. The waterfront unveiled signs suspended from two and three-storied hotels, restaurants, and boat repair shops. It still appeared as he remembered from the previous year, a large, congested city.

Drew looked out at the sleeping city. In a few hours, comforting silence would give way to a throbbing metropolis. The same held true for the darkened water of the Yangtze River. Sails, sampans, gunboats, and opium traffickers would cruise up and down the waterway, its surface sparkling like millions of diamonds just before the strong current forced it to flow out to sea.

Tearing his gaze away from a quiet corner of his ship, muscles in his jaw tensed. Everything above board appeared in perfect order. A new mast stood proudly upright, ready to challenge the next storm.

It felt good to dock. There was something nice being near Sui in the same city.

Sui replaced a black velvet display tray and slid the case closed. She rubbed her temples and gave her head a little shake. Dark hair escaped confining pins and fell to her shoulders in an array of curls. Sometimes she thought about getting it cut in a half-shingle, but she never found time to fuss with it.

Unconsciously touching the gold chain resting against her throat, she twisted it around her finger, studying a stack of receipts demanding attention.

Peripheral vision allowed her a glimpse of an unusually tall man. "I'll be right with you," she told the customer pleasantly.

Sui glanced at her watch. Forty-five minutes until lunch. She should have eaten breakfast. She would take time tomorrow. Gathering receipts into a neat pile, she lifted a smiling mask to the man expecting to be waited on. And she froze as he stepped forward in very slow motion.

"Drew."

For the longest time she didn't move, just stood looking at him from beneath sooty black lashes as if she were seeing a ghost. He stood just a couple of feet from her, so close she could see the jagged white squint lines on each corner of his eyes, contrasting with the bronzed tan of the rest of his face. Towering above her, he stood with legs spread. His gray eyes ran over her with a wave of emotions so powerful they threatened to consume all the practical barriers she had erected between herself and the pain Drew held the power to induce. Sui felt herself drawn to his hard strength. Just in time she straightened and took a shallow breath.

"Sui." He caught a hand and ran his thumb along the inside of her wrist. Her warm skin felt soft and smelled of apricots.

Sui let her hands slide out of his grasp. "Can I help you?" she whispered in a strangled voice.

Something tugged at Drew's heart so desperately it caused physical pain. His stomach tied in a painful knot that sent his mind reeling. He didn't know what kind of reception he'd expected, but certainly not the same impersonal greeting she gave all her customers. Before he knew what to say, Sui excused herself.

"I'll be back." If she said any more she would cry, so she fled.

Drew ran a distracted hand through his hair. His eyes followed her up the sweeping staircase. He felt a crushing weight deep within, putting pressure on his chest and lungs.

Sui slipped quickly up the private stairway. For a long time, unable to move, she stood there while waves of hurt and anger rippled through her like a flood. Fingering the smooth, weighty texture of Xhiang's imposing chair, Sui allowed the full import of Drew's return to sink in and then strike her with the impact of the entire world descending on her chest.

Tears filled her eyes and ran over. Shaking terribly, she sat down at the head of the table as though she couldn't bear to stand any longer. The hardwood table felt cool against her forehead.

She hadn't asked Drew to leave. She couldn't force him to stay. She wanted to be down there now, drinking in the sight of him, enjoying every moment of his company. Instead, she was feeling sorry for herself and wondering how she could best punish him for breaking her heart.

"Drew, oh Drew. Why did you come back?" she whispered to herself.

"I came back to see you."

Sui hadn't heard his silent tread and jerked quickly to pull herself together. She stared at him wide-eyed and shook her head. Her dark hair now entirely escaped its earlier sleek, simple twist. Turning her back to him, she concentrated on the view the window commanded. Busy sidewalks filled with people rushing about their daily tasks.

15

Drew looked down at her fingers and the quilled pen she rolled back and forth restlessly. "I guess you're upset with me."

Sui smiled politely and swallowed. It hurt. He could see she was in no mood to talk.

He touched her shoulder.

She flinched.

"Sui, I'm sorry."

"You left without me."

"Yes, I did."

"How could you?"

"I don't know." He stroked a finger beneath her chin and gently raised her face. "I should never have left without talking to you first. Forgive me?"

Sui found it difficult but she tore her gaze away from Drew long enough to look into the incensed face of the man who now stood in the open door frame.

"My, how touching. The boss's daughter shows her true colors."

They turned together. WuTsing stepped forward and slammed the door. Sauntering across the room, he surveyed the intimate picture they made, and sneered.

Drew looked from one to the other. In deafening silence, he measured the man before him, stepped forward, and bowed deeply. "Drew Bach."

WuTsing directly insulted Drew by ignoring him. His attention remained centered on Sui, who turned to the window and squinted into the sun, seemingly engrossed in activity below.

"It seems you have forgotten your place, Suiteiko. Customers wait for you downstairs. I suggest you leave, now!"

"I would appreciate a moment alone with Drew." Sui's face paled visibly. She knew who would pay if WuTsing felt crossed.

"Ah, but I do mind." Without taking his eyes off her, a flicker of anger quickened them.

Sui watched Drew as he stared at her in silence. He felt as if air had been sucked out of his lungs. His stomach tied into hard knots. Obviously, WuTsing held a claim on Sui. In his mid-thirties, WuTsing possessed a self-imposed air of command. Dressed in a tight, shiny black western-style suit, red shirt, and thin tie, his silver-rimmed glasses framed baneful eyes. Raven hair, secured neatly in a braid, hung nearly to his waist.

Drew loosened his clenched jaw, forcing himself to relax. His smile turned grim. Had he actually expected Sui to wait for him forever? His voice sounded more harsh than he would have liked. "Are you going to introduce me to your husband, Sui?"

WuTsing stared past Drew, stopped, and looked unerringly back. "Sui is engaged to me. We will be married, soon."

So, WuTsing finally admitted his design toward her, Sui thought. Well, she had no intention of exchanging a domineering father for a controlling husband. She looked at Drew with a strange combination of pain and anger.

"That is a lie. I have no intention of marrying WuTsing, now or ever. There is only one man I would ever marry. And *he* didn't care enough to stay."

Drew winced.

"If you'll excuse me, gentlemen, I have customers to tend to."

Sui turned just in time to see WuTsing give Drew a knowing sneer. His eyes grew cold, his features hard. He would steal from his mother, lie to his father, and even kill her if it meant he gained control of Xhiang's fortune. He proved himself a coward who feared both Xhiang and the price he'd pay if he got caught.

Suddenly Sui felt anger rise within her, unlike anything she'd ever experienced before. She tossed her head backward and got right in his face. "Don't look so smug, WuTsing. If I do ever decide to give up my freedom, it won't be for you."

A smile grew in Drew's mind and tried to attach itself to his mouth. He'd never seen this side of Sui. He liked her better the other way, soft and sweet. He felt grateful her rage was directed at WuTsing, and not at him.

WuTsing still sounded angry and eager to vent that anger on someone. If looking lethal were an offense, he would be incarcerated, which is probably where he belongs, Drew thought to himself.

WuTsing made a grab for Sui's arm. By twisting, he turned her to face him. Sweat trickled down her spine. She winced.

"Hands off the lady." Drew's voice struck like a threatening growl. He stepped rigidly forward.

WuTsing's look said he didn't like Drew's interference. He opened his mouth to reply, then shrugged arrogantly and dropped her arm. "Be careful, Suiteiko."

Sui swallowed back a sigh of relief. Drew might irritate her, but she couldn't deny the feeling of safety he provided. She lifted her chin.

WuTsing lifted his higher.

Her spine straightened.

WuTsing drew back a mere inch. "Shall I be forced to teach you your place, Suiteiko?"

Drew edged between them. He went tense and cold inside. Without willing it, his fist knotted. "What exactly do you consider her place, WuTsing?"

Without taking his eyes off Sui, WuTsing ignored the question. "Leave this foreigner to me. What do you know about him?"

"She knows enough." The question wasn't addressed to Drew, but he interrupted it anyway. "Are you in charge, of her life I mean? Are you in charge?"

Sparks snapped from WuTsing's eyes.

Drew's posture sent out a challenge.

WuTsing stiffened. His mouth pressed tightly into a thin line.

Something snapped inside Sui. WuTsing had no right to admonish her. For the second time in her life, fear of the man vanished, replaced by anger.

She felt more alive than she had since Drew first left, furious with WuTsing for attempting to control her life, and with Drew for leaving when she'd loved him so desperately.

"No one is in charge of my life. Now if you two will just leave!"

WuTsing favored Drew with a chilly smile.

Drew responded with the same. "What's your last name?"

WuTsing set his shoulders back and straightened. "What? My what!"

"Your last name, in case I see Xhiang. I'll be sure to put a word in for you."

"I will personally take this matter to Xhiang myself," WuTsing threatened.

"No one will be seeing Xhiang! The poor man is on his death bed." Sui exhaled a long breath, suddenly feeling sick. Outwardly, she stayed calm. Inside, fear shot through her like a bullet. Xhiang's existence remained her only hope of safety. Now that she'd exposed his condition, heaven only knew what WuTsing was capable of.

WuTsing's dead eyes brightened. His jaw dropped open. "Well, you should have said so."

Sui glanced at Drew.

He looked back rather curiously.

"What about him?" WuTsing prompted by pointing at Drew, "I could get real curious how a complete stranger shows up out of nowhere. And how that same stranger consorts with the daughter of a very rich man."

Drew retorted. "That doesn't take much imagination, does it? I could get curious about a great many things where you're concerned."

WuTsing stalked away, his hands clenched into knots. When he reached the stairs Sui heard Drew murmur beneath his breath, "Thank you, WuTsing, for making all my nightmares come true."

Anger vanished as quickly as it came. Sui took a deep breath and faced Drew squarely. Her temples began to pound with uneasiness. She looked almost ill, waiting silently for Drew to say something comforting, something promising to open the way for reconciliation. Anything but what he said.

"Be careful, Sui. That man spells trouble."

"Oh, really. Is there any other kind?"

He squinted intently into her eyes. "I'll forget you said that."

"Naturally. You would." She turned to leave.

Drew caught her by the arm and spun her around to face him.

"Why don't you just tell me what an unfeeling man I am. Tell me how little I care for you. Would that help?"

The abrupt endless silence became deafening. She forgot everything she'd rehearsed, everything she'd planned to tell him when they met again. Trembling, she forced herself to regard him calmly.

Drew crossed the span separating them. He rested his arm across Sui's shoulder and pulled her close. She longed to lean into him, to draw strength she so desperately needed, to breathe in his scent of fresh soap and lemony spice.

"I will never hurt you again, Sui," he whispered against her hair.

Sui nodded acknowledgment. "You're right, you won't." Sui blinked hard and shifted her attention to the corner of the room, refusing to look at him.

Drew reached out and tipped up her chin. "Okay, then. Let's go somewhere quiet. We have a lot to talk about. Maybe a walk? We used to do that a lot, remember?" His eyes begged her to go with him, to listen.

Remember? Did he really imagine she could forget curving walks and pathways of Yu Garden, or the ancient ginko tree where they shared their first kiss? No, she would never forget. Drew alone held within his power the ability to inflict pain she refused to risk. Her shoulders drooped as her gaze drifted to his feet.

"I've missed you, Sui."

Maybe, but somehow it didn't make her feel any more assured.

They stood silently for a long time, each with their own private thoughts. Uncertainty created a hard lump in his throat. Uncertainty made her worry that if she said yes, she would come to regret it months from now when he left again.

"Are you going to give me another chance, Sui?"

"I'm sorry. I can't."

He dropped his eyes to their joined hands. The expression on his face became so disheartened, she found it difficult to meet his gaze.

"Oh, Sui, I can't believe this is happening. Let's just talk, please."

Sui slipped her hand from his. "I'm sorry. I can't see you any more, at least for now."

"How long is 'for now'?" Drew asked in a hurt voice.

"I don't know. I just can't."

WuTsing hurled open a ledger lying on his desk. Figures went unnoticed as he slid a sideway glance in Sui's direction. Born and raised with meager peasants in the hills just outside of Shanghai, his pledge to attain wealth hinged on control of Xhiang's daughter.

WuTsing's face turned crimson. A spasm of rage gripped his throat. All five feet, eight inches of muscle stiffened. Gripping a knife-sharp letter opener in his right hand, he ran the fingers of his left slowly along his long, glossy black pigtail while he watched.

Drew was holding Sui's chin in his hand. And Sui allowed it!

Suddenly an idea struck him. He would take care of the foreigner. He just now realized how. Tossing a glass of wine down in one swallow, he pulled back the lid of his personal file. Drawing out a business card, he glanced at the Chinese characters. With a glint in his eyes, the marks etched beside his mouth showed a satisfied smile. With nothing to do immediately, he watched the foreigner and Sui talking together. And something within him laughed with glee.

Chapter 4

A nother sleepless night compelled Drew to the river. Before the sun arose fully, he jogged down narrow streets toward the original section of town with high priced shops.

He almost passed the Regency. On a whim he stopped outside the front of the building where he and Sui once shared dinner together. Vivid memories came before him. He could have reached out and touched them, could reach out and touch Sui, and smell her subtle fragrance. Everything was all right.

Close against the front window hung a curtain of strung beads to keep sun out. Faint light from inside allowed him a glimpse of the exact spot they'd held hands beneath the table and spoke of personal hopes and dreams for the future.

He remembered the quiet strains of their song and recalled the silver dollar he'd given the musician for playing it. The same night he determined their relationship advanced to a stage for which they may not have been prepared. He alone decided to sort out feelings about their commitment and her unbelief.

Too late he realized his mistake. A healthy relationship is shared by two. He'd made a life changing decision alone, without even giving Sui a chance to meet his God. At the time it seemed the right thing to do. Drew frowned, remembering what their life had once been like.

Jogging alone down cobbled streets, he counted on physical activity to ease his troubled mind, and it did for awhile. But in the end he simply felt colder. With some deliberation, he crossed the street to a local eating-house called the Café de Paris. By no stretch of the imagination did it resemble an establishment from Paris, but it did stay open all night.

Inside, smoke clouded the steamy air, settling on mirrors teeming with hazy reflections. Drew nodded to an old man who smiled thinly and pushed his way through the crowded room.

"Morning," they greeted one another as he brushed past. Workmanship on the man's gray-on-black outfit reminded him of apparel Sui wore when they'd visited a concert together. Everything seemed to remind him of Sui.

Drew took a seat at the only empty table. A heavy set woman in a black tunic and gray pants sat a tea pot and cup before him. Drew nodded his gratitude, then attempted to read what looked like gravy-covered chicken scratch. Lying the menu aside, he settled back against the seat. "Do you know how to fix bacon and eggs?"

The waitress answered with a paltry toss of her head.

"Then give me the house special."

The waitress nodded and left. From time to time she carried out plates filled with steaming food. Rice balls, quail eggs, and red cabbage she brought him smelled awful. Lately, nothing tasted especially good.

Patrons offered a certain amount of amusement. He could just make out a loud voice in the corner and back chat from a man with a Cantonese accent. They spoke eagerly, eyes bright, faces sweating, coats askew. Drew listened absently to their heated conversation. If he noticed dark looks directed at him from a tall figure across the room, he didn't let on.

Drew wandered over to the window, wondering about Sui. Did she hurt as badly as he? If only things had turned out differently. They may be somewhere in the middle of the ocean by now, headed for California together.

He tried to imagine a place in California where he might sit quietly, drink coffee, and mind his own business. And he couldn't. Towns were springing up in the middle of nowhere and being abandoned just as quickly. California no longer consisted of tidy civilized communities. Law and order were almost a thing of the past. Since the gold rush, many men left their wives and families to chase a dream.

It had been a long time since Drew felt such nostalgia for what used to be. One could never turn the clock back. Time had a way of changing things, forging ahead despite tragedy, mistakes, or circumstances. Avoiding mistakes before they happened wasn't always easy. Closing his eyes, he tried to blot out difficult memories, but they persisted.

For a little farm boy in Michigan, his life certainly had changed from a penniless orphan to the owner and captain of a fleet of ships. As an only child of only children, there seemed no one to turn to when tragedy struck his parents. At nine years old, his life became a constant shift from foster home to foster home, family to family. Big man tools thrust into little boy hands became a way of life. It didn't take long to understand that most couples desired a baby. Few settled for a boy of nine with the height and strong build of someone much older.

Only the knowledge that with God he never endured alone kept his heart from succumbing to bitterness, especially when abandoned in Chicago at age fourteen.

"Go on now! We can't afford to pay your way no more." Jude Rebedeaux had sat tall and forbidding aboard his expensive horse-driven carriage.

In his entire life Drew had never felt more alone. Given what had passed between him and Jude Rebedeaux for eight months, he should have been thankful to leave. Sixteen hours of labor each day in a smoldering foundry seemed unfair at the time. Now even that was gone.

Ordinarily he chose the path of silence, but looking about closely as waves of heat shimmered over the dusty street, Drew's sturdy limbs had trembled with fear. "Mr. Rebedeaux, if you'll..."

"Get on with ya!" With the flick of reigns, Drew had found himself alone in a strange city. He stood in one spot just long enough to mop his face with a rag.

On either side of the street, housewives shouted to one another from open windows, their fresh laundry snapping from lines overhead, reminding him of his own threadbare clothes. No one seemed to notice a deserted boy standing alone on the street curb, except three rough-looking street urchins. They eyed him strangely.

The guy closest dropped a ragged canvas pack and stuffed a dirty hand into the pocket of his worn khaki jacket. He caught his chum's eye and gestured. His companion nodded, blocking Drew's route like the well-trained hood he was. Maybe the guys weren't so bad, maybe they were. One couldn't tell until you got to know them. By that time it could be too late to try being nice.

Drew backed off a half block before hightailing it out of there. Exhausted, he slumped down among boxes of rubbish in an alley, awakening to the sweet smells of breakfast. One hotcake later he continued, unsatisfied and penniless.

After foraging in the streets for two days, he began to panic. He'd looked for work at a printing press, a meat packing plant, as a busboy, a cashier, and even a dishwasher. One look at his ragged condition guaranteed the side of the door leading out.

One night he got lost and walked along a bright part of Chicago, with theatres, bright lights, and plush restaurants. Couples strolled down streets, talking and laughing. Scuffed brown shoes, blue shirt, and small, frayed black pants were a far cry from what he witnessed in stylish Chicago.

Yeasty, fresh bread seemed almost an injustice. When an ill-tempered sales woman became occupied Drew considered snatching a roll. He was tempted. OH Lord, he certainly was tempted. But in the end he couldn't.

Young Drew slipped into the gloom of a smelly alley and lowered his head to wait for light-headedness to pass. Shafts of light tunneling between buildings nearly blinded him when he stepped back into sunshine nearly an hour later.

At first he didn't see the husky man to his immediate left. In his mid-thirties, broad-shouldered, of medium height, with a bristly mustache and bushy beard, Jackson Hurley's tangled black hair glowed almost blue in the light. He wore a giddy blue and red plaid jacket over a blinding yellow shirt. Long hair covered his grimy collar. A thick knot of gold chains around his neck didn't interest Drew. The handbill he tacked on the pole did. MEN WANTED—ALL AGES—FAIR WAGE.

Hurley stuffed the hammer into his oversized pocket. He chewed on a cigar, sucked hard, examined the red glow at the other end, and shoved it back into his mouth.

"Hi, what kind of labor you advertising for?"

"Looking for men!"

Drew didn't respond.

Hurley inflicted a hurtful dig. "You been bawlin'. Sissy, ain't ya?" He grinned smugly, chewed and sucked again.

"You think I'm incapable of hard work?"

"Maybe." Hurley held the cigar loosely and rolled it in his mouth.

"Put out that cloud of smoke and take a better look." Drew attempted to swallow his anger. He wasn't all that successful.

"Well, maybe I-"

Drew advanced.

The cutting edge to Hurley's humor died abruptly. He backed off. The boy looked solid, with that piercing look about his eyes one gets when fighting to survive.

"How old are you, boy?" Hurley twirled his mustache, eyeing Drew carefully.

"Old enough to do whatever needs to be done." Drew met his gaze squarely. God must delight in amusement if Hurley became the answer to his prayer. The man seemed full of himself. His type seldom knew they were being used. Drew relaxed while he watched God work.

"Everyone feels they can handle the job. Then they begin working." Hurley turned his back to Drew.

"Are you the captain of a ship, then?"

Hurley turned back with an unwavering stare. "Me?"

Drew didn't answer. The look he shot Hurley suggested patience for a child.

"Look, kid, I don't have time or the inclination to mess with the sort of stuff they do out at sea. I'm lead recruiter for a shipping firm." His hasty statement thinned the pressing crowd considerably.

"Can't take the heat, huh?" Several emotions, none of them pleasant, warred inside Drew. At last a chance for support presented itself. He couldn't afford to lose the opportunity. Cold, consuming anger, the kind that makes it tough to compromise, threatened. Years of pent up frustration and bitterness welled up inside him.

Hurley stopped dead still and stiffened. Something in the boy's eyes made him jumpy. Unable to scrutinize his stare, Hurley glanced down at the dusty weeds growing in the cracked, parched soil. He got paid for each man he delivered. If any one of them backed out before they arrived in California, he lost the price of a railway ticket, plus the trouble it took to get there.

Hurley's eyes went from Drew to the others, then back. He pressed his lips into a thin line. "You may be gone for months, perhaps a year at a time."

Drew nodded.

"Well," Hurley said in a resigned voice, "I hope you know what you're doing."

"I'm willing to take a chance." Drew still remembered signing the agreement that eventually led him here to Shanghai. Hurley dropped a copy into his case.

That was the last time Drew found himself at the mercy of another person, until Suiteiko. What would Sui want with a guy like him anyway? He ought to stop thinking about her, but he knew he couldn't.

Darkened storefronts looked dark and empty when Drew stepped outside. The wind quieted for the moment, with little traffic so early. Dark curls bounced against his face in the mornings soft breeze. He looked very young as he hiked up tangled streets and ducked down alleys. Drew came to Haukwang and turned off Komat'su. The architecture began to change as he headed west on Hankow. Wooden walkways gave way to stone paths, superficial modernity to ornamental enrichment.

He'd seen it all before but he still found changes that transpired since 1842 amazing. Britain compelled China to open their city to foreign trade, due mostly to Europe's victory involving the Opium War. Shanghai, no longer a small trading center, reflected those changes also. Britain, Japan, France, and the United States settled there, their influence responsible for a strange appearance by their arrival.

Breaking into a slow jog, Drew tasted the pungent combination of decay, fish, and garlic in the cold air. The smells set his teeth on edge. Shanghai's river made heavy trade a legacy, drawing people and creating a pollution problem. The heart of the city remained ancient and beautiful, spared from the urban renewal of foreign interchange.

When he passed the candle lighting shrine, a shiver creeped up his spine. He ran past one savage stone icon after another, an array of weather-eroded gods, gazing down vacantly from ramparts at passersby.

Gusty air off the river blasted chilled wind. Drew's lungs began to ache. On an impulse, he took a turn onto Miyung Street, walking for several blocks to a series of darkened commercial windows of Xhiang's Emporium. Standing alongside the dark street and knowing it as part of Sui's world, that she entered and left by those very doors, filled him with a certain measure of contentment. He felt close to her here.

Towering, methodically groomed hedges obscured intricate architecture that shielded the imposing structure. Completed at the turn of the century, the building boasted two stories of sloping lines, regal chimneys, and individual narrow windows. The entrance door with gilded dragons opened outward over a white marble staircase.

Drew recognized Sui's handiwork in the silk drapery hanging at the dimly lit windows, displaying to best advantage crystal chandeliers, ornate figurines, white jade carvings, glittering gems, and diverse impeccable pieces. The place looked deserted now. In a couple of hours Sui may stand on the very spot he stood now.

Drew turned away and settled into a jog, loping for miles. The existing trail became a winding path through the valley. Unexpectedly, an outstretched gnarled root of a tortuous pine loomed in front of him. With sleek magnificence, Drew leaped it, landing in stride on the other side.

Darkness began lifting its veil. Drew tossed about in his mind the idea of leaving Shanghai, with all its reminders of Sui. He stopped along the bluff. Glancing down at the yellow mud flat, he hardly noticed the man below throwing a patched fishing net onto shore, or his partner who followed quickly behind to remove their catch of fish.

His mind stayed set on Sui. There were times he worried about her. He knew very clearly that Xhiang didn't appreciate her, and Drew wondered if Xhiang's other employees were any smarter. When Drew met with the senior partners a year ago for a purchase agreement, everyone bowed to Xhiang. The associates congratulated Drew and one another. In the confusion of the group in the conference room, Sui became all but forgotten. No one made a point of telling her she had done her job well. Most of the others were engrossed in congratulating Xhiang and the other partners. Knowing that it meant a great deal to Sui to put together such a tremendous transaction, Drew watched her accept Xhiang's achievement without question. She was used to it, and it didn't surprise her.

Drew made a point of calling Sui's effort to their attention. "I feel Sui should be acknowledged for amazingly putting all this together." No one seemed particularly interested in what he was saying. And he felt so annoyed that if he could have he would have turned his back on the entire shipment. Sui put together a tremendous package, and she alone made all the connections. He and Xhiang made a hefty profit from her efforts while Sui took a back seat without even receiving recognition. She wasn't upset. She accepted it all as her place in life.

What would he do without her in his life? He would be lost without her wide, radiant eyes to lose himself in, or her soft laughter to charge his emotions. He knew he couldn't leave, not until he and Sui were able to talk calmly and rationally.

Chapter 5

Close to midnight Sui stepped out of Xhiang's Emporium. The empty streets had cooled and the traffic thinned, leaving the city as quiet as it ever got in Shanghai.

Pulling her bag close, she breathed in the night air and spotted a lone vehicle parked at the curb. When she reached it, Xhiang's guard, Makischuk, stepped out to open the rear door. Sui flung her heavy bag onto the seat and slid in beside it. Makischuk turned north onto Myauyotz, joining the scattering of traffic trudging past darkened store windows and closed shops.

Sui dug in her bag and pulled out a bulky folder. Packed inside were conference notes for a lengthy presentation on the company's economic growth. Sui flipped through a packet of papers, searching for a list of members, while mentally preparing for tomorrow's meeting. Ten minutes later she replaced the list in her bag, and removed another folder, this one less full but every bit as important.

Struggling valiantly to focus, she was no match for her wandering mind. Unbidden tears made the moon's light fuzzy. She concentrated on the velvety glow, wondering why life must be so fraught with distress and confusion.

Another rush of pain pierced her. Desire and agony battled, seemingly never-ending. For a year she'd strived to balance fear with reason, worried half out of her mind about Drew. He'd changed since the first time they'd met. If anything, he seemed more in tune with her feelings. She didn't know if she liked it. From the first moment, her reaction to Drew proved all she'd expected. Determined not to let it show, she would pretend he didn't exist, at least until after he left.

Her eyes rested on the folder she'd worked on so long tonight. Facts and figures so essential to the Treasury Minister were all written out neatly, she hoped accurately. Long hours and a quick mind gave Sui the edge on their competition. But tonight had been horrible, just horrible.

Unmistakable anger wore at Sui's spirit in the two weeks after her impassioned detachment from Drew. Playing at being boss to grown men who resented her became a game in which she no longer cared to take part. Creating the illusion that conferences were Xhiang's idea grew tedious.

She became brusque at work. She left customers in the middle of a sale. She snapped at Xhiang's employees, using leverage as his daughter to her own advantage for the first time in her life.

Thursday morning, shortly before they opened, Macao questioned her about a shipment. With her back to him, he couldn't tell she was crying.

"What do you mean, what happened to the shipment? Am I the only one who works around here? Why you can't look up a simple order is beyond me! Move out of my way!"

"I'll check the order if you allow me a key to the cabinet."

"Oh sure, now you want a key. Well, I've already unlocked it. Just move!"

Macao eyed her thoughtfully. Later that afternoon he heard Sui snap at WuTsing.

Drew's close proximity frayed her nerves. Time slowed to a crawl without the incentive of his company to speed it along. Separation robbed her of all reason, cheating her of the ability to perform adequately, to find fulfillment in her achievements. Work suffered without her usual concentration and concern for detail. She ignored her own despondency.

Her appetite became almost nonexistent. Meals reminded her of pleasant times she and Drew shared together in the past. Sui regarded food as a distressing from of torment.

One day she opened a glass case to replace a gold wedding band. It glowed richly against the black velvet, a reminder that she didn't deserve someone special. The case closed with a snap.

Many times, someone uncommonly tall walked past the window. Her heart would give a lurch that left her feeling longingly empty. She must stay cool and professional. She could not afford to think of Drew as anything other than a customer. But in the short time she'd known him, he'd become far more than that.

Nights became worse. Lying alone in bed, she wondered how Drew spent his time. Would he find someone else? Did he miss her as much as she missed him?

She fought the impulse to go to him. One evening she actually decided to meet him come morning. In the still of the night, she rehearsed what to say and how she intended to answer his questions. She awoke late with a throbbing headache and no time to carry out her plan.

The location of Xhiang's Emporium did not necessitate the route she now took past the Port of Shanghai. She intentionally walked past the *Marybeth* and glanced up, longing to catch a glimpse of Drew. But she never did see him. His men hastened about the deck, leaving a yearning that he alone could satisfy. Loneliness took on new meaning with Drew so close, and yet so far away.

Sui lay the requisition she'd been working on aside, feeling better for the first time in days. Effie always made her feel that way. It had been so long since they'd talked together. When Effie squeezed her hand, it felt right.

"Hello, Sui."

"It's so good to see you, Effie."

"How are things here at the store?"

"Busy as always."

"Did busy put those dark circles under your eyes?"

"Maybe. Do you have time for lunch?"

"I'd love it. I've been feeling a little blue lately. I wondered if you'd mind cheering up this old woman."

"You're not old." Effie's zest for life outweighed the sag of her satiny cheeks, the light sprinkling of gray streaking her soft brown hair.

"Evidently I am."

"Oh, Effie, I'm so sorry. You're not, are you?"

Effie knew what Sui spoke of and shook her head sadly.

"I just can't understand why God hasn't given you a little girl," Sui said. "Don't give up, though. He may yet. You and Elliott deserve it."

"Thank God, gifts aren't given based on merit. Perhaps I still have a chance."

"I'm praying, you know."

"Yeah, me too."

The waitress filled their cups with tea and left. Effie took a sip and looked Sui over thoughtfully. "Well, need I ask who took the sparkle from your eye?"

Sui felt her heart take a plunge. "Is it obvious?"

"It's quite clear you've come down from the mountain."

"The mountain?"

"The mountain. Remember the day you took Christ as your own?"

"How could I forget?" It was a pleasant moment, sitting there thinking back on the day she'd knelt at Effie's couch to ask Jesus to remove her sin, to take away the heaviness she'd carried for so long. And He had. When she stood up her heaviness had stayed down.

Effie remembered, too. She sat back and smiled. "A person who receives Christ as their own visits the mountain. Life tends to pull us back to earth after a time. What brought you back down?"

"Oh, Effie, Drew came back," she whispered.

Effie eyed Sui openly, not trying to hide her surprise. "Drew? Isn't he the man we've been praying for?"

Sui nodded. Tears she'd held at bay began stinging her eyes.

"And the problem is?"

Sui couldn't speak. She couldn't look at Effie and say what she felt. As much as she didn't want to admit it, she was affected by her feelings for him.

Effie covered her hand with her own short, thin fingers. "Sui, dear, we have known one another for what, a year? We've confided to each other almost everything. We have laughed and we cried when you describe Drew. How important is this young man?"

"I haven't given him much hope."

Effie released Sui's hand and lifted her cup. She sipped tea slowly. "It's not easy to watch your glow grow dim."

"He hurt me."

"I know."

"Drew could leave me again."

"He could. And we could all die tomorrow."

Sui smiled in spite of herself. The waiter brought their soup. Sui picked up her spoon and absently stirred. "I acted awful, Effie. I even yelled at him."

Effie nodded knowingly. "Humm, the unpardonable."

"You're laughing at me."

"Maybe, or maybe I'm simply viewing the situation more clearly than you're able to. Now drink your tea and stop looking as if this is the end of the world."

"What would you do?"

"I would certainly give him an opportunity to explain."

"I don't even know if he is still here."

"Have you checked the harbor for his ship?"

Sui nodded. Every hour or so. But she wouldn't admit it, even to her best friend.

"And?"

"The *Marybeth* was still there this morning."

"Maybe you should go see him."

"Oh, Effie, you almost make it sound like there's hope for us."

"Maybe there is. What are you going to do about it?"

"Nothing."

"What a shame."

"Eat your soup, and stop looking as if you want to beat sense into me."

"It's your decision."

"Effie Pepple," Sui said, smiling at her affectionately, "I am so fortunate to have a friend like you. You're the sweetest, most sensible woman in the world. I only wish I could repay you for all the kindness you've shown me."

"No one can give me the one thing I really want."

"I know. Shall I beg God to give you a little girl?"

"Why not? But only if I may beg God to knock some sense into you. Drew is a good man. You said so yourself."

"Let's eat."

Chapter 6

At noon Sui walked out of the building onto a crowded sidewalk. In Shanghai's usual state of calm chaos, groups of paralyzed traffic occupied the much too narrow streets. Today was no different. Street vendors wheeled their pushcarts into the open and hollered advertisements. Wherever you looked, people crowded the avenue on foot or aboard rickshas, plying the streets and fighting valiantly to make their way.

Heat increased as traffic intensified. A garbage wagon trudged along side streets, making daily rounds. A few blocks away, an alarm shrilled, followed by the scream of a police whistle.

Sui pulled the strap of her pouch onto her shoulder, breathing in Shanghai's humid noon air. She spotted her building two blocks away and headed for it, too confused to question the wisdom of her intended inquiry. If what she suspected was true, Xhiang could be in a heap of trouble.

Her hands clenched the pouch tighter, hoping the contract she'd happened across proved to be some ridiculous mistake. Fixedly, she forced herself to refocus. Now was not the time to analyze Xhiang's responsibility.

A new sound, more keen than the incessant background noise of the street, caught Sui's attention. Shifting her concentration to its source, she didn't know what she expected, but what she found was certainly not it.

In the midst of the crowd, an overstuffed donkey cart clattered slowly down the cobbled street. The coach wasn't an unusual sight, but the way the driver handled the vehicle looked comical. And the donkeys that pulled it were hilarious, attracting attention from the crowd. Long, floppy ears poked through the rim of straw hats they wore, each with a large orange poppy stuck to and teetering over the brim. Children were being raised to parents' shoulders for a better look, while stepping aside to allow the animals to pass.

Drew's leather-gloved hands drove a one-man circus act through a crowded street which allowed just enough room to make it through.

Reluctant to mingle with the noisy throng, the donkeys hee-hawed and sidestepped.

Drew's face wore a solemn expression that cut through Sui like a knife. She resisted. Regardless of how attracted Sui felt toward Drew, he was the man who left her by his own free will.

Her stomach lurched when the coach slowed to a stop. Drew stepped out.

Music from a wind instrument drifted across the street above the drone of the crowd.

Sui stood motionless, noticing Drew slowly and steadily moving in her direction. And then, in an awful moment, one of the donkeys brayed loud enough to wake the entire city.

Sui stepped around the carriage Drew hitched them to and into a clearing. Drew caught her by the shoulder.

"Wait, Sui." Drew searched her face with desperate longing.

She blinked away tears and concentrated on the animals.

"We need to talk, honey."

Long twitching ears set a hat in motion. Those ears never rested as they worried a wisp of fringe hanging loosely from the hat. The smaller animal jerked his head back. A poppy dropped just out of reach, before springing back into place. The shaggier of the two turned his homely head toward Sui. Large nostrils flared as he sniffed in her scent.

"Sorry, this wasn't my idea. They were all I could find at the moment."

Sui nodded sadly. Any progress she'd made in the past two weeks turned topsy-turvy from the moment she looked into his face and heard his reverberating voice. Her heart raced as she looked into his sad eyes. She sensed that Drew continued in the same lonely state as she.

They stood facing one another, looking fervently into the other's eyes while their hearts came alive. She didn't say anything or even smile. She simply looked at Drew from big brown eyes and bit her lower lip.

"Would you care for some company? I would."

"Drew, please don't." Sui allowed her gaze to drift. She found the deep V of his shirt, where dark hair escaped, and focused on it.

"Don't what, Sui?"

"Anything, everything, You know."

Drew shifted closer and murmured near her ear. "No, you tell me."

"You are relentless."

"Yes, I suppose I am. I won't force you to do anything you don't want to, Sui. I promise."

She surprised herself by pushing him out of her path to brush past.

Drew caught up from behind. As she moved through the crowd, Sui was surprised to feel Drew's hand close over her shoulder. When she turned, he glanced down. Couldn't she see they were blaming one another while looking for a healing balm, and angry because they couldn't find one. He suspected they were in for a long struggle. "Listen, Sui," he said

31

calmly. "We need a quiet place to talk. I want to listen to what you have to say."

"Maybe you should have listened a long time ago."

A lady passed them, pushing a bamboo stroller. She looked up and back down quickly.

Sui looked away. Unlike westerners, her people greeted one another impassively, even formally. They weren't in America where physical demonstrations appeared permissible. Hand holding and hugging were not permitted. Sui shrugged his hand off her shoulder.

Drew sucked a deep breath and blew it out slowly. He began to get impatient and knew that would lead them no where. "What can I say, Sui? It doesn't give me a lot of pleasure of satisfaction to know I hurt you. I was wrong."

Her face paled. She turned away.

"Oh, Sui, I didn't want to hurt you." His voice softened. "You mean so much."

She studied him thoughtfully.

"Come with me?"

"I need to get this contract to my lawyer."

"Great, we'll take it together. You can keep me company while I deliver this stuff."

A burst of laughter came from someone nearby. Sui glanced out at the crowd.

"Please, Sui, just this once."

"Drew, try to understand. I can't take being hurt again, not the way you hurt me."

He looked down at her from his great height, his face rough from beard stubble he hadn't bothered to shave this morning. "You won't have to, I promise."

She debated with herself for a long time. Finally she took a deep breath and said the words that could destroy them both. "Okay, I will go with you this one time. But only if you promise to leave Shanghai afterward, and never look for me again."

Drew braced himself, absorbing the impact of her words. "If that's what you want. But if what we have is going to end, let's at least remain friends."

It took nearly an hour to drive from Shanghai to Fusuma. Throughout the entire trip, Drew remained painfully considerate of her every comfort, helping her safely into the carriage, handling it responsibly, slowing for ruts in the road. He kept their pace to a moderate speed. He even reached out once to steady her when the wheel encountered a rough spot.

Sui attempted a glance in his direction and found his troubled eyes focused on her. She dropped her gaze to the floor beneath her shoes, knowingly aware of each breath he took, every time he moved his head. Thick curls tumbled across lean, hard features, unruly as ever. His mouth, inclined to turn slightly at the left corner, did just that now. She ached with emptiness that was certain to hurt with intense pain when he left.

Her heart throbbed. In her entire life, Sui had never felt more miserable. The desire to reach out and touch Drew became almost unbearable. There they sat, alone together, with mere inches separating them.

A hard lump in her throat swelled, cutting off more and more air. It pressed against her chest until she felt certain that not enough oxygen remained to support her. The carriage slowed, then stopped roughly one mile from their destination. She looked up. From where she sat, Sui could smell donkey sweat and even the hay they breathed.

Drew looked down at her linked fingers, searching for something to say that would break the awkwardness between them. The moment their eyes met, Drew's hard-held control broke and he gave up all pretense. "I can't do this anymore, Suiteiko. I love you." His voice trailed off. "And I think you love me."

Tears stung her eyes.

"I made a mistake," he said. "I admit that. We need to talk. I believe we owe that to ourselves."

Drew reached for her hand, felt the firm grasp of her fingers and the swift loosening of them as she drew her hand away. His jaw tightened. For the moment, he and Sui became cut off from one another, feeling the pulsing push and pull of their emotions. "You'd like to throw it in my face, wouldn't you?"

"Just leave me alone." Turning sideway, she leaned back so her shoulders would become a wall between them.

"No. I can't leave until we talk. I can't stand this anymore, Sui."

Sui eased her fingers through her hair and began to cry. "It isn't what I want. It's what I have to do. I thought our relationship meant something. How did you think leaving made me feel? I fought so hard to pull my life back together after you left. Now you're back, and it's all falling apart. I can't go through this again." She fought hard to keep her voice from breaking.

"You don't even want to try?"

Sui turned around. For a long time she couldn't think of the right thing to say to break the silence. "I can't," she finally said softly, taking a long sobbing breath.

"I understand." For Drew, hope vanished and resignation surfaced.

Sui couldn't bring herself to look at him. She focused instead on a muddy puddle left from last night's rain shower.

His voice diminished to a coarse whisper. "I'm sure going to miss you."

Her throat tightened. She tried to smile and failed miserably. "I'll miss you, too."

Drew sounded tortured. "Look, Sui, I'll always be there for you."

"Thank you."

Another long silence while he summoned courage. "Before I go, I promised myself I'd introduce you to a friend of mine."

Sui glanced at her watch. It read ten minutes past three. Time moved too fast. "Yes," she whispered sadly, "It's time to go."

"No, it's not only the people of Fusuma I want you to meet."

"Oh, who then?"

"Jesus Christ." Drew observed the startled turn of Sui's head, the blank look that replaced momentary surprise.

She smiled faintly, remembering hours of Bible lessons she'd taken with Effie. She studied Drew, the anxious lines of confusion back again. She'd built a shell around herself, making it difficult for Drew to tell what was going on inside.

"Sui," he began.

"Shh." Her eyes focused on his mouth and her finger. Her finger ran softly across his top lip. This time there were no questions, no accusations. This time she reached out to him with a soft smile. "I think I understand."

"You do?"

"I hope so. Are you telling me you're born again?"

Now it was his turn to be shocked. He'd planned to ask her the same question. "Are you going to tell me what happened while I was gone?"

"Not now. Later maybe."

Between them passed a silent message that went deeper than words could say. The quiet moment lengthened while Sui recognized a strength within Drew she'd never been able to put a name to. Now she knew, and it made all the difference.

In very slow motion he reached out and pulled Sui toward him. The world swam past his tears. He kissed the top of her head and made an amazing discovery. She didn't resist this time. A smile dawned slowly. He held her closer and swallowed.

Sui found herself wanting to reach out to him, to hold him near, to make promises she would keep. As Drew sensed her thoughts, she surprised him by leaning back. Something desperately sad showed in her eyes when she looked at him.

A fresh wave of dread struck. He pinched the bridge of his nose while an invisible band seemed to close around his chest. He wanted to tell her everything would be all right. He didn't. She looked as though she were inclined to argue with him. Waiting for her to speak became one of the hardest things he'd ever done.

"God is a spirit."

He nodded, his face pale.

"They that worship Him must worship Him in spirit and in truth."

"What are you saying?"

"You claim to know God's Son, Jesus Christ."

"And you want to know if I'm trustworthy," he finished for her.

"Yes."

Drew took her hands in his and linked their fingers together. The tip of his thumb stroked her thumbnail. He took a deep breath, considering his words carefully.

"I sure hope so, Sui. I attempt to live by the Word. That's the only reason I left you last year. I meant to do the right thing. I was wrong and we both suffered for it. Can you ever forgive me?"

Drew held himself still and studied their intertwined hands. "As God is my witness, I will always consider your feelings and weigh your thoughts. If you reconsider, I mean."

Sui smiled uncertainly. "I couldn't ask for more."

A muscle in his cheek twitched, becoming a short lived grin. "Even if I attempt to sway your opinion?"

"I would expect that, but only if you consider my judgment less than sound."

"God holds us responsible for decisions we make."

"I know."

"But, Sui?"

He lifted her chin. "I'm certainly not perfect."

"I know." Drew braced his arm against the back of her seat and laughed a booming, rolling laugh, filled with pleasure.

Sui linked her fingers behind Drew's neck and lifted her eyes to his happy face.

Drew cleared his throat. He pulled her to him, his lips feathering hers with light kisses. Without words, they exchanged silent messages that their feelings hadn't changed, their love lived on, the longing remained.

"I've missed you."

"I've missed you, too."

"Drew, I'm sorry," she whispered. "I wasn't sure I could trust you. I'm so sorry."

"It's been awful without you."

"For me, too."

"I'm glad we're together." Drew touched her hand, a half smile on his mouth.

"You never wrote," she attempted lightly. They exchanged a long, tender look. Sui felt tears burn behind her eyes.

"Yes, I did. I thought about sending letters sometimes, but it didn't seem right."

"I loved you then." Her eyes lowered, looking unseeingly at her fingers. "I love you now."

Drew leaned forward and spoke very quietly. "A marriage requires each party in that union to be built on the same foundation. We could have found happiness together for a while. Sooner or later one of us may have realized that we had no future together."

Sui looked confused. "No future together? Why?"

"Marriage bonds must be made of something stronger than feelings alone."

"And I didn't know Him then." She began to understand. "You could have told me."

"Yes, I should have, but I feared you would accept Him for my sake. Marriage rarely works out that way."

She didn't have to tell him how bad she'd hurt, how she'd lived with guilt for driving him away somehow. "You could have done something."

"I know." He nodded, catching her hand and holding it close. "I did the only thing I knew to do." After all they'd shared, did she imagine he desired to give her up? Since the day they'd met he'd fought for her persistently, on his knees.

"Yes, you did. But it hurt." Leaving couldn't have been easy for him. She wasn't all that certain she could have followed through by leaving him if their roles were reversed. He admitted that he'd prayed, and God couldn't have worked a greater miracle.

Hurt would heal. He would see to it, Drew thought as he held her face in both hands and looked into her eyes, long and hard. "I love you, Suiteiko Wong." He searched her face and found what he was looking for. "Will you be my wife?"

"I love you, Drew."

"Will you?"

"What would I do, Drew, without you?"

"If it were up to me you'd never find out."

"I never want to again."

His thumb made circles beneath her chin. "Then tell me you'll marry me."

Sui pressed her face against the bare skin just above the notch of his shirt. Tears sprang to her eyes as she melted into his arms. "Yes, I will. I'll marry you, Drew."

Chapter 7

Lavender breeze drifted through the air and cooled her warm skin. Sui changed her position so she could inhale the deep, flowery scent.

"Enjoying yourself?" Drew laughed. He knew what it was like to see the Bund for the first time. The mosquito-infested, yellow shore now grew lush gardens. Fertile earth produced thick vegetation along the edge of a wet marsh. It hadn't always been like this. Contrast to the region was just beginning.

Drew's hands grasped the reigns gently. Corded tendons strained against tight skin. Those arms made her feel protected, needed. Drew followed her glance, reading the expression before Sui could hide it.

If only he could think of something to say. Words seemed so trivial when trying to convey the heaviness of his heart when he thought of leaving Sui. Drew's hands tightened on the leather lead. The intensity of his expression flowed into her, matching her own.

"Do you know how much I love you, Sui?"

"I hope so."

Drew sat back slowly and caught the sparkle in her eyes. Thick hair fell across his forehead. He pushed it back with an absent gesture. "Do you get a kick out of making me beg for a response?"

"Maybe." Moving closer, she leaned against his shoulder. Tipping her head back, she looked into his eyes.

Drew slid an arm across her shoulders and resisted stopping the carriage to kiss her one last time before they reached town.

Sui shifted. Drew took his eyes off the track and regarded her thoughtfully. "Is something bothering you?"

Sui felt a tug at her heart. She would get used to life with Drew as an intricate part of it. They were a team and she had a great time with him. But what if he eventually felt different? And what if...?

Drew pulled the animals to a stop then. He put his arms around her and kissed her as he'd longed to since the last kiss. He ached to be with her all the time, to have her go away with him. But he knew it was too soon to set a date. He also knew Sui couldn't leave Xhiang right now, and he had his hands full dropping off orders and restocking his ship.

Sui looked a lot happier than she had a moment before. Drew stared at her with a silent question.

"What?"

A deep-throated laugh. "I asked if something had you bothered."

"What if your friends don't like me?"

Drew almost laughed out loud. He probably would have if she sounded less serious. Clearing his throat, he returned her worried look with a level one of his own. "What gives you the idea they won't like you?"

"They may think I'm not good enough for you. What if they think I'm too young?"

"Then I shall take their advice. I'll leave you here and go home alone."

Her dark eyes widened. Drew's attempt at humor went right over her head. "Would you really?"

Drew's heart pounded faster as he watched Sui's wide eyed face. "Not hardly. I meant it when I said I love you, Sui. My friends don't have to love you, but they will." His fingers squeezed hers. "Just wait and see."

"But if..."

"Trust me, Sui."

"You won't leave me, will you, Drew?"

"Never."

A hand-painted sign swung from a metal post, squeaking gently. Painted words identified the town they were entering as Fusuma. Tree branches crisscrossed, covering the trail with lacy shadows.

"Over there." Drew pointed. "If you look real close, you'll see bird houses attached to those posts. They help keep the mosquito population down. The marsh is being filled with dirt for the same reason, that and gardening."

They passed evidence of construction everywhere. Residents waved as they passed, taking a moment from back-breaking steps toward independence. Between clearing debris, building, and working the land, not a person looked idle. To Sui's experienced eye, the lush plants alone could help bring economic strength. If work could put a city on its feet, Fusuma should be there soon. "Fusuma is a rather strange name for a city. Don't you think so?"

Drew looked up from the donkey. "Because it means swinging door?"

Sui nodded.

"People come here out of curiosity, they rarely stay. For a while folks came and went so quickly the community adopted the name. Mostly they stay now."

"I don't remember seeing Fusuma on a map."

"Officially, the place doesn't exist."

"Why not?"

"Residents here are mainly maimed and crippled. Some folks don't care to acknowledge cripples."

"Why?"

Drew shrugged. "The crippled need a place to escape prying eyes." Drew's arm shot out to steady her. "Watch this bump."

Sui laughed softly. "This bump?"

"You're right. Like the town, this is not an official road."

"You took the difficult route. I should have known."

"If I attempted the river, I would have missed you."

"You were deliberately looking for me today?"

"Today, yesterday, the day before."

"You did, really?"

He turned to study her upturned face, from the tips of her sooty lashes to the fullness of her mouth. "The plain truth is, I found myself desperate to see you, Sui." His lips flowed across her hair, caressing the dark, untamed curls. "I must have passed your father's shop a dozen times."

"And I wore a path to the *Marybeth*." She reached a finger to the corner of his uplifted lip. "I do love you."

Amazed by the fervor in her voice, he held her tightly in his arms. Her response was exactly what he'd longed for. "These past two weeks have been awful. I didn't like the way things stood between us. I had to make things right."

"I know. But never again." Her voice was serious and low. Sui pictured years ahead, of loving and treasuring him. She looked forward to sharing his home, his people, and his God. "Never again."

They stopped outside a restaurant. Drew's boots kicked up dust as he headed for Sui's side of the carriage. Before he reached it, his eyes roamed the town's perimeter. Everything appeared quiet. Even the billowy clouds promised clear weather. Yet he couldn't shake off the impression that something wasn't right.

Just then, the door to the restaurant was thrown aside. A dingy, middle aged man stepped out. Drew wasn't sure why the individual caught his attention. At first he thought the man reminded him of someone he should remember and couldn't. Before Drew could put a name to the face, the man hesitated at the door, then walked down the path, apparently searching for someone.

The man walked upright with heavy steps. He advanced twenty yards when someone intercepted him. Their conversation lasted three minutes. And for most of that three minutes they studied Drew.

"This is rather nice, Drew. I certainly didn't believe earlier we would be together today." Sui stretched to work a twinge out of her neck and took a deep breath. "That carriage gives a bumpy ride."

Drew smiled in spite of a numbing chill seeping up his spine. He looked over the shadowed buildings, instinctively pulling Sui to his side. With a sense of disgust, he pushed apprehension away and prayed silently for safekeeping.

The door to the restaurant stood ajar. As they started up the steps, Drew sensed more than saw the dark blur following them. With a palm against Sui's back, he pressed her forward, away from the stairs.

Unexpectedly, something nudged his back. Drew's pulse raced. In one swift motion, he propelled himself to the ground, rolled to his left, pulled a knife from his boot, and bounded to his feet.

Drawing in half a breath, he faced his opposition. Without a glimmer of apology, the donkey's steady gaze rested on Drew. Drew's breath escaped in a rush. "Good grief, critter, I almost did you in. What are you two doing up here?" His less than friendly tone was aimed at two hairy animals now blocking the stairway. The heavy carriage they pulled slowed their progress up the steps. Drew returned the knife to his boot.

"A little edgy today, are we?" A faint smile twitched at the corners of Sui's mouth. She leaned over the donkey, flipped back a very long ear, and scratched. The opposite ear thrust up and quivered.

Drew nodded carelessly, swatting dust off his clothes. "I should have known better than to hire pets."

"Why did you?"

"They were available at the moment." Drew stood on the top step, glaring at the ugly beasts. "Shoo. Go away."

The animals stayed put, drawing the attention of a small group, their laughter electrifying the air.

A young man propelled himself through the open doorway on crutches. He settled himself on massive forearms.

"Drew Bach, you old goat." Myauyotz leaned on his crutches, his worn pant legs turned up and stitched closed where his legs stopped at the thigh. The late morning breeze played with Myauyotz's shoulder length black hair. He squinted in the warm sunlight and grinned happily.

"Myauyotz Xu, the garden king of Fusuma. How is it going, old man?"

"I'd say it's about time you-" Suddenly his eyes glazed over and gripped shut for a fleeting moment. When they cleared, a tic pulled at his cheek. With a lurch, he turned, placing his weight on one stub, then the other.

Drew seemed unaffected by the sight. Sensing Sui's growing concern, he casually dropped an arm across her shoulders.

"Suiteiko, this is my good friend, Myauyotz."

Myauyotz inched forward. "Where did you find her?"

Sui drew a shaky breath and smiled one of her golden smiles.

"She doesn't talk, Drew. I might just keep her."

"Can't, she's spoken for."

"They always are." Myauyotz opened his hands palm up, indicating the donkeys. "Where did these two come from?" Somehow the two managed to climb another step.

Drew rolled his eyes and moaned. The closest donkey opened his jaws to take Myauyotz's shirt between his yellow teeth. Closing his mouth again, the animal tugged.

"When did you feed them last?"

"Didn't. These guys think they're pet dogs. They may never leave if I feed them."

The room had a lunch counter built in front of the kitchen. Small tables were scattered through out the spacious room. Drew usually took a corner booth, but this time he sat at a table large enough for them both. They slid into sturdy, hand-made chairs, upholstered in burgundy leather.

"Andrew!" A young woman with a white, splattered apron appeared from behind the kitchen's swinging door, took one amazed look at Drew, and flung herself into his arms. It didn't take a genius to guess she felt comfortable with Drew. A growing nightmare persisted as Sui watched the two of them chat excitedly. She carefully studied the beauty of the woman and the laughter she sparked in Drew.

"Did you just get in?"

"Not exactly."

"But you brought me a present? How long do you plan to stay?"

"Woah," Drew told her. "Slow down, woman. Allow me to introduce you to a very special lady. Marissa, meet Suiteiko. Sui just agreed to become my wife."

Drew disregarded the awkward moment of silence. "Suiteiko Wong, I'd like you to meet a very dear friend of mine, Marissa Cheung."

It became clear Marissa didn't like the idea. Her lashes fanned upward. She smiled rather stiffly. Very young and pretty, she looked out of place in a greasy apron.

"Hello, Marissa," Sui said in a voice thick with emotion.

Drew nodded encouragingly at Marissa. The girl chewed at her bottom lip, then turned to look Sui full in the face. "How nice to meet you, Sui."

Sui gasped and choked down a breath. The entire left side of Marissa's lovely face was non-existent, including the eye socket. Nothing could prepare Sui for this. Color flushed her face as swiftly as it drained. She recovered enough to find herself babbling nervously.

"Cheung," Sui repeated. "My father does business with a Makischu Cheung. Mr. Cheung ordered a rather large supply of explosives a few years ago. You wouldn't believe the paperwork, the countless calls, the juggling, the time it took to find a company willing to produce the type of explosives he'd requested. It took another eternity to receive government approval to order them."

Marissa broke into a reluctant smile. "It happened almost exactly three years ago. Father cleared land to plant a grove. I chose the exact moment he lit a charge to bring him tea." Dropping her hand, Marissa turned a very unsightly scar toward Sui for her to view.

This time Sui felt prepared. She wanted to cry and probably would have if she thought it would help. "I am so sorry. I don't know what to say."

"Neither did my father." Marissa averted her face, deliberately turning the injury away from Sui's line of vision.

"It can imagine how difficult it must have been to leave your home and your family."

Marissa flinched as if Sui touched a raw nerve. "Father didn't ask me to leave. I left because he lost face."

At the same instant it occurred to them both what she'd just said, and Marissa must have thought it particularly amusing. Suddenly they were laughing openly.

"It is I who lost face...literally."

They laughed again and spent some time enjoying one another's company. Drew teased, the girls chuckled, and they talked for nearly an hour.

Drew pushed his chair beneath the table, surprised so much time had passed. "We'd better go, Sui. I have a few things to take care of before I take you home. The valley gets dark early."

Sui told Marissa, "I hope we can keep in touch."

"I'd like that, Sui."

Drew casually checked over his shoulder. "Tomoko 'Sata needs to talk with me. Will you be okay by yourself?"

"Actually, I think maybe I'll take a walk down by the water. I'm sort of stiff after our long ride. Would that be all right?"

"Certainly."

"Drew?"

"Hmm?"

"I love you."

"I love you, Suiteiko Wong." Drew loved the sound of her Oriental name and teased her about how everyone would change her spelling to S-u-e when they arrived in America. He reached out and touched her hair. It felt soft, like cool silk between his fingers. "I shouldn't be with Tomoko 'Sata too long."

Sui watched Drew walk away and stared after him until he disappeared into one of the buildings.

I love you. The words reverberated in her heart and mind as Sui wandered down the path to the river. A few yards from shore she found a large rock jutting into the water. Discovering a dry spot, she sat down, breathing deeply of the fishy smell. In the distance, she could hear hammers clanging against metal and the joyous laughter of children.

Sui brushed back a stray hair with her fingers. Fusuma proved to be an idyllic place, filled with order and basic values. Where a new house became finished, the old was cleared away. Various dwellings were scattered about, built with whatever could be found, metal, stone, and occasionally wood.

Physically impaired humanity worked industriously at various jobs. The more hardy ones occupied themselves with the various tasks of mending nets, striking, bending and forming metal, while others boxed equipment. From a distance, Sui watched a woman hanging clothes from bamboo poles stop to greet her neighbor.

In the midst of what could have been termed despair, everything seemed peaceful and so right with the world, as if it always would be. Sui knew too well that *always* never happened. This world forever startled you with upsets when you least expected it.

No one had ever warned her that such deformities and human suffering existed. Discarded by society, they banded together, preferring the security of those in a similar predicament.

Drew must have introduced her to the entire population. With each introduction they were made to feel special. How Drew kept their names and details straight remained anyone's guess. In a very short time she began to comprehend the significant importance Drew played in their lives.

Myauyotz does a remarkable job of gardening.

Kudoh cooks the fluffiest rice.

Youki discovered a distinct knack for catching fish.

Kyn is a marvel in the kitchen.

Chima is a very obedient child.

Sata grows the sweetest corn.

Moto exhibits a tendency to attract snakes, followed by a long explanation that brought a great deal of laughter.

Sui had been surprised to see Woznau, Xhiang's niece by marriage. A large growth beneath her throat brought Woznau to Fusuma.

"You'll get used to it. Wait until you get to know them," Drew had whispered.

Sui wasn't so sure she ever would, but she didn't say so.

The day revolved around a scope of emotions, a series of ups and downs. What she and Drew shared left them ultimately closer. Drew observed Sui's reactions with quiet eyes, appreciating what he saw.

She'd discovered a new side of Drew and fell in love with him all over again.

The city looked well organized with a medical office, supply tent, library, chapel, and two large unmarked buildings. Beside a large house tucked well behind the park, a group of elderly gentlemen were going through the motions of *tai ji quan* exercises, the slow and steady movements of a cat stalking prey.

Chickens ran freely about a farmhouse to the east, pecking at the ground. In the distance, bamboo scaffolding contrasted starkly against an unusually clear blue sky. The community created a very different life from the one she'd grown up in, the majority having been built within the past twelve years.

"A penny for your thoughts."

Sui tensed. "You scared me, Drew."

"Sorry. You were so deep in thought you didn't hear me. What were you thinking just now?"

"That it's very beautiful here in a rugged sort of way," Sui said softly.

"It is pleasant. I'm glad we came together," Drew whispered close to her ear.

"So am I." Her eyes drifted back to his and he reached for her hand. His masculine scent and the feel of his warm breath fanned her face. Drew tipped her head, pressing his lips to hers so tenderly she felt the whisper of his breath against her mouth. They stayed like that, lips barely joined, leaning slightly toward the other until Sui wavered a bit. Drew reached out to steady her, set her back gently, and took an unsteady breath. His eyes leveled on her, seeing all he was looking for, and more. His head went back, his shoulders forward. "Oh, Sui," he moaned.

"Hmm?" she murmured, lazily circling his chin with her index finger.

"Please, hon, don't do that."

"What?"

"That." He caught her hand and brought it to his mouth.

"Why?"

"Because I like it too much."

"Oh."

He looked away, forcing his attention off her and back to the city. "What do you think so far?"

"Mmm." Sui saw his smile and smiled back.

Drew laughed softly. He cupped her shoulders, positioning her so he wasn't able to look into her face. "Fusuma, what do you think of Fusuma?"

"Oh, Fusuma is nice, too."

"Right." Drew offered his hand and Sui took it. "Come on, I'll show you the rest." They wandered past the medical facility and the library. Children waved shyly at them. Three little girls struggled to quiet their giggles when Drew waved back.

"They like you," Sui whispered.

"They like the candy I bring them."

"I'm sure they do."

"You surprise me."

"I do?"

"You've picked up the same typical language style as Americans. You learn quickly."

Sui caught her breath. His simplest compliment could make her heart race. It would be difficult to find anyone who didn't respect Drew. In the past year, her love for Drew had never cooled, in spite of their heated exchange over his departure and return. She was hungry to learn everything about his career, the country from which he came, the political implications of his various transactions. Her love knew no bounds. For the first time in her life she began to include the thought of sharing a family with Drew. "I haven't seen many children playing outside. Do they attend school?"

Drew nodded. "Children are taught through the fifth grade. Those who care to go on are sent away."

"Who finances their education?"

"A percentage of all Fusuma's income is divided into a reserve. The town began an education fund three years ago. It's working quite well, really."

Sui stuck hands into her pockets and hunched up her shoulders. "This town obviously took a lot of thought and planning."

"You're right. Diplomats do not recommend that Shanghai or China intervene in Fusuma's struggle for independence. You see firsthand what people can accomplish in spite of circumstances. This is the real Fusuma, the community ambassadors don't care to acknowledge."

"I will never forget their kindness and generosity. I am just sorry I have to leave so soon."

"Maybe we can come back sometime."

"When?"

Drew shrugged resting his arm across the back of Sui's shoulder. "I don't know, sometime. What time is it?"

Sui glanced down at her watch. "Five-fifty, our time."

"Good. We're expected for six o'clock chapel. It takes about ten minutes to get across the compound. Everyone wants to meet you."

"You mean there's more? My head is spinning with names."

Drew nodded and returned her smile.

In the quiet commotion of the chapel, Sui was treated as if she'd belonged forever. She wasn't used to fitting in so easily and she liked it. In a country still troubled by acknowledging women, it meant a great deal to be included.

The service began with a scripture reading, followed by a hymn. Voices joined, weaving the group together in a strong bond. The chorus ended with a long moment of silence.

The woman to Sui's right began to hum a tune of which Sui wasn't familiar. An elderly gentleman picked up the melody. When the woman grew silent he tipped back his head, closed his eyes, and broke into a song of his own making.

> *"God sure did something when He saved this old son*
> *I'll walk streets of Heaven with two legs, not one,*
> *For there won't be a cripple who stands before Him*
> *And all that I did was ask Him to come in."*

The song would have been beautiful in itself, but the man clutching a wooden crutch balanced himself on one leg. A woman blended her voice with his. Marissa's voice rang out harmoniously. In a matter of seconds, you could have heard the people singing half a mile away.

The people were serious as they sang hymns. It was a lovely service. Sui glanced at Drew once or twice and he smiled at her. His was a rich, melodic voice. Their voices rose in unison.

Singing stopped. The place grew silent. Sui knew it wasn't unusual. Effie often spent a moment in silence following worship and took the moment to seek God. In her heart, Sui cried out for His guidance.

Myauyotz must have sensed her sincerity. He stepped forward boldly. "In honor of our visitor, Suiteiko here, I feel we should allow her to close the service in prayer." If he wanted to do something special for the girl with the golden smile, he couldn't think of a greater privilege.

Sui could. She lifted her eyebrows in surprise. Suddenly unsettled and very shaken, she licked dry lips and peeked out from between squeezed lids. Expecting every eye in the place to be centered on her, she discovered they weren't. All but her own remained closed.

Her mind raced and her heart nearly pounded out of her chest. Not one prayer she'd learned as a child would come to mind. Sui shivered with cold born of fear.

Then something amazing happened. The Spirit of God washed over her and settled deep within. She enjoyed talking to Him, listening to His voice, watching things around her change, and knowing He was responsible.

Drew stood directly behind her. She could hear his whispered utterance of praise to the Father, and wondered what he expected of her. Hopefully, not much. She didn't have the experience or the know-how to pray as she would have liked to. So she simply dropped to her knees and spoke from her heart, trusting Drew would understand.

"Father God, we're truly beholden to you for so great a salvation. We thank You for what we received today-good things to eat, friends to warm our heart, these people's faithfulness, and a better understanding of what friendship truly means. In the name of Jesus, we thank YOU. And in Your name we all say, amen."

Sui cast a quick eye about the crowd. They acted quite natural. She directed her glance at Drew. He didn't look embarrassed at all, nor anxious about how spiritually undeveloped she sounded. No shock or grieving silence came from any direction, just a simple amen of agreement. For the first time in her life, Sui felt total acceptance.

Tuesday was perfect and over too soon, almost as soon as it began.

Chapter 8

It had been an absolutely horrible couple of days and nights, Xiaoping Deng reminded himself, rubbing a hand over his face. Beard stubble gave confirmation that he'd neither shaved nor slept during his thirty-nine hour wait for Andrew Bach and Suiteiko Wong to arrive. He knew the foreigner would arrive eventually. His sources assured him that Bach visited Fusuma routinely.

From outside, the groan of a rubbing axle caught Deng's attention. He stood anxiously.

Their carriage stopped before the hollow wooden door Deng threw open. A steady hum of voices and the scent of garlic wafted from the restaurant.

Deng had barely identified Suiteiko when the foreigner leaped to the ground. Deng paused in the doorway slowly and deliberately, signaling Aki Pav with a nod. Pav stepped into the shadows of a darkened alley.

Deng took the path straight through town, walking as quickly as he thought he could get away with. Even before he neared the alley, he could smell the overpowering scent Pav wore.

"What happened? I began to wonder if you made a mistake."

Deng paused in the act of brushing a fly from his shirt. "They're here. I knew he would bring her."

"Yeah." Pav slipped the front of his jacket open, slipped his new magazine into his chest holster, and scanned the area. "Did you get a good look at her?"

"It's her."

Pav became silent as he considered the plan. He had to admit he found it attractive. In short, he found his plan nothing less than ingenious and daring. One shot earned a year's wages. "Let's make this fast. We have important things to tend to."

"More important than Miamoto's matter?"

"Come on, man. Miamoto is a conspiracy terrorist, always sniffing around international capital men. Xhiang's involvement with all manner of evil pricks his interest. But why Xhiang's daughter?"

"A warning."

"So she gets snuffed out to prove a point."

"When you have a daughter one level removed from the head of Xhiang's pursuit, and trying to connect Miamoto to what just went down, he has a problem. Their association promises trouble."

"You and I both know they work as a unit."

"Stop and think! They work as a unit, yes. Miamoto has been skimming from the top. Get the picture?"

Pav shrugged. "So they go down together."

"We all go down together!"

"That won't happen. We won't let it."

"Suiteiko went through her father's personal logs."

"But you...Are you certain? I mean-"

"Who cares? We were told to carry out an order!"

"She may put two and two together."

"That's right. Miamoto can't take the chance."

"Xhiang gives her too much authority."

"Tell Xhiang that." Deng shifted the point of a pistol from where it stuck against his ribs.

"Does Xhiang know we're bringing his daughter down?"

"Not unless you told him."

"Not me!"

"Suiteiko's association with the foreigner is a threat to us all. He has certain connections in the States." Pav studied the couple.

"I thought we were agonizing over Britain. Where do the States fit in?"

"Now isn't the time to debate the issue. Do you want to follow through with the assignment...or not?"

"Consider it done." Pav paused to let the promise of a job harden his soul. He heard the distant voice of Sui. A wild tremor ran up his spine. Beneath the shadows of the stone building, each man looked into the dark face of the other. A flash of excitement leaped between them, making them an abhorrent unit.

Deng backed up. Pav studied bulky lumps beneath Deng's clothing. An arsenal of weapons were held snugly in hip holsters he'd strapped to his legs. Pav knew Deng well. The knives beneath his arms and around massive ankles would be razor sharp. A shoulder harness encased a hefty pair of massive pistols. And Deng's uncommonly broad chest hinted at a bullet proof vest.

Before Pav could suggest that Deng remove a portion of weaponry for quicker response, Deng threw out an order. "I'll have horses ready. Make it quick," he said over his shoulder. Deng walked with startling speed without looking back.

Pav looked closely at Deng's retreating figure, regarding him with fated hate. He would give Deng an attitude adjustment at a more opportune time.

Sui stepped from the carriage and stretched.

Pav dropped to his knees. He laid the magazine over the edge of a slab of granite, raised cold steel to his right eye with both hands, and pointed the barrel at her head. His hand steadied as he drew back his thumb.

"That's it, Suiteiko," Pav whispered. "One step...two steps...good girl." Pav held his breath. His hands pressed the handle with steady assurance.

Sui drew closer to the entrance.

"Steady. That's it. Turn. Keep going, Suiteiko. One more step." His left eye closed. His right focused her in his sights.

Suddenly a set of donkeys stepped in his way of a clean shot, and Suiteiko and Drew dropped from sight. On the other side of the gathering crowd, Drew stepped to his feet and pivoted. He stopped short when he saw the animals, and shrank back. A moment later the scene became a laughing match, with shouts and friendly jesting.

Having worked himself into a fury, Pav's voice sounded raspy to his own ears. "You got away this time, Suiteiko. You will not escape me again." Something touched his arm. Pav yanked it free and spun around.

"Watch where you point that thing!"

"Don't go sneaking up on me!"

Deng slammed a fist into his palm. Anger joined his fervor, making inactivity that much harder to take. Deng pulled a weapon from beneath his jacket. His bullet clicked as he drove it home. "I understood you were the best, Pav. Guess I heard wrong."

"I had her in my sights."

"If you wait long enough, something always happens. Guess I'll have to take care of the problem."

"Hey, I tried."

"Miamoto doesn't pay for failure. In your case he just might. Goodbye my friend."

Deng heard a fish slap the surface of the river. A five minute cautious walk down an incline, and he moved cautiously into a dense area. A log he stepped on crumbled beneath his weight, setting off an army of ants. Deng muttered a muffled oath, then clamped tight lips against corrupt words.

Suddenly he tensed. For the first time all morning, Suiteiko actually headed straight for the tree he leaned against, alone. Deng smiled a humorless smile and glanced over his shoulder. When he discovered her alone, Deng slipped behind a fallen log he'd vacated earlier. Sui passed so close he could smell her silky scent, could almost reach out and touch her.

Sui stopped suddenly and sniffed the air. When she continued on, Deng lifted his left arm. He took a deep whiff and wished he hadn't.

Sui half turned, then continued toward the river.

Deng followed her into tall brush growing along the track. The cloying smell of damp dirt and rotting vegetation reached him. He muttered an oath, silently shifting through thinning trees, each step taken with stealth.

When he found her, Sui was sitting on a rock that jutted into the Yangtze River. She brushed back stray hairs with long, thin fingers.

Dent's depraved mind ran through options. He shot a hard glance up and down the river bank. No threatening foreigner in sight. He would love nothing more than to take care of them both. Suiteiko would have to do for starters. His lips thinned into a wicked grin. With hands wrapped around the cold metal of his pistol, he took aim and pulled back the hammer. He stopped. A gun shot would be heard for miles, arousing suspicion and inviting pursuit.

His eye swept a stretch of yellow mud along the quiet flow of the river and into a stand of trees in search of a silent weapon. Then a thought occurred to him. His smile began small and grew in width. A quiet drowning offered more than Deng could hope for.

Seemingly, Sui didn't notice him as he inched toward her. Her attention was focused on the remains of a dead fish covered in flies. When Deng drew close enough to smell sweet perfume, he surprised himself by a compelling temptation to run fingers through her halo of curls. His eyes, glassy with madness, waited expectantly for her to turn around, to smell her fear. With a steady hand, Deng leaned in and reached for her.

Then his keen ears picked up the hint of rustling brush. Fastening the gun to his side, Deng took a step back and dashed for cover. The stand of trees would take too long and he had neither time nor inclination to dig a trench. He became desperate.

Deng stepped into the river quickly, slipping silently beneath the smooth surface. Too late, he considered the arsenal of weaponry strapped about his chest and ankles. His oxygen level dropped quickly. A struggle to the surface proved impossible. His mouth's stubborn set line opened in desperation.

Weight held him down for an eternity while his body twisted and hands flailed. Arteries began to throb, his chest heaving. Every fiber in his tissue strained. Reaching into his sleeve, Deng pulled the tip of a knife from his wrist, slicing unsuccessfully across stubborn fabric. Fumbling, he succeeded in loosening his pistol belt. Thick leather slid harmlessly to the sandy bottom of the river.

Snug trousers caught and held to his ankle holster. Deng drew and cocked his magazine almost without realizing it. The gun trembled helplessly in his hand as he struggled against concentrated weight that pulled him under and held him captive.

Chapter 9

Heavy footsteps grew in momentum. Sui recognized who they belonged to even before WuTsing flung open the door to her office.

She held her composure, surprised not that he sought her out, but that he'd waited so long. The foreclosure note on his property wrought no compassion in her for his current financial problems. He'd caused his own problems with a combination of illegal activities and poor investments.

"Where is he?" WuTsing clenched the edge of her desk, his dark face twisted in anger.

"I presume you mean Xhiang."

WuTsing leaned close and Sui caught her breath. Garlic nearly overpowered the potent smell of alcohol. She shifted rigidly, fighting queasiness.

"You know who I mean." His eyes narrowed into slits. "I won't stand for it! You will not take my estate from me!"

"You're right, I won't."

WuTsing stood back and breathed deeply. "That property is mine. No one has the right to take it, especially you."

Sui pushed her chair back and stood. "Xhiang's lawyers handle his business."

"His lawyers?"

"They were instructed to handle his affairs while he recuperates."

"On whose authority?"

Her response came immediately. "On Xhiang's authority. You don't really expect me to be given control? I mean, a woman has so little comprehension of business matters."

For the first time WuTsing looked at Sui, really looked at her. She appeared the same, soft, almost fragile, except her eyes. A sort of strength and anger lurked in their dark brown depths. And they both knew she was needed now to tun the business end of Xhiang's affairs. More than that, he needed her. She held the key to all his finances.

"You will not take what belongs to me!"

"Simply pay the balance of the sum you borrowed from my father. The land will automatically revert back to you."

"I can't get my hands on that much money, not before the beginning of next month. I'll need more time."

"I'm afraid time is something you've run out of, WuTsing."

His eyes darkened. "You think you're important around here, don't you? Well, you're not. You are both unfeeling and repulsive, Suiteiko. No wonder you never married. Even your father abhors you."

Pain struck swiftly. The type of pain only a daughter can know when her father refuses to acknowledge her. Pain increases over years, rather than lessens, just as Xhiang's seeming disapproval of her grew daily. Unable to dispute WuTsing's injurious allegation, Sui straightened. "I fail to see any connection between your arrears and that unfortunate remark. My relationship with Xhiang has absolutely no bearing on your debt to him."

A cocky sneer creased his mouth and fanned the corners of his barren eyes. "Oh, really? Don't be too certain."

Chapter 10

At 7:15, night shift bloomed into full swing. Streets thronged with those waiting to enter low-priced eateries and affluent restaurants. The restaurant Drew led Sui into shut out street noise and smelled of spice and English roses. They stood for some time, enjoying pleasant strains of woodwind instruments while waiting for tables to empty and fill again.

"Bach?" The stern fellow who called them wouldn't pass a cute test, Drew thought. His sunken eyes gave Sui a sideways look, inspecting her as he would an insect. In the tumult of men in the waiting area, the host acted as if nothing would please him more than to intentionally forget her.

Drew heaved a sigh and grinned weakly. Sui refused to catch his eye, directing her eyes toward the tips of her shoes. "Smile, love," he whispered tightly.

"This way to the woman's section." The man's voice remained devoid of emotion.

"The lady and I prefer being seated together." Drew's piercing gray eyes and a ten-dollar bill guaranteed a quiet spot in the corner. After they ordered the house special, he turned to her with a smile, and was surprised when Sui made a statement he hadn't expected.

"I don't think the man likes me." She was used to it, and it didn't shock her. Shanghai remained a patriarchal society, an alliance which still had trouble acknowledging women.

Drew followed the direction of her focus. He could see very clearly that in the eyes of the host, women were especially detested. Drew wondered if the other domestic staff were any smarter. "I can't imagine he likes anyone. That old charmer likes nothing but money."

It meant a great deal to her that Drew felt differently. She wouldn't waste time considering a stranger's attitude. She and Drew had too much to make up for, too much to discuss. She felt especially thrilled that they were together again.

Drew reached to clasp Sui's hands. "Let's talk about something else."

Sui recognized the people at the tables on either side of them. One was a group of very successful loan officers, one English, one Japanese, and two Shanghainese. At the table on their left sat a market director and jeweler who often visited Xhiang's. If they recognized her, they didn't let on.

Sui gently withdrew her hand. "Maybe we shouldn't."

Drew looked startled by what she said. Her face grew red as she looked away.

"I'm not sure you understand what I'm trying to say."

In spite of himself, Drew laughed softly. "I understand perfectly. You think holding hands is a huge mistake."

"Perhaps. You wouldn't want to shock old charmer into kicking us out," she said with a smile, still thinking of the time they'd spent together, and their lovemaking on the way to Fusuma. It already seemed like an eternity since Drew had kissed her. Their time apart seemed an injustice.

"I enjoyed being together yesterday."

Sui nodded slowly. "I shall never forget the beautiful service." She wanted to sit there for a moment and remember. Then she looked tenderly at Drew. "It breaks your heart though, doesn't it? I mean the people we met in Fusuma."

"Yes, it does. They all do. But they're making the most of it."

Drew knew their plight well, the limbo caused by not belonging, hunger without the promise of food, intemperate weather without shelter. "They'll make it. They know what's important. The real heartbreak is for those who never discover they will be made whole someday. Hope keeps them going."

Sui was struck again by how little credit Drew took for himself. "Marissa admitted they used to live in fear. How did you change all that? You are responsible for the improvements, aren't you, Drew?"

Drew stretched his long legs out beneath the table. "I wish I could boast of something so selfless as setting out to change their world. The tragedy is, I stumbled on those people with a totally selfish purpose in mind."

"You'll never make me believe you meant to take advantage of them."

"It's called employment. Have you heard about the California gold rush, Sui?"

"I think so."

"A certain Mr. Sutter discovered gold in California a couple years ago. Gold offers endless possibilities, a lure for even the most wealthy. Everyone wants a share."

"That, I understand," Sui teased.

"Like everything, there's cost to be considered. Men leave their families. Children become orphans."

"And all for hard, cold metal."

"That hard, cold metal buys warm houses and food."

Their tea arrived by then, and the waiter poured it for them.

"I thought about going after gold," Drew said. "Actually, I did for a while. Those became the longest two months of my life."

"Did you find any? Gold, I mean?"

"Sure did. Worked past dark every night and dragged myself out of bed before daylight every morning. I impressed even myself." He smiled again. "Water froze stiff the day I left the icy river to go into town. I expected to come away with a bank account the size of Mount Everest."

His deep, husky laugh seemed forced. "Prices became outrageously steep. I couldn't even afford staples."

"So you gave up."

"I didn't have a choice."

"And you came here."

They paused when the waiter slipped a vegetable tray quietly in front of them.

"How *did* you end up here?"

"Aboard the *Marybeth*." He grinned at her, looking much younger than his twenty-seven years.

"Funny. You know what I mean."

"I intended to contract a company willing to build reasonably priced gold-mining equipment. You know, picks, pans, axes, shovels."

"Why Shanghai?"

"Yes, why Shanghai?" How could he explain his ties here without sounding pretentious? "My concept got turned down flat in several other ports. I figured someone may be willing to break the trend. Why not Shanghai?"

"The day I set foot in Fusuma two children were fighting over a scrap of rice. It was awful, Sui. The adults were too tired to care."

"They needed food," she surmised aloud.

"With a river at their doorstep, you'd think fish and seaweed would become a stable diet. Those people didn't know what a net or hook looked like. And housing?" He shook his head.

"So you provided them with jobs."

Drew looked into the small teacup, all but dwarfed in his large hands, and carefully sat it on the saucer.

"Raw materials alone must amount to an enormous sum of money," Sui said. "Who provides the material?"

"That's what we delivered yesterday."

"Ahh, that's where those donkeys come in."

Drew groaned. "I told you, they weren't my idea."

"They were kind of funny."

"You weren't laughing."

"Yes, I was."

"Next time let your face know. A smile would have been very welcome."

In a moment of silence they stared at one another, each realizing what he may have lost in the other. "Those animals weren't number one on my priority list at the time. Hey, are you laughing at me?"

"Maybe."

"Well don't. Next time I'll travel at night."

"Wouldn't it have made more sense to take off their hats?"

"Now, there's a thought."

"Mining equipment came back with us, didn't it?"

Drew nodded. "It's all loaded and waiting to be shipped."

"And everyone benefits."

"Exactly."

"They love you, Drew. Those people love you."

"They're good people. How is your tea?"

"Yummy. Orange pekoe."

"It's your favorite."

"You remembered."

"Oh, I remember. How could I forget the love of my life?"

"Tell me about her. What is she like?"

"A lot like you as a matter of fact. This woman is very intelligent."

Sui couldn't keep the laughter from her dark eyes. It flowed over to her mouth forming a charming smile. "Ah, but I'm beautiful *and* smart."

"Smart enough to come in out of the rain?"

"Absolutely. I've never been particularly fond of rain."

"Oh? I seem to remember a certain evening with a certain lady."

"We did have fun, didn't we?"

"If I recall correctly, it happened just across the street."

"You didn't forget."

"Orange pekoe tea. That's what you ordered the night we met, the night you threw yourself into my arms."

Sui gasped and shook her head. "Is that what you believe, that I intentionally threw myself into your arms?"

Drew looked amused now. "But you did. Yes, you did."

Her face reddened as though he'd delivered her a shocking blow.

"Are you telling me our meeting was strictly accidental? Because that would be a cruel blow to my ego. All this time I thought..." His voice trailed off. Her reaction was immediate.

"I didn't even see you!" But now laughter lighted her eyes as well. "I slipped in the rain, remember?"

Sui remembered. She hadn't been paying close attention that night. At the time, she wanted to find a dry place to get out of the shower. The protective awning had seemed a likely spot. It also happened to be the spot Drew was waiting out the weather. When she would have fallen, a powerful arm reached out to grab her. Before she knew what happened, she was cradled against his chest, her mouth practically touching his cheek.

His deep voice had startled her. Sui looked up into gorgeous, deep gray eyes, framed by dark brows and lashes. They turned down when he smiled. His sun-burnished skin and wet mahogany hair looked even darker in the shadows at night. He hadn't shaved recently. She liked his raw appearance. A wide jaw, strong chin, and imposing brow, along with substantial strength, height, and broad shoulders made him the most powerful, most breathtakingly masculine man she'd ever met. And his wet clothes had made his pleasant scent impossible to miss. She still remembered every word they'd said.

Drew had grinned. "I don't make a habit of holding strangers."

"I should hope not. Why haven't I seen you in Shanghai before?"

"I'm from the States. My ship is harbored at the dock. Name's Drew Bach."

Her heart had lurched in her throat. The States wee so far away. "I am Suiteiko Wong. You may call me Sui."

"S-u-e?"

"No, S-u-i. They are pronounced the same."

Sui remembered straightening her clothes. She wished she'd worn something other than her yellow cheungsam. It plainly showed water spots. And her hair had become a riot of curls. Did Drew remember as well?

"I asked if you were all right."

"And I told you I was fine."

Her thoughts were all too easy to read. His face relaxed into a teasing smile. "You thought I was really handsome, huh?"

She did, but she wasn't about to admit it that easily. "You looked like a drowned puppy, so tired and very wet. That's why I let you hold me so long."

"Is that right? I don't remember getting wet until you stepped into my arms." He made her laugh.

"Well, maybe I was the first to pounce, but you spoke first. I should have waited at the Emporium until the storm passed."

"But then I would have missed rescuing you. I'm glad you came out on a wet night." He said it with such solemnity that she laughed again.

The following day they met, and several days after. They got to know one another better and Drew cared for her anyway. She'd believed that very thing until he left so unexpectedly a year ago. Now she knew why.

"And to think, I almost didn't go out that night."

"Why did you? You never told me."

"Noah convinced me I would pace a path through the floor."

"Were you pacing the floor?"

"Probably. When you've been out to sea for months there's something very comforting about the feel of solid earth beneath your feet."

"You almost felt earth under more than your feet when I ran into you."

"I reacted quickly."

"Quick reactions can be good." Sui laughed, fingering the brim of her cup thoughtfully. "There's something I don't quite understand."

Drew nodded.

"How do you know so many people from Fusuma?"

"I spent three weeks with them."

"Working, I imagine."

Drew grinned, but he didn't deny it.

"If Fusuma doesn't exist on a map, and the government doesn't recognize it, how did you find the place? I mean, it's not exactly on your way to anywhere."

"You're right." Drew lay his napkin aside. "The warehouse opens early. You can imagine how crowded the aisles are that time of day."

Sui stirred her tea and nodded.

"With all the noise and commotion, people poke and jostle from all sides. I began inspecting a bolt of silk when a young boy worked his hand into my back pocket. The little guy's eyes turned big as saucers when he discovered that wallet chained to my belt."

"A pickpocket?"

"Exactly. Li-Tou bolted out of there so fast I almost lost sight of him before he reached the door. I lost him at Tak's Apothecary."

"Tak's Apothecary is way on the other side of town."

"Tell me about it! It's probably a good thing I didn't catch him." Drew sat back into his chair, grinning all the while. "I may have strangled the kid."

"Did he get your wallet?"

"No, he didn't. I happened across him later and watched the kid at his game. He's good! In less than a half hour he picked three pockets, filched two apples, and slipped a gold ring off a man's finger."

"What?"

"That's not the half of it. The child only has one hand."

"He lives in Fusuma," Sui speculated out loud, looking at Drew with serious eyes.

"You guessed it. I followed him home."

"Is that how you discovered the shelter?"

"Over several years time the place had become poverty stricken. Li-Tou found a way to help feed his little community. Those people are really great folks, nicer than some. They stay to themselves mostly."

"Because they feel different."

Drew lowered his voice. "Even the blind aren't oblivious to gasping reactions."

Sui traced the placemat's engraved initial with her finger. "If Fusuma is commonly accepted, why isn't it being supported by families of those who live there?"

"From time to time, gifts are left on a doorstep."

"From time to time. What do they suppose happens in between?"

Drew shrugged. "Try to forget?"

"Is Li-Tou okay?"

"Li-Tou is fine. I'll admit I half expected him to be rather slow, but he possesses a brilliant mind. The youngster simply needs guidance. That's why I placed him in a school for boys."

Sui smiled a slow smile. "I don't suppose he liked that."

"Believe me, he made quite an impression on the other residents. The man I left him with will give Li-Tou proper guidance. Elliott doesn't tolerate nonsense, but he's fair."

"You can't mean Elliott Pepple?" She knew of only one man named Elliott in Shanghai.

"Did I say something wrong?"

"I'm just surprised, that's all. You left Li-Tou with Elliott Pepple, didn't you?"

Drew nodded. "I met Elliott last year. I've never met his wife."

"Effie is very vivacious and sweet and charming, and she likes lots of children everywhere. You'll know what I mean when you meet her. She has a way of making things fun."

"Perhaps I'll meet her when I stop in to visit Li-Tou tomorrow."

"Perhaps." Sui looked at him thoughtfully. "You certainly have a number of friends."

That didn't really surprise her. Drew's easygoing, friendly nature attracted people. He never boasted about possessions. He gloried in the One who allowed him to enjoy them. Sui would never forget what he once told her, that the purpose of a Christian was little more than one beggar showing another beggar where to find bread. And hadn't Effie implied the same thing?

As the evening progressed the waiter unassumingly took note of what should be replaced. They sampled savory dishes, and grinned like conspirators when Sui reached for another crabmeat rangoon. She bit into a crunchy wrap and creamy filling oozed out the crisp edges.

Drew raised both eyebrows. He wanted to laugh and Sui wanted go giggle, but they couldn't. It wouldn't be proper.

"I just know Effie would love these," Sui said.

"Did you tell me the Pepples came from Kentucky?"

"An accident at a coal mine took the lives of a young Chinese couple. Elliott and Effie brought the couple's son back. They were never able to locate the boy's grandparents."

"Where is he now?"

"He's the reason they stayed, to keep the boy with them. The government granted them permission to open a school for homeless boys, the same school you left Li-Tou at."

"That's quite commendable." Drew settled his cup. "Does the school house girls?"

"Girls? Heavens, no. Their inferior minds are unable to comprehend characters or numbers. Occasionally the wealthy are presumed intelligent. Girls walk with bound feet, selecting words as smoothly as they select their steps."

"Do I detect a touch of sarcasm?"

"Perhaps. It's difficult having to do twice the work to get half the credit. A husband is chosen for a woman. She is taught to accept his authority in silence."

Dean leaned forward.

Sui quickly interrupted him. "I know what you're thinking, but don't get any ideas. I refuse certain teachings." She lifted a size seven foot from beneath the table. "See for yourself."

His outburst of laughter confused her.

"What?"

"You are a rebel, Suiteiko."

"Mother encouraged me to think for myself."

"And you father?"

"Xhiang had little to do with my education."

"Why do you call him Xhiang, and not Father?"

"At his request. So says Xhiang."

Drew moaned, loving it. "Your mother didn't originate from the east, did she?"

"No, Mother came from England."

"I guessed. You look so..."

"Un-Oriental? I know. Mother received her education in England. I watched and learned."

Drew looked across the table, imagining Sui a tiny, dark-haired little girl in a fuzzy nightgown snuggled against a caring mother, her clever mind hidden behind a soft, smooth face, all innocence and purity of heart.

"...so from a man's point of view, would you?" Sui tipped her head to one side. "You weren't listening were you?"

Drew's eyes, warm and alive, caressed her face. "You're right, and I'm sorry. What did you say?"

Sui plunked her chin against a hand. "I'm boring you."

Drew looked at her in a way that convinced her otherwise, so she repeated herself. "Effie wants a daughter. Would you want a child at Elliott's age?"

"Having a child at any age would be wonderful."

"Good," as though that settled the matter, "because I've been praying they get their daughter. No two people deserve it more."

Deeply affected by her mother's death, Sui felt the need for another woman to relate to, someone she could talk to in a way she could never talk to Xhiang. Effie filled the void.

"Three months after I lost her, I sat in Effie's garden looking at her rhododendrons and talking about Mother. For the first time, I didn't cry. I even told Effie an amusing story about Mother. We both laughed. I survived the loss, thanks to Effie. I owe her so much, with no way to repay her kindness."

"Does Effie feel the same way, that you owe her?"

Sui shook her head. "She wouldn't take anything if I offered it. But I can pray God repays her with the one thing I know Effie wants more than anything else in the world, a baby girl."

"That is very nice of you, Sui. You make me happy, happier than I have ever been. I'm sure you make Effie happy too."

"I hope so. Effie's home is very different than the house where I grew up. The Pepple's house almost seems to open its arms to you."

Drew's mouth twitched. "A house that opens its arms."

Sui nodded. "It must be the lace curtains."

"Lace curtains?"

"When the sun comes up in the morning, it peeks through lace curtains, painting all sorts of pictures on the wall. When I have a house I will make lace curtains just like Effie's."

"Do you like to sew?"

"Not always. I was ten years old when Xhiang's third wife ordered me to do her mending. No matter how tiny the stitches or how straight the seam, she found fault with my work. I got angry. So while my fingers darned, I pretended to be married to a wonderful man. The clothing I mended belonged to our children."

"Yours and mine?"

His question and the simplicity of it caught her off guard. She recovered quickly. "Are you intruding on my fantasy?"

"I wouldn't dream of it. Go on."

"With tiny stitches, I worked a patch on San Wen's dress and almost jumped out of my skin when she stepped behind my chair to scold. I became so mad that I forced my eyes to remain downcast and counted to ten. I didn't want her to witness my anger. I looked back up, smiled sweetly, and apologized. But I left a small hole in one of her pockets so her power and wealth would trickle away, very slow and very steadily."

"I knew it. You are a rebel, Suiteiko."

"I'm not always submissive."

"I'll make it a point to remember."

Sui cleared her throat. "Okay, your turn."

"My turn?"

"Confess. You must have done something you're unwilling to share with the world."

For the first time in a long time, Drew allowed himself to remember. His childhood seemed so long ago. At times it became difficult to recall what his parents looked like. Yet there were things he remembered as clearly as if they'd been together yesterday. "My father was a big guy. Wholesome, he was wholesome."

Sui's eyes rested on Drew's broad shoulders, slowly wandering back up to his warm gray eyes. "Like you."

"They named me after him. Dad wanted me to be a doctor."

Sui rested her chin on folded hands, her eyes crinkling upward at the corners. "He believed in you."

"I hope I wouldn't have disappointed him."

"Not a chance."

"Maybe." Drew chuckled. "I put plenty of holes in my jeans. Remind me to fix them myself."

"It's a deal."

"I think I just got took. Xhiang doesn't stand a chance against you, does he?"

"Andrew Bach! You sound as if you feel sorry for him."

"Of course I feel sorry for the guy. With two wives and all that disgusting money to take care of, poor man."

"I suppose your father was perfect."

"I used to think so. I would reach up and squeeze his sinewy muscles. Dad pinched my peewee arm back and faked amazement, as if my muscles would lift me. My muscles grew before his eyes. I wasn't so sure, but I wanted to believe him."

A unseen hand squeezed at Drew's heart as he remembered things long forgotten. "For such a large man, Dad's hands could be gentle. He lifted me until I towered above the floor. A couple of times I walked across the ceiling upside down. The last time Mother made us wash it.

"I must have been about five years old when I got really sick. I moaned and Mom cried. Dad came out of their room and whispered something to her. He lifted me in his enormous arms. I felt like a little boy."

"You were a little boy."

"Don't ever admit that to a five year old."

Sui looked at him with a smile and a look in her eyes that made it easy to talk.

"Dad's solid chest reverberated a husky roar as he crooned a senseless song. Things like that mean a lot when you're five and not feeling good."

He hadn't intended to burden her with memories. "Sorry."

"Sorry for what?"

A lop-sided grin. "For rattling on."

"Rattling on? You still haven't confessed anything I can hold against you."

Two waiters approached their table bearing silver platters topped with Zhu-rou, bean curds, calamari, eel stuffed wild mushrooms, pea pods, and preserved duck eggs. There was something very pleasant about sharing it together.

Sui couldn't remember a time in her life when she felt so comfortable with another person. She wasn't forced to be formal or solemn, forever prepared for and guarded against mood swings. Being herself seemed to please him, and sometimes when she said something witty, Drew laughed.

The creamy hue of her silk dress made her eyes glow darkly, adding a gentle radiance to her lovely face. But it wasn't outward beauty alone Drew admired about her. Since the day they'd met, he'd been convinced Sui maintained the simple quality of honesty and unpretentiousness. She showed inner strength that withstood the hardships life threw her way. And she never complained, in spite of adversity. When life handed out difficulties, she wasn't afraid to meet them head on. That was good, because his life wasn't always easy.

"We've had some wonderful times together, haven't we, Drew?"

"Suiteiko, what I want are wonderful years together."

When she made no reply, Drew traced her chin with his finger. "I don't want to leave you."

"You promised you wouldn't."

63

"I'm responsible to the men who work for me."

"What are you saying?"

"They want to go home." His eyes warmed her. "Will you go back with me this trip? As my wife, I mean."

Sui's eyes shone with the heat of her emotions. "You have a responsibility for your men. I have a responsibility to my father. Where does that leave us, Drew, you and me?"

She was right. He could offer her everything materially, but he couldn't give her peace of mind where Xhiang was concerned, or sever ties that bind a child to her parent. He wouldn't want to. "I left before because I love you, not because I didn't."

"What are you saying, Drew?" Her eyes were big and sad, and more lovely than ever.

"I will always love you, Sui. You lived on in my mind when we were separated by an ocean. Nothing can separate the way I feel for you."

Sui gulped on a sob. "Is this your way of telling me you're leaving?"

He bent close to press something into her hand.

"What is this?"

"Open it and see."

The box held a gold ring, the first ring she ever designed. Elegant and small, chips of ruby surrounded a large diamond.

"You're a very nice man, Andrew Bach. How did you know?"

"That you wanted it?"

She nodded.

"I came into the shop last week," Drew said.

"I didn't see you."

"I knew you needed time."

"You should have let me know."

Drew raised a brow.

"You're right, and I'm sorry. Go on," she said.

"You must have waited on a dozen customers."

"At least."

"Do you remember the gentleman who came in to buy an anniversary gift for his wife?"

This time she laughed. "I talked him into an emerald brooch."

"An emerald frog!"

"His wife loves it. She came in to thank me."

"That's good. I would have purchased the ring."

"I couldn't part with it. Now I'll never have to." But she would part with Drew, Sui thought.

"Drew-"

"Sui-" he said at the same time. "Sorry, go ahead."

"No, you first."

"Xhiang is your father, I think I can understand your need to be here for him. I wish I could stay here for months. The thought of leaving you again..."

"Drew, I'm sorry."

"You don't have to be sorry, honey. Your loving kindness and compassion is a part of the reason I love you. Your day and mine will come. I'll wait forever if you want me to."

"You would do that for me?"

Drew wiped a stray tear from her eye. "You don't mind?" he asked.

"I never said that." Sui laughed softly, hoping silently he meant it.

"I promised I would wait. And I will."

"I don't want to take a chance of losing you, but-"

"I know." He managed a faint smile. "I'm going to be at the Pepple's house tomorrow, at noon."

Sui looked up. Her eyes held a mixture of anguish and hope.

"If things don't work out, if you change your mind, meet me there. Will you do that, Sui? Will you?"

"Maybe we should say goodbye tonight."

"Maybe we should get married tomorrow."

She raised big brown eyes to him. "Tomorrow?"

"It's up to you, honey."

"I wish it was. Up to me, I mean."

"Let's not worry. God has a way of taking care of things."

Drew covered her hand. Smooth warmth of gold pressed against his palm, a reminder that she consented to spend the rest of her life with him. They would be together, forever. Hopefully soon.

Chapter 11

Armed guards spotted Drew long before they arrived at the boundary of Xhiang's court. On either side of the path, lookouts held modern magazines. How had the latest weapons reached Shanghai, to fall into the hands of Xhiang's hired defense? A true message of Xhiang's strength flashed to him across the falling darkness.

Drew heard a shout and a muttered answer. The guards made a bit of noise in discussion. Roaring clicks of cocking pistols certainly proved a distinct sound, yet Sui paid no attention. Drew took advantage of the chance to case the perimeter, with its shadowed trees and imposing army.

"Father holds title to all this," Sui explained. "The valley path we follow begins in the city and progresses to this fence. Those trees shade flowers. Flowers drop seed over that barrier. In summer, mounds of blooms grow where black dirt settles between those rocks."

Unaware of the heavy accent she'd reverted to in the past few minutes, Sui uncharacteristically prattled as they drew close to the house. Drew suspected that she felt uncomfortable about their encounter with her father.

"The kitchen garden surrounded by that stone wall? In summer, flowering hedges separate it from flower beds."

Drew's eyes searched the settling night, locating the guards Xhiang would have posted strategically along the perimeter of his property. It wasn't difficult. He stood for a moment beneath a banyan tree and breathed deeply. He not only inhaled the aromatic scent of humid earth and green foliage, but a far more pungent smell, the stench of liquor and seasoned sweat.

The noise he heard might have come from any direction. But it seemed that it must have floated from a place nearby. He turned slowly until he faced a stand of shadowy trees. Nothing moved at first. A moment later something flashed through the impending darkness.

Then he saw it. WuTsing lay out on his stomach, his head cushioned in folded arms as if waiting for something. But what?

The wise thing would be to go straight to Xhiang and make inquiries. But Drew considered Xhiang's condition. He scanned the darkness farther beyond the place WuTsing lay silently watching them, making a conscious attempt to compose himself. Nothing could be gained by confronting WuTsing, he told himself, except to give the man a chance to become defensive. He had come too far to give up his effort to gain Sui without further battle.

Sui seemed oblivious to it all. But suddenly she looked tired. Tiny lines showed between her eyes. It had been an amazing, yet very long day.

"This is the *ting*," she said, "I mean the summer pavilion. Xhiang had it built here in the *yuan* years ago." Sui cleared her throat. "The garden, he had it built in the garden."

Drew reached out a finger beneath her chin, forcing her to meet his steady gaze. "I'm well aware of what a *ting* is, and a *yuan*."

In spite of herself, she did smile. "I seem to get a little crazy when I'm tense."

"That's one of the things I like about you."

"The usual stuff? That I'm crazy?"

Drew reached for her hand and grinned. "No, that you are honest and very sincere."

"I hope you don't expect perfection, because I'm not. Perfect, I mean."

"We'll both do our best. That's what matters.

Sui nodded, trying to believe him.

"And we'll never give up," Drew said. "You and I will stick together forever."

"Together." Sui ran a trembling hand through her hair. Dark curls fell free and spilled to her shoulders. "I ran away once. I couldn't have been much more than a little girl. I fell asleep in that pavilion."

"And why would a little girl run away from all of this?"

"The usual reason. I felt the need to prove to myself I would be missed."

"Were you?"

Sui grinned. "No one even realized I'd left."

"How disappointing."

"It was at the time." Suddenly she laughed, thinking how senseless it all seemed now, the self pity, the vying for attention. "This is the main house."

Hideous dragons framed each doorway of the house. They walked in silence. Drew glanced at Sui and rolled his eyes comically. She knew what he thought. The very notion of introducing evil dragons to scare away evil spirits seemed contradictory.

A carved stone fountain was the focal point of the patio. Clear water flowed from a length of bamboo and emptied into the sunken bath below. It bubbled invitingly as they approached the house.

Her stepmother was the first to greet them. San Wen looked fit as usual, with beautifully done hair and a striking pink *cheungsam* that showed off her trim figure. She clung lightly to a white silk bag and matching pouch, and gave Sui a cautious greeting, looking past her to Drew. "I am just on my way out. Check on Xhiang, will you?"

"How is he?" Sui asked her stepmother cautiously. But Xhiang's wife cut her off almost as soon as she spoke, complaining how little time there is in a day. Nothing had changed.

"Make yourself at home while I check on Xhiang." Sui told Drew, smiling uncertainly. She had no idea how like a frightened little girl she looked, with her eyes large as saucers.

Xhiang owned a house, not a home, Drew thought. Something about it made him feel uncomfortable. Perhaps the armed guard standing in the doorway had something to do with the chill working its way up his spine. Drew looked past broad shoulders to where Sui slipped through transparent doors shutting the kitchen wing from the patio.

Or maybe the ornamental fire-breathing dragon mounted on the east wall set his nerves on edge. No matter what other operations were performed on the place each day, that gold fire was burnished until it blazed brightly like a flame. He'd seen one similar only once before. On special holidays, the hollow mouth served as a stone basin into which hot coals were poured to cook delicacies.

Only the kitchen held a semblance of being lived in, though the atmosphere didn't compel one to relax over a hot cup of coffee. The room smelled of pork, turnips, bok choy, ginger, and garlic. Slivered food was scattered on the elevated table, two feet from the stone floor.

A glance the guard gave him was as brutal as the oath he murmured with it. Drew ignored him, pretending he couldn't understand the language. Shouldering past him, Drew surprised the man by holding himself erect. When his solid stance threw the guard off balance, Drew smiled broadly and bowed deeply. The guard responded by slamming back the door with enough force to drive it off the frame. Drew could just make out a loud voice and the answering chatter in the back yard.

He looked for the nearest exit and found one off the dining room. Sparsely furnished with a low black lacquer table, the room boasted a rich, polished floor, covered with woven rice mats. Opposite the room, an arched opening into Xhiang's office led to another door, allowing the master of the house freedom to come and go without knowledge of the household.

Xhiang had furnished the place carefully. The mural itself was a ponderous structure, surrounded by a heavy gilt frame. Designs of a frenzied tiger, muscles undulating sinuously while stalking through a dense thicket along a swift river, seemed to leap out of the wall.

Drew frowned, thankful for the home where he'd grown up. Clean and sort of cluttered, a fishing pole could be found leaning against the rose papered wall. Jackets hung on a wooden peg beside the kitchen door. He could still hear wood popping in the fireplace on a cold winter night, imagine the pleasant smells of supper cooking after chores were finished.

His family came together like clockwork around a heavy oak table. Against the soft tapping of spoons and forks, they took turns describing their day and making plans for the next.

Xhiang's house boasted frangible beauty, a splendid museum. Each icon carefully displayed considerable detail. Changing even one object would unbalance the entire room. Drew felt an urge to throw back shutters, to let sunlight filter through the darkness, but he couldn't. He had intruded on Xhiang's storehouse of wealth. He could merely peek into Sui's lonely past by soaking up the sterile atmosphere.

He found Sui crying softly in Xhiang's room. Drew joined her there. Warm, pungent air closed about him like an imprisoning barrier. Drew would have turned to leave, but something made him stay. The light that filtered through open cracks in the drapery struck the wall, trailed across the bed, a bureau, a chair, and then glazed the face of a very ill Xhiang.

Sui went to him, burying her face against his chest. She cried for her father. She might never again have a chance to tell him how she cared. She cried because he wouldn't be pleased if he did know. She cried because she loved him. And she cried because she wanted him to love her, too.

Drew rocked her back and forth in his arms. "Shh...What do you want, Sui? What can I do?"

"I don't know what I want."

"I won't do anything you don't want," he whispered. "Just tell me, and I'll mind my own business." But he felt Xhiang was his business, too. He had a concerned interest in every aspect of Sui's life. He didn't want to push her. She looked so unhappy. It was all he could do to leave her, even for one night. He felt terrible as he watched her wrestle with her conscience.

"I don't know what to do, Drew." She raised her big brown eyes to his. "Two months ago, I considered Father invincible. Now I look at him, and I know he is just as susceptible to illness and death as the next man. Life as I knew it is probably over. And in the midst of it all, here you are, someone I can depend on. I want to be with you," she whispered.

"I don't know what I will do, or what's going to happen next. I just don't know. I'm a mess." Her voice drifted of in confusion.

"You're not a mess." He kissed the tip of her nose and cocked his brow at a crazy angle. "Well, maybe a little."

Sui smiled, and suddenly life wasn't so bad again.

"It's okay. You don't have to do anything." Drew took her in his arms. He wanted to hold her and kiss her. He pressed his lips softly against hers.

His mouth was soft and warm at first. When Sui felt her breath catch, Drew pulled her closer. She was overwhelmed by what she felt, and unsettled at the same time. He took her breath away as they kissed again. "Maybe it's a good thing Xhiang is sedated," she giggled softly, looking at him like a small child. "What are we going to do?"

"You'll decide in due time. Things have a way of working out." He struggled to look solemn, but he couldn't. "Did I mention I would be at the Pepple's tomorrow at noon? If you come to me, Sui, we will be together, forever."

His voice became husky. He began kissing her neck. Sui closed her eyes, relishing the moment. "I really think you should reconsider. But I don't want to..." he kissed her earlobe "...rush anything."

WuTsing slapped at a droning mosquito. Hatred brought him down a strange trail. He stood silently in the shadows, waiting for Drew. His long, hostile face grew grave as he watched from a distance. All the while he wondered what the foreign devil wanted of Sui. He would find out, and he would deal with the situation.

Chapter 12

Sui stayed up late reading again, touching on specific points for the presentation. There were a few things she wanted to emphasize, and she needed to present it as if the idea had come from Xhiang and not herself. It would be easier just talking to the group, but there was no point. If she shared her own ideas they would be disregarded, and Xhiang couldn't afford that.

She dreamed of Xhiang for the second time in a week. Mental images seemed complicated, a glimpse of him laying on his back in bed. WuTsing pilfered through his things. Xhiang's eyes followed WuTsing while his body remained paralyzed.

During those few seconds before she totally awoke, Sui sensed Xhiang's health taking a turn. She entered his room and touched his face. His forehead felt warm and moist to the tips of her fingers.

And then, not for the first time, a thought occurred to her. She considered her father's condition and his reliance on her. Who would oversee his business if not her? Certainly God wouldn't honor selfish behavior. Conviction pressed painfully against her heart. She should make things right before she sought her own happiness. Tears flowed unchecked down her eyes. She reached out, took Xhiang's hand in her own, and held it for a moment.

His hair fanned out across the pillow. In sleep he looked so helpless, so harmless. An empty bottle of sake lay loosely in Xhiang's hand. In his unconscious state, a small portion of the liquid had spilled, staining the sheet. Sui reached for the bottle and placed it on a table nearby. He might have been mistaken for a corpse if not for the menacing rattle struggling in and out of his shrunken chest.

Sui observed his unhealthy yellow cheeks and thought of all those times Xhiang had been spared from death.

Seven years ago his ricksha collided with a runaway horse and buggy. The ricksha collapsed, talking the life of the puller. Xhiang remained unscathed.

At a business dinner, four associates died of food poisoning. Xhiang hadn't been especially hungry that particular night. His food was nearly untouched.

The war had claimed numerous lives, but not Xhiang's.

During the Cultural Revolution, he had nearly starved to death along with so many other children.

Her eyes grew sad. If she closed them, she could make believe he would be all right. She still wasn't sure why she felt so indebted to him. He had never seemed concerned with her needs or how he played on her sense of obligation, her fears, her emotions. None of that mattered. He was her father. Sui reached forward to kiss his feverish face, and a raspy cough broke into her thoughts.

All her feelings showed in the way she moved. She tucked the blanket beneath his chin, her eyes touching Xhiang tenderly. For just a moment she pretended to be precious to him. He would never know.

Her attention was drawn to a photograph hanging on the wall above the lacquered oriental screen. A gaunt boy of seven years, Xhiang stared from the portrait with hungry eyes. Skin stretched across his bare chest so tightly you could count each protruding bone. His slight frame looked so small, his clothes so ragged, that Xhiang had become the brunt of other children's torment.

His heart had grown hard. His greatest aspiration was to refrain from tears in the presence of others. The few times he did cry, his were not tears of defeat. They were born of bitterness and a growing sense of indomitability. The image hung in plain view as a reminder of where he came from and where he intended to arrive.

Only those closest to him really knew Xhiang. He never discussed or even hinted at his past. Sui painted the picture of his orphan upbringing from bits and pieces of servants' gossip.

Xhiang had been born just north of Shanghai. When he was fourteen years old, the Communists came into their small town and took away his parents. With little education, hope for a better life gnawed at him. Foreigners, scholars, and the most corrupt were those who lived beyond a mere existence.

Then the unforeseen happened. Xhiang met a man who offered to teach him to read and write fifteen hundred characters in a month. That would allow him to read ordinary books and write letters.

Xhiang worked hard, refusing to stop at fifteen hundred characters. He sought knowledge until he became capable of passing an examination that allowed him into University.

He could hide his past from the world, but almost nothing from his daughter. Her glance said she loved him. Sui hoped he knew how proud he made her. He'd overcome insurmountable odds and done something with his life. She really was happy about his accomplishments. She just wasn't certain he'd used his knowledge in an ethical manner.

The ornate clock ticked off seconds. She glanced around Xhiang's room at his acquired wealth. He possessed so much, and yet so little. So many depended on Xhiang. Yet so few would ever miss him.

Long, dark hair hid her face as Sui kneeled beside Xhiang's bed. She whispered his name and stroked wisps of raven hair from his forehead. As if in answer to her prayer, Xhiang stirred.

"Xhiang? I need to speak with you."

Xhiang fell helplessly against his pillow. Just before he closed his eyes he emitted a low cry. Sui waited a long moment before his chest rose and fell. A minute passed. She heard his next breath, this one more shallow than the last. In his unresponsive state, Sui felt free to expose her heart.

"I'm worried about you." The truth brought tightness to her throat.

"Do you miss Mother as sorely as I do? It's been awful since she died. I met someone special at Mother's funeral. Do you remember Elliott Pepple? He officiated the service?"

No reply came, only the ticking of the clock, and finally the wheeze of his breath.

"Probably not. You seemed quite uncomfortable at the time. A Christian burial isn't something to get angry about. Christianity is helping me. Before I met Christ, my life was tossed like fog on a windy day."

She paused.

"Father...I hope you allow me to call you that, just this once." She cleared her throat. "I'm worried about you, Father. I look at you and wonder what will happen to your spirit if your heart stops. Where will it go?"

Again, Xhiang didn't move.

"There is a place called heaven. God lives there."

Xhiang groaned.

Sui stood.

Xhiang relaxed.

She sat back down.

"Remember when Aunt Aki wanted to come for a visit? You welcomed her."

The room swelled with silence.

"But you refused to allow her dog inside the house."

Sui licked dry lips.

"God would welcome everyone into heaven. But He will not allow sin to enter his house."

Sui leaned forward.

"There is only one way to get rid of sin, Father."

Sui shifted restlessly. "We have all sinned and come short of the glory of God. Do you know what that means? It means He knows all about you."

Her eyes widened.

"I mean...I didn't mean to imply that you are...you know...you haven't..."

Through thick, sooty lashes, Sui watched Xhiang carefully. Waiting for an intense response that never came.

"He gives us power to become His if we receive Him. That means you, Xhiang. Christ died for you."

Sui leaned closer. "You're always looking for a bargain, Xhiang. This is the deal of a lifetime, because you have more to forgive than most."

Suddenly she realized what she'd said. "I mean, there's no sin too great for Christ to forgive."

She swallowed uncomfortably.

"Not that you've done anything all that bad." But he had, and she knew it.

Sui closed her eyes and realized there were tears on her lashes. She took a deep breath and forced it out in a rush.

"The wage of sin is death, Xhiang. Can you hear me? The wage of sin is death."

There was no answer, of course, only the enormity of her concern and an immense hopelessness.

How could one's heart acknowledge its sin, while that person goes on smiling at customers, buying groceries, making beds, pressing clothes, cooking meals, pulling weeds, all the time knowing the wages of sin is death?

Sui leaned forward and whispered in his ear. "The gift of God is eternal life. If you can hear me, listen real close. Let Jesus take your sin away so we can spend eternity together, you, me, and Mother."

Sui blinked away a tear.

"Just ask Him."

She choked on a sob.

Another hushed silence crawled by, filled with longing hope.

Sui dropped into bed, torn. She ached with emptiness that would surely hit her even harder when Drew sailed away. The large yellow moon that shone through the window showed a shadowy glimpse of her room. Everything looked so familiar, almost safe.

She'd cried this hard once before and she'd lived through Drew's departure. Surely she would live through it again. Only this time felt worse. This time she chose.

Over and over she relived Drew's parting kiss, watched him turn to her with expectation on his face, heard the lilting song he whistled as he walked away.

Come morning, she would break his heart. With a broken heart of her own, she tossed about in bed, sobbing so hard that the stern guard opened her door a crack.

"Are you okay, missy?"

He sounded almost concerned, which made her cry harder. She couldn't force words past her lips, leaving the guard to wonder.

Weeping racked her for hours. She wondered how she would get through the lonely days without Drew. There would be no one to hold her when she needed holding, to understand when she needed a shoulder to cry on, or to share laughter during good times.

Sui turned to her right side. Her head throbbed. Her eyes hurt. She couldn't breathe without trembling.

Sui awoke with a start and lunged upright. A large hand clamped her mouth to still an alarmed cry. She turned her head. Then she looked into WuTsing's hard eyes and her heart nearly stopped.

"Quiet!"

Silence caught her attention. No one seemed to be moving through the house. "When Father finds you..."

WuTsing's fist came out of no where. When it connected with her jaw, her cry was silenced. WuTsing stood over her, watching her reaction while Sui watched his in return. If he'd looked crazed before, he really looked wild now. A chill ran up her spine. She had to do something. Oh, God, she prayed, help me.

Sui wanted to shout, to run for help, but she couldn't move. WuTsing must have known the guards wouldn't help or he wouldn't have felt relaxed enough to walk calmly about her room, looking at her over his shoulder. Sui suspected this had something to do with the repossession of WuTsing's property.

WuTsing sat down on the side of her bed and gave Sui his mild, deadly smile. Leaning forward, he looked at her as a parent looks at a very slow child. "Suiteiko."

"Get out!"

He stiffened. "Are you asking me to leave?"

"No. I am telling you. Leave right now and I will not tell my father you were here. If not, you will answer to Xhiang."

WuTsing rubbed a sweaty palm over her throat as if he might squeeze. He must have thought better of it, because he smiled faintly and drew a finger over her cheek. "I am willing to marry you."

"You are willing to marry me," she repeated in stunned disbelief.

"It's okay to feel that way," he said gently, leaning closer to her. WuTsing silenced her by raising the palm of his hand. "I know what you are thinking. And you are at least partly right. You are not what I would have chosen if things were different."

"I'm not."

"No, you're not. But you do come from a reputed family. Under the circumstances," he shrugged, "there's little choice."

"For you maybe. I do have a choice."

He ignored her words. "I believe I found a solution to our problem."

"I don't have a problem."

"Sure you do. But you and I will beat Xhiang at his own game."

"I do not care to play games."

"Of course you do," WuTsing said so bitingly Sui looked away. "Your father will know nothing until the deed is done."

"I can't marry without his permission."

"You're right." Suddenly it was all he could do to keep from laughing recklessly. "I have his signed permission here in my hand." WuTsing swung a legal-looking document in Sui's face.

"That's forgery. Xhiang is in no condition to sign!"

"Xhiang is in no condition to deter our marriage either. Our union will place me in a position to take control of his assets immediately. As his son-in-law, I stand to inherit."

"Not while he is alive."

"All in a matter of time."

"And if I refuse to go along with you?"

"You have no choice."

"Are you serious?" The words were barely a whisper.

"Am I serious!" WuTsing stood abruptly. "In time you will come to your senses. But time is something I do not have. I will be back in two hours to get you. Be ready."

Sui did not answer.

WuTsing grabbed her arm and forced her to face him. "Don't look so upset. It's perfect."

"For whom?" she whispered to herself. Sui felt delighted suddenly, and frightened at the same time. A very difficult decision had been taken from her. With no other option, Sui knew what she had to do, for Drew, for Xhiang, and for herself.

Chapter 13

On Thursday, at twelve o'clock noon, Sui knocked and waited. The handle turned and Drew stood before her in dress uniform, his black shoes newly polished and shining. He allowed his eyes to wander to her hair she'd pulled back into a semblance of order, down to her full lips, back up to her puffy eyes, and rested on the bruise that was beginning to purple on her cheek. His eyes narrowed. "Your father?"

Sui covered the injured cheek with an unsteady hand.

Drew stiffened. "Who then?"

"It really doesn't matter."

"It does matter. No one has the right, Sui." Gentle hands grasped her shoulders and pulled her to his chest.

Sui allowed herself to let go and be comforted. She felt utterly drained. Her cheek rested against the cool fabric of his jacket. Drew's left hand spread lightly against her back.

Sickening fear made her waver. "Can we talk about it later?"

Drew set her away from him, and the grim lines on his face softened. "If we must."

Sui straightened and pushed a wisp of hair from her face.

"Did I tell you how beautiful you are?" he whispered.

Bright red crept up her cheeks. "My hands are damp with sweat, my knees are shaking, and you think I'm beautiful."

Bending his head toward hers Drew kissed her uplifted lips possessively.

The garden smelled lovely with a floral array of riotous color and the sweet scent of gardenia. As Sui looked around, she realized she knew very few of the guests. With no family and few friends present for her marriage, she approached Elliott People looking rather pale. The impact of the day began taking its toll.

"Everything will be fine," Elliott whispered softly when she and Drew stood before him.

And it was. Sui would always remember their wedding as simple and intimate. Her only attendant, Effie, beamed affectionately as she watched the couple from where she stood in her place of honor, thinking of how perfect Andrew and Sui looked together.

Drew looked very solemn in his black uniform. Noah served as best man. With earnest blue eyes, silver-streaked blond hair, and a full face of wrinkles, he beamed at the couple, sensing a special reverence of the moment.

Elliott spoke calmly, trying desperately to hide a grin. Drew couldn't seem to take his eyes off their Sui. At forty-two, little lines traced Elliott's mouth and framed his eyes in creases. But the years hadn't faded the dusting of freckles across his broad face.

"Answer the questions I present you with honesty. Afterward you may speak to one another of what's in your heart."

Drew's encouraging smile calmed Sui. While Drew made promises, she took in his well-etched features reveling in his hint of possessiveness toward her.

Elliott spoke solemnly to them both. "Marriage is a sacred union instituted by God, between a man and a woman. You will share your hopes, dreams, joy, sorrow, pain, and pleasure. You will belong to each other and to God. With God's help, our faith in Him and in each other will grow stronger each day. I assure you, He wants to help."

Elliott turned to Drew. "Drew, until today you've had only yourself to consider. Now you'll have a wife, and perhaps someday a family to care for. Are you willing to accept these responsibilities?"

Without taking his eyes off Sui, Drew answered, "I am." Pressing her hands between his own, he spoke from his heart. "I earnestly promise my love to you, Sui. I will protect you and stand beside you through the good times and the bad."

"Sui," Elliott continued, "you will be expected to love Drew, to work beside him, and have his children. Are you willing to take on these responsibilities, to forsake all others for Andrew Bach?"

Sui lifted her eyes to Drew and pressed the tips of his fingers. "I am. Andrew, I will stand beside you, have your children, comfort you, and gladly share your life with joy."

"Considering this, will you, Andrew John Bach, take Suiteiko Itsi Wong as your lawful wife, to have and to hold from this day forward, for better, for worse, for richer, for poorer, in sickness and in health, forsaking all others, so long as you both shall live?

"I will." Drew blew out a long breath that held a trace of laughter because his part of the vows was over.

"Will you, Suiteiko Itsi Wong, take Andrew John Bach, for your lawful husband, to have and to hold from this day forward, for better, for worse, for richer, for poorer, in sickness and in health, forsaking all others, so long as you both shall live?"

Sui felt her breath catch in her throat. "I will," she answered softly.

"Andrew and Suiteiko, you have chosen to bind your lives together, to share whatever comes your way. By the authority vested in me, I now pronounce you man and wife. What God has joined together, let no man put asunder. Drew, you may kiss your bride."

"I will." Drew reached for Sui and pulled her into his arms. Theirs was a gentle kiss, a kiss filled with promise and longing.

"Thank you," he whispered into her hair.

A lovelier bride never lived. Drew would remember the moment forever. The warm flush on Sui's cheeks made her dark eyes glow with a hint of rapture. Shining brown hair lifted away from her face, cascaded down past her shoulders. She looked radiant. The significance of the day enhanced her beauty. At one point Sui felt Drew tremble beside her.

"I love you, Drew." It sounded barely more than a whisper on her lips.

"I love you, Suiteiko." As if words were necessary, Drew said them in a way that left her with no question of his devotion.

Everything seemed perfect. A day that began so frightening suddenly wasn't so bad again. Drew's crew introduced themselves to pupils from Sun Yat-son School for Boys during a simple celebration afterward.

Sui never looked more beautiful than she did today, Drew thought, as they exchanged a veiled glance from across the yard where she said goodbye to Effie.

"Well, Boss, I'd say you found a keeper." Noah's deep, booming voice startled Drew from his absorption.

Drew pressed his brows together and nodded.

"We thought we might fix up your cabin while you're gone. What do you think?"

Drew straightened and frowned. "What do I think? I think you're crazy. No, you can't mess with my cabin."

"Okay, but-" He didn't finish. Obviously his suggestion didn't make Drew any too happy.

"What exactly do you consider wrong with my cabin?"

"Nothing's wrong with it."

"Then I don't understand the problem."

"Some of us guys thought it could use some frilly things to make your wife feel at home. Women like that sort of thing."

"Some of you guys," Drew repeated. Then Sui turned to face him, smiling one of those smiles that puts the sun to shame. "You could be right. I suppose Sui might appreciate that."

"What about you? Would you appreciate that?" Noah asked.

Drew shook his head, but he wasn't paying attention. He looked at Sui as if for the first time. "I don't care what you do, so long as everyone leaves us to ourselves."

"You think you'll be okay? Without me, I mean... to go along on your honeymoon?"

They both laughed, but Noah was only half joking. He'd heard rumors that someone had it in for Drew. But that wasn't unusual. There would always be a crazy out there who didn't like to see someone become more successful than themselves. Their captain possessed integrity and character. He was liked by everyone, almost.

"I'll try to manage a honeymoon without you, Noah. We'll be thrown together for an awfully long time when we cross the sea again. We can visit then, after Sui and I get back."

"When do you suppose that will be?"

Drew sort of smiled and shook his head. "I'm beginning to think you ask an awful lot of questions."

"I'm just looking out for you."

"I know. You're a great friend."

"But you've taken care of yourself long before we met," Noah finished for Drew.

"We should be back a week from Monday. That gives us just a little over a week. We'll travel upriver and stop," he shrugged, "wherever."

"Sounds like a plan. If you're sure..." Noah stopped mid-sentence, and they both laughed again.

Chapter 14

$\mathcal{S}ui$ paused for a moment to get her breath. She glanced at the watch on her slender wrist. It was nearly three o'clock. They were making good progress, with only two blocks to go.

Drew stopped and motioned for Sui to follow him. "Come on. The boat for Nanjing will leave without us."

"Hey, it's not my fault. You'd think a place as well-known as Nantong's cotton and textile mills would have a clock that keeps proper time."

"Next time we'll consult our watches."

"Next time we'll wear a mask. I thought that little lady would have a heart attack when you sneezed." Sui laughed and dabbed at the corner of her eyes with a handkerchief. She couldn't remember having laughed as much as she had in the last forty-eight hours.

"You did your share of sneezing, too, my darling wife."

"I was having trouble just breathing."

"Admit it, woman. You sneezed as often as I did."

"But I didn't cause an earthquake."

"Speaking of earthquakes, are you ready to put some earth beneath your feet?"

Sui moaned. "You start. I'll follow."

"Give me your hand or we will never make it." He took Sui's hand and pulled her along. Their boat was scheduled to leave in less than five minutes.

Tucked against the hillside, Nichiren Inn overlooked the Yangtze River, glowing obscurely in the early evening dusk. From inside their room, Sui gazed from the window. Lofty masts of ships laying at anchor could be seen beyond the bay. Soon she and Drew would sail back to Shanghai, then on to California.

Hearing the door click behind Drew, Sui turned away from the beautiful view. It was useless to plan what might be until they got there. Where they were going did not matter. What was important is that now they could travel and build a future together.

"Hungry?" Drew whispered, his hands wrapping snugly about her waist and pulling her back against the strength of his chest.

Sui shook her head. The motion tugged at a pin holding her hair. It fell to her shoulders, cascading against her face. Aware of the effect she was having on him, her soft skin flushed with happiness, her heavy lashes casting shadows over her eyes and darkening them. Drew was only too aware.

"I love you, Mrs. Bach," he whispered.

His words held such promise. Phrases from their wedding ceremony echoed through Sui's mind. *Marriage is instituted of God...to have and to hold...and two shall become one flesh.*

Slowly, Drew turned Sui and drew her into his arms. His gentle kiss gradually deepened. The waiting and longing, the uncertainty and frustration that had been buried for so long became evident.

Sui waited quietly the next morning for Drew to awaken. She remained very still, dreaming dreams of their future. The wedding had worked out perfectly. For a moment life seemed almost too perfect. She turned her head and watched Drew in quiet sleep, happier than she could remember ever having been. They were deeply in love. And they knew what they wanted out of life-to be together, to build a home and a family, to share with others. She almost wished the moment would never end.

She stretched languidly.

Drew reached for her.

"Good morning, darling. Are you-"

They were interrupted by a soft knock on the door.

Drew closed his eyes, then opened them again. "Yeah?"

"Breakfast on table," a boy's voice said in chopped English.

"Thanks." Drew grinned, moving closer to Sui. "You are incredible, do you know that?"

"So are you, love," Sui replied, pulling away a little and pushing back the sheet. "But we can't disappoint our host by letting breakfast get cold. Besides, I'm famished."

Drew dropped back against his pillow and groaned. Sui laughed and threw clothes at him. "Please hurry, Drew. I'm starving."

Nanjing resembled a small version of Shanghai. They were content to stroll, and eventually ended up at an *Owyang* shop they discovered. They went in and browsed through racks of ready-made garments. Drew purchased whatever caught her eye. After an hour, Sui refused to look. But that didn't stop Drew. He found an imported Regency hat and jacket. The high-crowned hat, trimmed in sealskin, had an ostrich feather attached to the right side and pulled across the crown to droop over her left ear. The long-sleeved matching jacket, with rich fabric and epaulet shoulders, was trimmed in identical sealskin.

"You must have them," Drew told her. "It's what affluent ladies are wearing in California." So while Drew was busy paying for their purchases, Sui couldn't resist buying him an elegant outfit. The clerk promised it was the rage of men in China. She also purchased matching *geta*, a Japanese pair of clogs.

"Where will I ever wear these?" Drew asked, laughing. Yet he seemed very pleased that someone cared enough to buy him something. He was touched and considered it a very special thing for Sui to do.

Later that afternoon she came across a pea jacket and a pair of white jean pants, imported from America. Drew thought it silly to purchase them in China. They would be in America soon anyway. But he felt pleased because of his wife's generosity toward him.

With overflowing arms, they walked into an elegant clothing emporium, immediately noticing veiled stares directed their way. Sui watched in fascination. Should she inform them that Americans weren't so strange, after all, that feelings and basic emotions were the same in people no matter where they lived, or what they looked like? Even as she considered mentioning it, she smiled to herself and walked along, wondering suddenly if Chinese faced the same discrimination living outside of their own country. Possibly.

But she didn't take time to dwell on her musings. Drew filled his arms with women's garments again. Sui protested that once they reached California she fully intended to dress in western wear. But the shop was very pretty and they loved it.

It was romantic being alone together. They rowed boats and went for long walks. Sui even taught Drew to play *fan tan*, a game of chance.

Like two children without a care in the world, they wandered down streets, between buildings and along sun-drenched walkways. Pressing between shoppers, they made their way through the door of a rather large warehouse, or *godown*. In a hive of activity, they were formally greeted by the head of the trading house, the *tai pan*, and his wife, the *tai tai*. The couple received many interested glances as they stepped over and picked their way between crates, casks, and piles of boxes. Drew's hand cupped Sui's elbow to keep her from being forced into the throng of people.

Inching their way along the aisles, they observed booths piled high with fish nets, bean curds, green grass snakes, various silk fabric, food stuffs, and every sort of geegaw. Vendors all but lived behind crates and boxes. Forced voices shouted out everything from noodles in thin broth to thick creamy sauces, awaiting someone to stop long enough to listen. The area remained smelly, noisy, and bustling. In the main body of the swarm, three men shoved massive crates filled with squawking chickens along the congested aisle, urging the crowd to allow them through with grunts and frowns.

Nowhere else in the world was shopping taken so seriously as China. Hawkers on the street were generally willing to go just a little lower than their original price. The dull clamor of scraping feet and low-voiced conversations became deafening. But Drew and Sui escaped safely, laughing all the while.

Later, they enjoyed the balmy afternoon, just warm enough for a picnic. Except for a few boats moaning and inching their way along, the river remained nearly deserted. From where they sat along the bank, dinghies and skiffs bobbed on gentle waves.

Sui spread lunch out on a white cloth. The hotel kitchen supplied them with crispy chicken, bok choy, and mixed vegetables in a lightly seasoned garlic sauce.

Drew talked for a while about the *Marybeth* and about his holdings, which were extensive and encompassed a wide area. In addition to three ships, he owned two houses, three riverboats, and a small fleet of fishing boats. And two years ago he'd purchased a sawmill in Michigan as an investment.

"Recently I hired a foreman to manage the business. It was struggling when I purchased it. The place is beginning to turn a tidy profit again."

"Do you think you'll ever go back?" Sui asked. Then she yawned. The sun felt warm, the food tasted good, and she felt very content propped against Drew on a blanket.

"I might. It would be a nice place to raise a family."

"Better than California?"

"I think so. There aren't nearly as many people. With all the commotion caused by the gold rush, you can't hear yourself think."

Sui laughed. "Is that a western term?"

Drew rolled onto his side so he could look down at her. "Are you laughing at me?"

With a small smile, she nodded. "I guess I am."

"Well, don't." Then he bent forward gently and kissed her on the tip of her nose, his breath fanning her hair intimately. Sui kissed him back, thinking how nicely she fit in his arms. Murmuring his name, she slid one arm around his neck, the other across the broad shoulder. Deep scar grooves crisscrossed his back. She'd noticed them before and wondered what could possibly have caused such brutish marks, but she hadn't wanted to embarrass Drew by mentioning them.

Drew positioned himself so he could look into her face and smiled sleepily. Her eyes radiated that soft glow she saved for only him, and it pleased him. But he also recognized the question on her face, raised a brow, and shifted. "What?"

"It's your back. It looks almost as if someone shredded it. What happened?"

Drew rolled over without taking his eyes off her. "Which time?"

"Oh."

"Foster homes aren't always what they're cracked up to be. But some were actually quite nice."

Sui lay stretched out on her back with her hand resting beneath her head on Drew's lap. She swallowed lumps of emotion while she listened. When he stopped talking, she rolled to her side so she could look into his face.

"You were a very lonely little boy."

Drew chuckled softly. "Hey, what's this? You're not crying?" He raised Sui's hand and touched it to his lips.

"Yes, I am," she said very softly. "It's just so sad."

He took her face in both hands and held it tenderly, his thumbs stirring softly just beside her mouth. "We all have a story, Sui. Some things are better left in the past, so let's forget it."

Sui knew she never would. But she would spend the rest of her life trying to make up for all the pain Drew ever suffered.

"I love you, Drew."

He sighed and pulled her closer so her head rested on his chest. "I love you, too."

"You know, don't you, that I began to love you the first time we met?" She whispered in his ear.

"And I became haunted by you every minute I was gone. I love everything about you. Your intelligence, your nature, your kind heart." And when she pulled his head down and kissed him, he knew she felt the same way he did.

Sui saw their trip come to an end with a combination of regret and excitement-regret that they would no longer share the intimacy a strange city allows, and eagerness of traveling to the unknown. They'd had a wonderful time.

On their last night, they paddled a boat out to a tiny fishing island and had dinner beneath a bamboo shelter. After dinner they walked along the line of huts. From inside, they could see musicians tuning up their instruments for the festival that would begin the moment the sun went down.

With hazy twilight, torches were lit. Firelight sparked all around them. Spicy fish and hot bread whetted their appetite. Far away, a glistening ocean hid the world beyond their hideaway island, giving the impression of leaving the real world far behind, and all responsibilities with it.

Because of unseasonably warm weather there was no need to seek shelter. When the festival broke up, they found a place to make themselves comfortable on the beach.

Drew teased, Sui laughed. They talked for hours, and they fell asleep together. But something awakened Drew several hours later, in the darkest part of the night. Lights had been extinguished. Glowing embers of earlier brilliant fires remained, smoldering with an occasional flare.

Drew lay on his side and pulled Sui protectively against his shoulder, her face buried in his chest. While his gentle fingertips stroked her dark tendrils, she stirred drowsily. Drew watched her chest rise and fall, breathing comfortably in her sleep. Lightly he caressed her smooth skin with the tip of his tough, callused finger. Then taking her hand in his, Drew pulled it to his mouth, lightly kissing each fingertip, his mouth slowly trailing a path across her face until he came to her ear. He lazily nipped her ear lobe.

Sui stretched and yawned contentedly, opening first one eye, then the other. "You're looking very contented, Mr. Bach."

"I have reason to be. I happen to be married to a very lovely, very wonderful woman."

She leaned back to admire him and found herself being drawn closer. "As wonderful as my husband?" Nestling in his arms, she enjoyed his gentleness, his warmth, and the feel of his hair as it wound around her fingers.

Drew's mouth curled in a lazy smile. He chuckled. The deep rumbling in his chest sent a tingle rushing through her. He had waited twenty-seven years for a special afternoon in Shanghai. Thousands of miles from home, he had taken Sui for his wife. And it was good.

Chapter 15

$\mathcal{D}rew$ turned his head and his heart stopped. Something stirred. From the corner of his eye, he chanced a glance into the shadowed rocks and brush. Nothing conspicuous moved. He looked from bush to bush. A shadow moved. Drew saw it. Turning his head sharply, he watched a wild cat stalk across the road.

Drew eased around a bend in the road, keeping as hidden as possible. The same ominous forewarning that began when he opened his eyes this morning returned. It grew and gathered strength as the wagon ate up miles.

Bright day darkened to make way for a cool night. A quarter moon hung low, illuminating the waterfront so far below. Ships swayed hull to hull, their lights glowing through portholes to silhouette darkly against a pale sky.

Drew hitched the reigns, reminding the sluggish donkey it wasn't time to stop yet.

Sui pressed close beside him, lifted his right arm, and slid beneath it. "Cold?"

"Kind of."

Drew leaned behind the seat and pulled out his jacket. Much too large, it trailed below Sui's hands and knees. She pulled it tight and breathed in Drew's manly scent. "Do you realize we'll be aboard the *Marybeth* in less than an hour?"

"Are you going to miss China?"

"I will miss having you all to myself. I'm going to remember our honeymoon for as long as I live."

He drew her fingers to his lips and kissed each one individually. "There will be more honeymoons, I promise."

Sui cuddled closer. "But they will never be like our first. The first time is always more special."

In a terrible instant, Drew's earlier apprehension became reality. The blast didn't come from anywhere in particular. It simply erupted, the deafening burst alarming the donkeys who were trudging along half asleep. As they reared into the air, Drew reached for the terrified animals. He tried to straighten. Another explosion threw him off balance. He tried to grasp Sui. His body shot through thin air.

Sui saw his fingers spread wide. They reached for her.

His hand closed inches from her own outstretched fingers. Another eruption. The buggy gave a mighty lurch. Propelled into the night air, the couple came back down, glancing off rough ground. The ravine's edge hastened forward. Suddenly they were spinning in air, over and over. While in horizontal freefall, Drew heard Sui scream. The desperate sound never stopped. It kept ringing in his ears.

Six airborne seconds didn't allow a lengthy prayer. Rushing air stole his breath. Drew's spirit pleaded for Sui's protection

A limb slapped his slick, sweaty hand. He reached out frantically for a gnarled branch. It snapped, holding an instant before it gave way. Clumps of coarse grass showed no mercy. They ripped at palms, tore away fingernails, and forced him into another downward plunge over the embankment.

An angled tree rushed past him. Drew reached out and caught a branch. The sudden stop pulled at his arm in a great thrust that stopped his descent and snatched him from certain death. His left arm snapped. Angry darts shot up his shoulder. After what seemed like a lifetime, Drew came to an abrupt halt.

He struggled up the embankment. Within inches of reaching his goal, he slid, going into a second gut-wrenching drop. His skull connected with a slab of granite. Consciousness exploded like a pressurized volcano. Fiery molten lava spiraled away from the center and dimmed. All went utterly black.

Drew lay face down on an outcropping boulder, held by unconscious thought.

Chapter 16

Gravity played a cruel game. Sui could do nothing to avoid stones raining down on her. Outcropping rocks struck her a battery of blows. Arms and legs bounced off jagged edges, reaching out to tear away. The abrupt halt happened so suddenly, it startled her. Gripped with pain and the need to draw a breath, agony clutched and held her prone like leaden weight.

The slightest movement proved torturous. Sharp pain in her head grew with intensity, radiating across her cheek, to encompass her left ear. Fiery darts shot up her neck and seized the base of her skull. Her stomach rolled with the taste and smell of blood. She gagged. Her tongue encountered a gaping hole tunneling through her cheek. She heard the sound of her own gulping shallow breaths. Voices faded in and out of her consciousness, the words echoing as if whispered from inside a canyon.

The sky that appeared a considerable distance from earth earlier, began to flow downward, closer and closer, until she was able to reach out and touch it. For a long time she floated on rings of light into space. Sui fought a battle for life and felt herself losing. Slowly, light faded into darkness.

WuTsing found Sui cradled on a slab of hard stone, a bloodied hand pressed to her torn cheek. With supreme effort, he pulled himself back from guilty thoughts pressing in on him. His fingers roamed her aimlessly, assessing damage as best he could. The uneven rising and falling of her chest did little to reassure him. If she died, his designs to infiltrate Xhiang's trust, and eventually his business, died with her. She alone held the means of continuing his success.

Rolling her over, he fumbled for a position across his shoulder. The trip upward went slowly. Weight made him pant with each faltering step. By not looking where he placed his feet, he inadvertently lost a foothold and fell to his knees. His cursing ripped the air as his own blood mingled with Sui's, his pant leg and shirt now drenched in both.

WuTsing shifted Sui's dead weight and straightened up. Intent on reaching the top, not a sound registered in his active mind. WuTsing continued forward.

Chapter 17

The police officer flicked his cigar into the dark, the glow shooting a red light against the dusky shadows. He cupped his hands to his mouth and shouted an order to the retreating back of a junior officer. Wind combed through his black hair restlessly. His glance moved suspiciously from Rob, across the other men, and rested on Noah.

"Name's Li Zhao. What are you men doing out this late?"

"We're looking for a friend of ours. That's his ship, anchored over there. He should have been back hours ago." Noah climbed down from the vehicle and patted the closest sweat-streaked mule. He remained too anxious from the adrenaline rush of the recent explosion to notice the oppressive humidity in the air.

The wind picked up speed, but Li Zhao seemed content to watch them intently. He stood big and powerful, straight and tall. His face showed no expression as he studied each man individually with penetrating eyes.

"You'd better pray your friend had nothing to do with this. Some crazed lunatic not only dynamited this bridge, he took out the entire south road." The officer's face showed nothing, but he gave Seth and Peyton a hard and measuring look, with no give. "You don't know anything about this, do you?"

"Only that we didn't do it." Being under suspicion in Shanghai could be as dangerous as being found guilty. Shanghai made rules where foreigners were concerned. Peyton sensed the atmosphere becoming charged. Officers began drifting away from their posts.

"Very creative, aren't you?" A glow of triumph lit Li Zhao's eyes and brought a satisfied curve to his lips.

Seth sighed, his expression turning very serious. "I know how this must look, a group of men wandering the streets after dark. We came here to check out the explosion. If our duty to Drew-"

Li Zhao cut in. "Drew?"

"Andrew Bach. He hasn't arrived from a trip he went on."

"When do you expect him back?" Li Zhao looked impatient and irritated.

"Any time. We felt the explosion and rushed over."

"I don't suppose you happen to be carrying explosives, or maybe weapons?"

Jeff shrugged. "Nothing but a revolver."

"Why do you carry a gun?"

"Protection."

"Under normal circumstances there would be no problem. We received this bit of excitement tonight. I'm not taking any chances."

Noah pretended not to mind the long seconds that dragged by while Li Zhao's men made a careful inspection of the wagon.

"Fortunately for you, we haven't found anything indicative here. How about your friend, is he in the habit of messing with explosives?"

"Not at all." Noah held his position until the officer dropped his grave demeanor.

"What reason do you have to check out the blast, besides your, ah...missing friend?" Li Zhao gave them a long, considering look.

"A man in Drew's position gathers his share of enemies."

"A man in his position?"

"Andrew Bach is captain of the *Marybeth*. Men with his wealth and power become the target of jealousy." Noah swatted at an insect whirring near his face, faintly conscious of the loud sound.

Sweat trickled down his chest. Li Zhao wiped at it. Two weeks ago he'd been out fishing. Thick fog had rolled in quickly. He paused to get his bearings. One minute he had pulled in his laden net, the next he was lost at sea. Certain his boat would capsize with him in it, he gave up hope after hours of fog as thick as mud.

The dark frame of a ship had appeared out of the gray mist. He shouted. The *Marybeth* made a wide arc, came back, and slid up along side of his teetering craft. Drew manned the ship that had taken him to a storm-darkened shore, where reeds twisted wildly beneath the wind.

Now Li Zhao faced Drew's group squarely and pulled himself to full height. Conditions suggested their guilt. Under ordinary circumstances, Li Zhao would take them in to stand trial. Not these men. Guilty or not, he owed Drew his life.

"I could take you in." He raised his palm for silence. "It looks as though you win this time. Follow me."

Within minutes of leaving the bridge, they reached a point in the road where it forked sharply to the left. Noah braked to a stop next to an abandoned wagon. It looked out of place parked on the grassy shoulder.

Except on foot, they would never get past the large rift in the road. Obviously the bridge hadn't been the only area destroyed by dynamite. Drew's men climbed the embankment and paused to look beyond the rising terrain. Wind whistling through rock clefts competed with dead silence. They heard no shouts, no footsteps on crunching gravel.

That didn't reassure Noah much. "I'll be over here." Noah crossed the road toward the chasm on the other side. Rob followed.

Freshly rutted ground between clumps of grass formed a twisted path. Darkened earth revealed tracks, corroborating his suspicion that someone had been there recently.

Rob slowed his steps when Noah did. Wind blew at his back through the thin cotton of his shirt. He was the first to spot the shattered cart below, held precariously to a fallen tree branch by the metal tongue. "I'd say we found the boss."

"I guess we know what this means, Rob."

They moved in single file, slowly, through broken branches. As they neared the rocky ledge, Noah heard a sharp crash of falling rocks. A shout of pain followed. He and Rob hit the ground instantly.

"What do you think?" Rob's voice lowered to a whisper. After making a swift glance of the area, he slid forward on his belly. "It doesn't sound like Drew. Maybe it's an injured animal."

"That settles it. Animals don't make that sort of noise. I have a feeling we'll find the boss here."

After a deep-throated laugh, Rob whispered, "You know it really ticks Drew off when you call him 'boss'."

"Yeah? If only he was here to hear me now."

"What do we do?" Rob rolled along side of him.

Noah had been wondering the same thing. Gravel rumbled below again, kicking up powdery dust just to the left of where they lay crouched.

"I'm not certain." With Drew's disappearance and the deplorable explosion, there was no telling what other unexpected calamity might add to the scene.

Stooping low and using the branch of a young tree for support, Noah inched his way closer, moving past Rob. Jeff, Jason, Seth, and Li Zhao stayed some thirty yards away, busy checking out the abandoned wagon.

Noah pressed a hand to Rob's shoulder. "Stay here."

"Where are you going?"

"Over there." With a jerk of his thumb, Noah indicated the direction they'd heard movement last. "If there's any trouble, cover me."

"Wouldn't you say that's Officer Li Zhao's job?"

"Do you see him offering help?"

"You're right. I hope he finds what he's looking for in that beat up wagon."

In spite of the wind, sweat trickled down Noah's back as he worked his way through weeds along the rocky border. With a likely location fixed in his mind, Noah made his way toward it. From his immediate right, he heard shuffling. It sounded close. A great deal closer than he expected. Cautiously, he stepped toward a clump of tall weeds. Through leafy foliage, he watched a man hunched over and leaning against a rocky wall. His attention remained focused on the incline and the woman he carried. He didn't see several men pilfering through his wagon.

Noah withdrew a step. When the man topped the rise, he became clearly visible. From where he stood, nearly hidden, Noah studied the situation close up. He had a vague memory of having seen the Chinese man, but he couldn't remember where.

Noah wet his lips, aware of heavy pounding in his chest. When the man stood panting directly in front of him, Noah waited a second, then reached out and tapped him on the shoulder.

WuTsing had a spot of white in the middle of each flushed cheek. His black eyes flashed. He jerked away from Noah, taking Sui with him. Noah grabbed an arm in one hand, spinning WuTsing around to face him.

The impact of his rescue paled to the jolt WuTsing received when he looked into the hard eyes of his enemy. Fear of discovery reached out and clutched him. He lacked an alibi during the explosion. His mind raced to find a plausible excuse for being there.

WuTsing stood boldly facing Noah, his skin crawling. He knew all about the man with the bushy eyebrows. He felt a shiver go down his spine and uneasily shifted Sui.

She was wet with blood. The limp swaying of her head made Noah sick in the pit of his stomach. He swallowed to stave off a wave of nausea. Even so, he couldn't take his eyes off the grisly sight of her left cheek nearly torn from her face. Finally he lifted his eyes to avoid looking at the once beautiful hair, now sticky and matted to her head. Her eyes appeared glassy and unseeing.

"What did she ever to do you?" Noah's steely eyes threatened. Li Zhao crossed the intervening distance, and the scene erupted in a commotion of frantic action.

"I found the woman. She is dead," WuTsing explained, hoping it wasn't true. A strange kind of anger twisted his face.

"Are you a member of the medical team then?" Noah demanded. WuTsing's detached intensity grated Noah's composure. "Do you make a habit of climbing down the bare edge of nothing to bring up dead women?"

"What's going on here?" Li Zhao's glance ran from the unconscious Sui to the blood-covered hands of WuTsing.

WuTsing slouched onto his right leg. He grunted and rolled Sui around in his arms.

Li Zhao struck a match, sheltered the flame in his hand, and calmly lit a thick cigar. "You can go lay her in the wagon if you want."

Under Li Zhao's watchful eye, WuTsing headed straight for the vehicle he'd left parked on the shoulder of the road. His horse stood beneath a tree he'd tied her to earlier. She fidgeted nervously. The smell of fresh blood disturbed her. WuTsing let Sui slip from his hands and tumble onto the rough floor of the wagon. The dark blanket he tossed her way hid a pulse alongside a very bruised throat. Disheveled hair lay in damp ribbons. Arteries pulsed rapidly close to the surface. WuTsing's hands came away wet with blood.

"Now, tell me what happened." Li Zhao blew a cloud of smoke, giving his men a silent signal with a nod. They closed in.

"She is dead." WuTsing's eyes darted from one officer to the other.

"That's not what I asked. What are you doing out here?"

WuTsing hesitated and ran a hand across his suddenly dry mouth.

"You just can't stay out of trouble, can you, WuTsing?"

WuTsing's tension went up a notch. "You can't possibly be serious. You would never trust one of these foreign devils over one of your own countrymen."

"I'm deadly serious." Li Zhao tossed his cigar into the dirt and ground it beneath his heel. "Where were you when this road and bridge were blown up?"

They watched WuTsing go still and knew Li Zhao had struck a vulnerable spot.

"You insult me. If you're so devoted to your own country, you would think twice before daring to question me."

"On the contrary, WuTsing. What kind of leader would I be if you were allowed to blow up the country on a whim? Now, where were you when this road vanished?"

"Xhiang Wong sent me to find his daughter. And I did."

Li Zhao froze. A sense of dread surfaced with a rush. Far too experienced to let it show in his expression, his face remained blank. But it reddened. A rush of color briefly eliminated the sudden pallor of his skin. You didn't cross Xhiang Wong, not if you were smart. To become his enemy meant certain peril.

"Take the woman to her home immediately, and WuTsing-"

"Yes."

"Send my regards to Xhiang."

"As you wish." WuTsing smiled in silent understanding, a faint gleam of triumph in his black eyes. Then, with impeccable manners, he bowed before Li Zhao.

Noah stepped back before saying something he would have been sorry for later. Bracing solid arms against his broad chest, he waited for his eyes to adjust to darkness.

"What happened?"

Noah relaxed a tightly clenched jaw. He hadn't heard Rob follow him.

"Li Zhao just allowed Suiteiko's killer to escape."

"Welcome to China," Rob answered.

Noah shook his head. "Welcome to the world."

They found Drew wedged between a crevice in the rocks. It took nearly an hour to remove him in one piece. His crew cheered silently when he reached the top. Their pleased looks faded when they witnessed the limp look of death. Drew's breathing made an awful set and raspy sound. With his face hidden in shadow, they didn't see hair matted slick with blood.

Noah ran his fingers along the back of his head. He felt the spongy fracture. A finger alongside Drew's throat held a small degree of promise. He still breathed, but just barely.

"He's alive!" Li Zhao shouted. "Someone bring an ambulance!"

Noah's stomach lurched. "Forty men are counting on you to take them back home, boss. And don't you be forgetting it." Noah pressed a hand against his shoulder. He felt better reminding Drew of things he'd accomplished and everything for which he had to live.

Crouching low and using what cover the tall grass offered, WuTsing watched Li Zhao kneeling beside the foreigner. He glanced at the blood seeping from a broken arm and trickling down Drew's crushed skull. Some part of his mind registered satisfaction. The foreigner would always be an interloper, a provoking stranger who deserved all he got. It made him sick with disgust to see the way people worried over Drew.

Chapter 18

Through the entire ordeal, WuTsing remained stunned. His feet dragged as he eased Sui around and through Xhiang's doorway. Dropping Sui into bed, he arranged the necessary changes in her position, made a fast examination of her pulse, checked for respirations, then drew his first truly comfortable breath.

He took another, this time his brow drawing together in a frown. Satisfaction and pride replaced initial apprehension. Xhiang seemed to believe Sui's present predicament purely chance.

While Xhiang ordered Sui to her previous room, he poured himself a drink, waiting for WuTsing to explain what happened. So much can be said by a person's body language, he thought. WuTsing limped into the library. Xhiang deliberated on his fixed eyes and lack of facial expression. Nervous fidgeting told their own story.

"Thank you for allowing me the honor of returning your daughter, Xhiang," WuTsing bowed deeply. "I trust you find no fault with my ministrations."

Distaste glimmered through Xhiang's expression. He banished all signs of it from his face, sensing the man's desire for praise. WuTsing's pleased look faded with Xhiang's continued silence.

"I did everything in my power to assure your daughter be returned to you. I realize now I should have been more aware of Suiteiko's activities. I do accept the blame for that. I beg you do not hold it against me."

Xhiang reddened. Rapid color hid the sickly pallor of his skin.

"Under the circumstances, I trust you consider freeing me of the debt I owe. As you may be aware, I became Suiteiko's protector during your, ah, while you recuperated."

"In that case, I am disappointed, WuTsing. As her protector, I would have thought you possessed more control over Sui. I've been told Suiteiko ran off with another man, a foreigner."

Xhiang continued to gauge WuTsing, resisting the overwhelming urge to order the man from his house. He restrained his impulse, making a loath decision to hear him out. His facial cast didn't change, but an icy spark glimmered in the dark depths of his eyes.

WuTsing shifted restlessly. If Xhiang was pleased to have Sui home, he certainly kept it to himself. "May I suggest that given the authority, Suiteiko would never have caused you this embarrassment." Immediately his eyes flinched at his ill-chosen words. "I mean, I didn't mean that to sound..."

Xhiang's eyebrows raised slightly. He looked WuTsing over with cool thoroughness. At times it became essential to think like one's adversary. Xhiang did that now. He looked inside WuTsing's mind, calculating his next move. "Of course. Be that as it may, I am still her authority."

WuTsing took the moment to wipe the light film of perspiration from his brow with a silk handkerchief, choosing his words carefully. "I am pleased you are looking well."

"Are you really? Does it gladden your heart that I am able to take charge of my concerns once again?" The corner's of Xhiang's mouth twitched and thinned to a knowing sneer.

WuTsing didn't respond. In between darting his eyes across the steel gray of modern Chinese art, he looked out the window at blank darkness. He didn't know Xhiang had only just discovered his part in the attempted take over of Xhiang's business long before and during his illness. Had WuTsing known, he would have fled with his life.

Xhiang's fingers curled tightly around his glass. He still couldn't figure out how WuTsing could have deluded him for so long. He wasn't easily misled. The man had deceived him, and he had to pay for it. Xhiang only regretted it took so long to find out. If the rest of the world found out, he would not only lose face. His reputation would suffer, opening the way for someone with more intelligence to attempt the same.

Xhiang cocked his brow at a sinister angle, shooting the other man the kind of withering look he would give to an insipid dolt. "Have you any idea who Suiteiko stayed with all week? It wasn't you, was it?"

"I would never take your daughter...without your blessing, of course."

Xhiang listened to the lie with a blank expression while silence stretched uncomfortably. When WuTsing bowed, Xhiang resisted an overwhelming desire to strike out at him.

"We are not wed."

Xhiang cocked his head. "Say that again."

"What?"

"You are not what?" Xhiang demanded.

In that moment, WuTsing realized his mistake. His eyes opened wide. It suddenly occurred to him that he might have been handling Xhiang wrong. Changing his approach hit him with a force that snapped his head up. "We are not wed. Out of respect for you, Xhiang, I am willing to take Suiteiko off your hands."

Xhiang stood there stunned.

A very surprised WuTsing gave him a knowing smile. "I know ways to break her spirit, to still her rash tendencies."

"Oh, and how exactly do you plan to do that?"

"I don't think I need explain to a man of your wisdom." WuTsing drew a calming breath and forced it to escape slowly. He must stay focused on the solution, not his problem. Suiteiko held his ticket to Xhiang's fortune. After going out on the limb with drug lords, he would need Xhiang's good will if he expected help to further his ambition.

Xhiang regarded WuTsing with dormant, seething anger. "You speak as a fool!"

WuTsing clenched his jaw. "I thought you would be grateful for the rescue of your only daughter."

"There you go thinking again, WuTsing. How fitting that you brought her here then. How fortunate for Sui," Xhiang said unfeelingly.

"She may have died if I hadn't found her."

Xhiang raised a inquisitive brow and stared at WuTsing intently. "How did you find her?"

An ice cold hand began squeezing at WuTsing's heart. "I told you, I-"

"Ah, yes. You just happened to be there when she encountered trouble. How touching."

"I didn't hurt her," WuTsing voiced raggedly, running a trembling hand through his hair. This encounter was becoming more difficult than he'd imagined. WuTsing wasn't blind to Xhiang's unwavering composure and unperceiving cruelty. He would make an appalling opponent. Xhiang proved capable of coercion.

"Did I accuse you of being responsible for Sui's misfortune?" Xhiang asked calmly, pouring himself another drink. "The girl deserves what she got." He stood up then. "I'm tired," he said, walking from the room.

The most uncanny thing happened next. On his way out the door, Xhiang stopped, turned, and silently stared at WuTsing. Then, as if he could read WuTsing's mind, he answered the man's unspoken question.

"I assume you realize you are no longer in my employ."

WuTsing's mouth dropped open. Frustration made his dead eyes come alive. He'd expected a promotion. Now he found himself without a job. Contemplating Sui and her connection to Xhiang's fortune, he grew frantic when Xhiang jerked his thumb toward the door as a silent order to leave. WuTsing backed away slowly.

"Oh, and Suiteiko is out of the question. Even she deserves better." His tone implied WuTsing didn't have a choice.

WuTsing straightened and braced a fist on the door frame. But Xhiang didn't witness his most dominant assertion. While blazing eyes bore through him, Xhiang calmly closed the door between them.

Chapter 19

Doctor Jind Wu shook his head slowly. "No more do. Wait, see." He waited to make sure Noah understood. He hadn't been born in Shanghai. His family owned a small stable of milk cows. Raised in the farm community of Sikh, his Cantonese accent became rather hard to follow. His voice grew loud. He slapped the palm of his left hand on the right.

"Arm..." he shrugged. "You see head. Big in front. On other, nothing."

In his sixties, his small frame slightly stooped, Jind Wu possessed an unusual enthusiasm for life. A quick glance at his gold timepiece indicated that two hours had passed. "I go to clinic. Patients so impatient."

He paused and looked at Noah with a grin. Long ago, Jind Wu Tsing had put away thoughts he might have had about the humorous side of life. Lately he had begun looking at life differently. Humor felt good, and he'd just made a funny play on words. He began to repeat it and abruptly sobered. Noah's grave concern for Drew deepened lines on the man's face.

"I come back tomorrow," he assured Noah. But he was quite certain there would be no need for a doctor by then. The only service Drew would likely have need of was that of an undertaker. But you never knew. The patient was still young, in his late twenties. And prior to the accident Drew was in healthy physical condition.

"Thank you for coming on such short notice, doctor." Noah couldn't remember a time he'd ever felt quite so tired. His eyes burned and his head ached. While they stood there talking, a gust of cool air awakened and refreshed him.

"I do more, but...." the doctor shrugged hopelessly.

At a loss for words, Noah nodded. It was hard to believe Drew had been breathing when they'd found him in the valley gorge, considering his concussion. Added to the severe fracture of his arm, his cheeks were sliced with

100

cuts and abrasions. But his head concerned them most. They'd had to shave it, exposing a particularly deep, oozing gash. If the concussion didn't kill him first, word of Sui's death would likely finish the job.

Noah had been tempted to go to the authorities for proof of Sui's demise. But an investigation would force them to remain anchored for who knows how long. At a minimum, he would be answering questions for days. And he wasn't excited about dealing with a powerful foreign government.

Noah gazed into the distance. "Drew doesn't deserve to die yet. Maybe God will be merciful and spare him. The man is an extraordinary person," he said, unable to meet the doctor's eyes, to witness hopelessness there.

"I be back," the doctor said with a sad smile. He knew how hard it was to lose someone special. And it was plain that Drew's entire crew shared a special bond with their captain that was hard to find.

"No need. We'll be pulling out momentarily."

"As you say," Dr. Jind Wu agreed politely. Then he bowed and he left.

It became an unending night for Noah, a night of hope and despair. For Drew, darkness overflowed with fever and delirium. In his hallucinations, Sui called his name. A strong undertow pulled her beneath the water's surface and out to sea. Frantically he reached for her. His hand came back empty. He watched helplessly as her body disappeared beneath an opening in a rock foundation that separated them. He followed her beneath the water's surface. The need for air filled him with urgency. He sucked in salt water. His lungs ached, and then they burned.

Drew longed to end the struggle. But if he gave up, Sui would be lost forever. With a powerful thrust of his legs, his body lunged against the undercurrent. And suddenly he joined her through a hidden gap. With great relief, they ascended together.

The noise of waves lapping at the hull of the *Marybeth* roused Drew from disturbing sleep. He opened his eyes to darkness. Disoriented, he sat up quickly and was attacked by waves of nausea, dizziness, and sharp pain that shot up his arm and centered in his head. Drew held his head with one hand and squeezed his eyes shut, but the painful burning continued.

As memory returned, Drew realized he was in his cabin on the *Marybeth*. Why couldn't he remember coming aboard? Stretching his aching limbs, Drew moaned and fell back against the pillows. Something pricked at his arm. He touched the splint and remembered his arm breaking in the fall. It hurt almost as much as the knife twisting in his heart for Sui.

He felt the gentle sway of the ship and knew they had set sail. Eventually he allowed himself to relax, confident Noah would never leave the shores of Shanghai without Sui. She was probably in the galley now, making the cook laugh with her spontaneously naïve ways.

Drew awoke two hours later. His face flushed bright red with fever. He blinked hazily and groaned. Pain exploded from his arm and the back of his head. He heard someone mutter something about lying still and he did. A pair of hands released him, then another. With tremendous effort he braced himself on his left elbow, attempting to raise his head. But even the most simple action brought forth a scream of protest.

He muttered something to Sui. He couldn't hear himself speak. Just before he gave in to welcoming darkness, he reached deliriously to the oppo-site side of his bunk, automatically feeling for her. When his hand met cool, empty sheets, he opened one eye, knowing with a sinking heart she wasn't there. Lowering his head to the pillow, he stared into the darkness, wonder-ing where she may have gone and trying to remember why.

It may have been a moment or it could have been days later. Drew thought he heard a familiar voice speaking as if through a tunnel. His temperature remained far from normal. Through a feverish haze, he recognized Noah's voice. "Easy, boss. You're going to hurt yourself thrashing around like that."

A shadow passed over Noah's usually cheery face as he tried to think of some sort of treatment he hadn't already thought of. Drew's fever returned in the late afternoon, followed by chills and hallucinations. What continued to surprise Noah was that Drew's heart kept beating when his respiration's remained so arrhythmic.

By morning Drew seemed to have left them. The ship became unusual-ly silent as each man grieved. Prayers made their way to the throne of God. Even those who had never believed prayed to a God they'd never believed in. And God must have agreed with their requests. By noon Drew began breath-ing peacefully.

When Drew halfway came to three days later, he was on his side. His head felt as if it had been used for a battering ram. For hours he lay in silence and didn't hear so much as a whisper. But over time, the sweet sound of water slapping against the ship's hull became a dull roar. It sounded like music to his ears. And the gentle sway of the ship lulled him to sleep.

Some eight hours later he awoke and became conscious of heavy foot-steps and voices coming from the main deck above. Everything looked dark again. Drew immediately assumed something was terribly wrong. The entire crew remained awake in the darkest part of night.

Forcing himself into an upright position, Drew sucked in air and moaned. A wave rocked the ship and threw him back. Jagged shafts of light danced in front of his eyes. Unaware of the passing of time, Drew awoke to the squeak of a chair and words that came at him from above and behind.

"About time you woke up," Noah said through a tunnel. He touched Drew's forehead and rested it there for a few seconds. "I think you might just make it."

Drew clamped the edge of the mattress and rolled on his side. His voice rasped beyond recognition. The water he was offered did little to restore it.

Drew asked about a light. Too low and garbled to understand, Noah didn't pay much attention. Drew may still be delirious. After bouncing his head off rocks, that was understandable. Within seconds he was out again.

As he dreamed, Drew relived his dreadful encounter with the rocks.

The bright day darkened to make way for a cool night. Ships along the waterfront swayed hull to hull, silhouetted darkly against the pale sky. Light glowed through portholes, illuminating the waterfront they headed toward. The moon hung low, just bright enough to illuminate the peaceful scene below.

Drew hitched the reigns, reminding the forgetful donkey not to stop. Then the explosion. In his nightmare, Drew relived the rearing of the animal, the shrill shriek of metal as the jolting wagon separated, and the forward momentum propelling it askew. With a mighty lurch, they were thrown free of the wagon. They slid across loose gravel. The ravine hastened forward.

Over and over Sui screamed. Drew reached for her. Just short of touching his hand, she flailed helplessly in the opposite direction, hurling into thin air. His head seemed to explode. He took his last breath.

Drew awoke with a start, immersed in sweat. He lurched up in the bed. The rapid drumming in his heart slowed. He rubbed his forehead and looked out the porthole. It still looked dark out there.

He tried to stand on his feet. Muscles ached from the battering they'd received. After several attempts, Drew felt his way to the bathroom. Awkwardly unbalanced, he began to shiver. Pain across the back of his head worked its way around and down. Then he coughed and began to retch. The spasm passed after what seemed like hours. Drew staggered back, lowered himself into bed, and lay weakly trembling.

A storm hit unexpectedly. Swells came from the west as if preparing for an onslaught. Undulating crests effortlessly lifted the ship. Gravity dropped her deep in surging waves. The intensity of the ocean's force created an understanding of the power of God deep in the heart of every man aboard. They witnessed a turgid wave lift them a full fifteen feet, to then drop the *Marybeth* with a force beyond reason.

Drew wiped sweat from his face. Pushing the blanket back, he raised himself to his feet, grabbed the door frame, braced his good arm against it, and hung his aching head. Everything not attached hurdled about freely. With the ship's next plunge, downward momentum forced a massive wooden table across the cabin. It crashed loudly, knocking Drew off his feet. He looked deliberately around the room, too weak to do more than whisper a prayer.

The ship rolled and lunged awry over the next hour. Gradually the wind calmed. Drew listened carefully to feet trudging across the upper deck, along with shouts from his crew. No one had been washed away in the storm. He would know if they were. A muscle in his jaw relaxed. Fifty miles from the nearest port, equipment became scattered among waves and swollen rain. But his men were okay.

Drew edged his way to the chest at the foot of his bed. He felt for his binoculars. From inside the cabin, he held them closely to his face and watched a sheet of darkness loom out of the water like a drizzling, dark wall. There were no boats nearby. Even if there were, he wouldn't have seen them through the impenetrable darkness. He began feeling almost as if night would never end. Glancing at the clock, he frowned, trying to shake off a shadowy thought. Then he turned his attention to bed.

Drew wasn't sure what woke him next. He sat up and had to admit he felt better. The pain in his head calmed to a dull ache, and he was famished. He tried out his legs, half slumping against the wall, his long arm reaching the door handle where his trousers hung. He got into them and slipped on a T-shirt. The hatch opened easily when he pushed against it.

"So, you're awake," Noah said, startling them both. "You had us all worried, boss."

"Worried myself. I feel like I've been beat up, battered, chewed up, and spit out."

"You were, almost."

Drew exhaled a long breath, hitched his hands in his back pockets, and stretched muscles in his lower back. "Well, I'm up now. I might even be tomorrow."

They moved in single file, slowly down the companion way.

"When you see Sui, will you tell her I'm looking for her. I'd like to have lunch together."

Noah sucked in his breath. He didn't know how to answer Drew. How would he react to the loss of his new wife? It seemed much safer to talk about basic things. "Cook just made stew and biscuits. Feel up to it?"

Drew nodded toward the galley. "I'll be in there. You get the lights squared away. I'll pick up whale oil for this end. I can't see a thing."

Noah's smile vanished.

Drew felt his way down the brightly lit hall.

For the first time Noah admitted that Drew's eyes seemed unfocused. And he wanted to cry. For three weeks, he had feared his friend might never recover. Now he could only hope what he had to tell Drew wouldn't make him sorry he was on the mend.

Sui was gone, and Drew was blind.

Chapter 20

In the two hours after Xhiang's demonstrative victory over him, WuTsing's desire for revenge grew out of proportion. Again and again the verbal exchange played over in his raging mind. His character in regard to such things, his actual inner battle, became more and more intense.

For some time WuTsing continued to deliberate his dilemma. It was in him to plan a strategy, when provoked to such mad desperation. But Xhiang was not just any man with whom to contend. To challenge Xhiang equaled certain destruction. It was inevitable Xhiang would see to it if he lost face. But to simply ignore such an adversary proved inconceivable for WuTsing.

He'd thought of going to his new quarters, but he needed solitude, utter quiet to formulate a plan. WuTsing stepped down from the wagon. Across the river, lamps were lit, their flames doing little to dispel the darkness engulfing him.

Then, just like that...the answer came plain as day, almost as if it fell from the sky. But it hadn't. Dynamite still remained from his first job. It had been there all along, lying in the hidden floor compartment of his wagon.

It still lay there all right. WuTsing didn't question the plug's intensity, or if he did he paid no attention. He simply connected dynamite with Xhiang's destruction. He scarcely took time to lift them from the wooden box before he bunched three together for easy handling and smiled knowingly. If two sticks were capable of blowing away an entire bridge, three sticks held the potential to erase Xhiang and his entire household from the face of the earth.

There at the river, the air felt cool because of wind and moisture rising from the water. Yet a thin film of sweat collected on his face. For the second time in days, he camped out at night with fresh air all around him, planning how he would attack Xhiang and his annoying daughter in a rush.

But as he considered his situation he met with a certain degree of doubt. A fast drive with combustible explosives could prove risky. Besides, after tonight's confrontation, Xhiang might be waiting to trap him.

That much decided, WuTsing gathered sticks and dead brush. He piled them into a fire to warm the cool night air. Then he squatted on a log, uncorked a bottle of whiskey, and waited for clouds to uncover the moon. It proved a picturesque spot, north of the main district, quite near the old part of town. Across the river a temple rose, silent and somehow gaunt.

It may have been a few minutes or it could have been a few hours later. Tired as ever, WuTsing awoke. He lay shivering. The fire had died down to glowing embers, his bottle of whiskey empty.

WuTsing stretched, slowly waking up for the attack. With his mind in a drunken stupor, he slowly fed the fire from a pile of sticks. Suddenly WuTsing let out a shrill whoop. Too late he realized his mistake. Thrusting his fist into the fire, he jerked out a stick of dynamite, gripped it tightly and laid it right in his lap.

Except for his ragged breathing, WuTsing was silent. No sound came from the cool river air except for an occasional crackle from the fire and a faint hiss. He sat still, with his dark narrow face and gold earring, looking confused and uneasy. Too late he saw sparks following the path of the dynamite's wick. There was no way for WuTsing to see his own destructive finish. His death headed on a straightway course. Fear showed in his eyes a split second before his portion of the world blew up with him in it.

Chapter 21

Sui fluttered open swollen, purple lids and breathed in stale air. Her room felt close. The pain that shot through her head with every pulse made her squint.

"Suiteiko!" Xhiang repeated her name. She whispered a soft moan. Then she groaned, louder this time, and he knew she was coming out of the coma.

The voice sounded familiar. Sui ignored the pain and looked desperately around her. But the room remained dark, and all she saw was the indistinct shape of a man.

"Drew," she whispered through a bulky bandage and dry, cracked lips. But it wasn't Drew who greeted her. Xhiang's pretentious stance and fierce face made her heart sink. Only for the most ruinous missions did Xhiang make himself available. For lesser tasks he employed hired hands.

"How nice of you to come back, Sui," said Xhiang tenderly. "Are you in much pain?" She groaned. Deception became a way of life for Xhiang. She knew his gentle voice meant annoyance. Getting words past very swollen lips proved extremely difficult.

"You're alive," she mumbled softly. She was surprised to see her father looking so well. She had all but given up hope the last time she'd been with him.

He gifted her with contemptuous amusement instead of reaching out to comfort her as she hoped he would, and it hurt. "Are you terribly disappointed that I'm still alive?"

Without thinking, she shook her head and emitted a shallow cry. "It hurts so bad," she whispered, closing her eyes. As she gave in to darkness, she wondered again why he loved her so little.

When next Sui opened her eyes sunlight flooded the room. Xhiang stood in the same place he'd stood the last time, staring down at her.

"I am pleased you are looking...so well, Father," Sui whispered faintly. She felt shy and awkward with him. One silent minute turned into two. Given the opportunity for such a rare moment, she plunged in. "I visited you. Do you remember?"

When Xhiang remained silent, Sui continued.

"I wished then I'd said things I hadn't, things I wanted to thank you for that I wished I had." Her voice sounded so humble and sincere. Something unfamiliar tugged at Xhiang.

He stiffened and turned to stare out the window, allowing time for the moisture in his eyes to clear. "How touching. But you must know that men like myself do not die."

She tried a weak smile, but it hurt to badly. "We all die, sometime."

"You didn't," he said, as if he disapproved. "Where have you been?" he asked in a flat, icy voice. He wanted to hear her version.

Like someone who struggled to survive a battle camp, Sui drew from her own private source of strength before she told him about her experience with and marriage to Drew.

"And that is why you didn't leave word you were leaving?"

"You seemed too ill to care at the time."

"Did you fear that I may die and leave you penniless?"

Sui nodded hesitantly. "The thought did cross my mind. I'm a daughter, remember? I cared for you. I cared for your business. But there wasn't a thing I could do about being a girl."

Xhiang had to admire her courage to speak honestly. But she didn't seem at all remorseful for the shame she brought him. "So you gave yourself to a strange man. Do you really suppose this...Drew fellow would have stayed around, that he would not have grown tired of you?"

Her voice was whisper soft. "It's not like that at all, Father. Drew loved me. He loves me still." Sui breathed a shaky breath, trying to control the tears threatening to spill over. Fiery pain stopped her short.

"What do you know of love?"

"I know I care deeply for you. I was concerned for you, Father."

Xhiang hesitated and shook his head slowly. "Surely you don't still believe I am your father. Look at yourself. Do you see any resemblance to me at all?"

"Paternity doesn't hinge on similarities. Nature is funny that way."

He dismissed her comment with a wave of his hand. "This is me you are talking to, Suiteiko. Who are you mocking here? We both know I am not your father." Xhiang turned away so he didn't have to witness the unmistakable sorrow in her eyes.

"Is this your idea of punishment, Father? Because if it is, it's working." Sui shifted stiffly. "I'm a little old to be disciplined, don't you think?" Sui could have laughed, except she wanted to cry.

Xhiang ignored her comment. "So you have been with a man," he said matter of factly.

"Not any man, my husband," she said, feeling very confused now.

"Then it's just as well he's dead. Without my approval, any marriage on your part is not legal."

Sui was stunned into silent pain. "Drew is dead? You don't know that for sure."

"I assumed you knew. WuTsing witnessed his death."

"WuTsing? How does he fit into this?"

"That doesn't matter. You are responsible for a man's death. Maybe next time you will think before you shame me."

"My husband is gone. Drew is gone." She sounded so abandoned, so alone that Xhiang turned away again. He couldn't bear to look into her eyes. "Are you absolutely certain?"

Xhiang spun back around and looked at Sui squarely. "I'm not going to play games with you, Sui, not now, not ever. The chances of him being alive are one million to one."

"Then there is a chance."

Xhiang eyed her with an icy smile. "Even if the man is alive, he is not your husband, not without my approval," he reminded Sui harshly.

"Without your approval?" she asked, puzzled.

"A father's approval is required for marriage."

"But you just admitted you're not my father. So which is it?"

"Legally, you have my name."

"Twenty-two years is a long time to believe someone is your parent. It's rather a shock to find out they're not."

"Your mother should have told you."

"Or perhaps my mother believed you were."

A muscle in his cheek went taut. "That's impossible."

"I hardly think so. You were married for twenty-three years."

And then he delivered the final blow. "We were married in name only."

She wanted to ask why. She chanced a glance at his face. His remoteness stopped her. It struck her with something of a shock that he'd never spoken of her mother so freely until now. All at once she realized that as a child he'd concealed his innermost feelings. He'd maintained the custom throughout life. Now he found it difficult to break down barriers he'd built around himself and certain areas of his past.

Sui felt stunned that he would admit something so intimate. But it explained so much. His lack of feelings and total indifference weren't unusual. Until that moment, any approach to him had been made through Mother. Xhiang remained the traditional father, unapproachable and feared. Now he came at last to the expressive side of fatherhood. But suddenly she wished he wouldn't. She wanted to disappear. Xhiang didn't accept her and never had.

Silence fell between them. Some uncomfortable seconds dragged by.

"I never knew," she finally said very softly.

"Of course not. How could you?"

"You could have told me."

"I just did."

"Yes, you did," Sui admitted, choking on a sob. "I almost wish you hadn't. At least I had an identity. Now I have nothing."

Xhiang's revelation released her of responsibility, but it didn't hurt any less. "Did you ever care for me at all?"

"Care? You ruined my life. You destroyed any hope of a relationship with Elizabeth," he accused, seemingly unmoved by her tears.

"A baby shouldn't be held responsible for a relationship between two adults."

"I made progress with Elizabeth before you came along."

"You made progress? How exactly did you do that?"

"When I brought her home, she..."

Sui groaned the instant she moved her head. "Home from where? Where did Mother come from? I mean, I know she was born in England. Where did you meet?"

Xhiang scowled darkly, his eyes filled with accusation. "Does it matter where I got her?"

Sui attempted to nod. Shrouds of pain shot through her head and settled in her back. "It matters a great deal to me."

"The ship she traveled on was overtaken. I found Elizabeth at WooHoons."

Sui shook visibly now. "But, isn't that..." she began hesitantly.

"Precisely, I paid dearly for your mother," Xhiang stated unkindly. "If you hadn't come along when you did, she may have learned to care for me. You, with your English looks and personality. You became a constant reminder of what she lost."

The acknowledgment became almost too awful to cry about. Sui huddled in a corner, trying not to breathe too hard for fear the pain would hurt too badly.

"What did she lose?" When Xhiang didn't answer, she realized sadly how much her mother went through, and how much she kept to herself. The thought suddenly occurred to Sui that her mother must have had a husband when Xhiang took her. That answered so much. "Do you have any idea who my biological father is, Xhiang?"

Xhiang stared out the window. He couldn't bare to witness the pained look in Sui's eyes. It bore through him like fiery coals. "Your father died on the same ship from which your mother became a captive."

"I see."

"Do you? Do you understand what it's like to be despised and overlooked by the only person you ever really cared about? Sometimes I almost wanted to leave everything behind, to run away with Elizabeth and begin a new life."

"Perhaps you should have. Who knows what might have happened."

A deep weariness settled on Sui. She felt so spent she could hardly move. "Sometimes I wanted to run away too. But then I would worry about what would happen if I did. Who would care for you? Who would see that the Emporium ran efficiently, the house kept clean, your meals prepared. I thought nothing would run smoothly if I disappeared. It isn't true, I know. But I chose to believe it."

After a long moment of silence, Sui whispered sadly, "I will leave in the morning."

"Where will you go?" Until that instant Xhiang hadn't realized how much he might miss her pleasant nature and gentle smile. If he really thought about it, he would acknowledge Sui as the only person in the world who ever really cared about him for more than his money.

"Somewhere. I don't know." She struggled with tears. For the second time in her life Xhiang had talked directly to her. She was grateful. "It seems I owe you so much."

Xhiang stiffened. "You owe me?"

"It couldn't have been easy having me around for so many years. You said so yourself."

"You will leave when I tell you to go." Something tugged at his cold heart. Xhiang felt ice begin to melt away. Why had he been so desperate to hurt her? As he looked into her sad face, the plans he'd made for her seemed very daunting.

Her somber face, staring at him wet with tears, followed him out of the room. For the next several days he stayed away from Sui, trying to forget how much she'd come to mean.

Life is strange.

Chapter 22

$\mathcal{S}ui$ recognized the package even before she touched it. The box had disappeared from the top shelf of her mother's closet the day of her death. Sui held the box for a long time, allowing her emotions to settle. Faded blue ribbon secured the lid and felt cool and soft against her fingers.

It mysteriously showed up now? Why? Was the box an unexpected act of kindness from whoever had laid it outside her bedroom door, or did it contain something painful? Sui suspected the latter. So she set the package aside while she dressed and forgot about it as she stared out the window at the garden beyond.

Had her mother suffered this same deep sense of loss? That would explain so much. There remained so much about Mother she could only guess at, so much she never knew, so many secrets only Xhiang retained knowledge of. She regretted not having asked Mother about her life while she still had the chance. Because of her own excessive self-indulgence, she had simply assumed things were as they appeared on the surface. Now she felt ashamed. She never considered the feelings of her parents.

Xhiang, with his biting tongue and snapping eyes, regarded her as an encumbrance, an imposition. Very cold and constrained to others, now she knew why he abhorred her so. No wonder he'd never cared to understand who she was or where she hoped to go. Sui had assumed herself his child, created of his flesh. But he made it clear that wasn't the case. She wasn't his daughter.

Now Sui wondered if he lay awake at night, tossing and turning as she did. Would he ever let the past go and simply accept her? But even as the thought crossed her mind, Sui realized such a concession proved too much to hope for. Anything beyond a civil existence was far too much to even conceive of.

When her mother had died, she'd taken all the answers with her. Mother seemed a serious woman when in the company of others, a woman of few words and inaccessible emotions, seemingly indifferent to the affairs of Xhiang's kingdom.

Dispirited as Mother seemed, when the door closed behind the two of them, Elizabeth became a mother first of all, with warmth and softness. She filled Sui's life with enchantment, touched her heart with loving kindness. When her mother died, Sui had missed laughing at Elizabeth's humorous stories and listening to romantic songs.

She loved Mother, would always miss her. But she missed Drew most of all now. Her heart cried out desperately to Drew, wondering how she could bear living without him, knowing perfectly what she'd lost, what she would never treasure again.

Sui bowed her head, thinking of what Xhiang had said to her, and she sighed deeply. Her own childhood hadn't been so extraordinarily different than that of most girls, she supposed. Certainly Xhiang didn't love her. But no person alive was promised love, except by One. She'd grown up most fortunate, if wealth is a standard to base happiness upon.

Disheartened, Sui stared at the four walls that protected her from the rest of the world. By choice, she'd stayed to herself for weeks now, waiting to learn what Xhiang had in mind for her. In turn, Xhiang hadn't sought her out, allowing the sting of discovery to dull.

Then Sui's eyes rested on the box. Slowly she walked to it and gently picked it up. The faded blue of the ribbon matched her somber heart. She held the box in her hands for a long moment. Then she dusted off the lavender cover and sat down, wondering what to expect. It took a few minutes to unravel the delicate ribbon.

The tissue peeled back. Tears came to her eyes, and for the first time in weeks, she grinned sadly, remembering a happier time in her life. The tiny dress she lifted carefully in her hands was just as she remembered. Except now the lace had yellowed, the ribbon frayed from age and wear. It was her own dress, a dress her mother made for her when she was what, six? Seven? She couldn't remember.

There were other things in the box as well-a plain gold wedding band, a stack of books, a music box, a newspaper clipping about an accident that took the life of a Christopher Wells, emerald earrings, faded lace gloves, and a gold locket.

Opening the locket, a man stared out at her. The striking picture had been painted with infinite care. He looked very handsome, with a high forehead and a well-trimmed mustache. His dark, laughing eyes caught and held Sui's attention.

The eyes looking out from the picture looked vaguely familiar, as if she'd looked into them before. But that was ridiculous, she thought. He probably just reminded her of someone.

Then she found a daguerreotype of her mother. The same gentleman in the gold locket stood beside an incredibly happy Elizabeth. He looked down at her with all the warmth and affection of someone very precious. Sui guessed easily they must have loved one another dearly.

Everything lay neatly on her bed. Not until she began putting everything back did Sui discover it. Partly hidden in the corner of the box she found a letter. Sui could see at a glance the letter had been sent from England. From the careful way the faded yellow ribbon bound the letter, Sui guessed it must have been very important to Mother.

She didn't know how she knew, but Sui was quite certain as she opened the letter the answer to her questions were written on the worn sheet of stationery she held. There was no hiding from the truth that had been concealed from her for a lifetime.

Dear Mrs. York,

Upon receiving your letter, I regret to inform you that your husband, Michael York, has been declared dead.

When I read your letter, I was grieved to learn of your tragic circumstances. Piracy is illegal, but it is difficult to prove. Sadly enough, there is no way we can patrol the entire ocean. There is good reason to believe, however, that we can secure your freedom from Xhiang Wong if you were coerced into a marriage against your will–without your daughter, of course.

It is unfortunate that your daughter was born outside of England, as she becomes a citizen of China upon her birth in that country. Your husband, Xhiang Wong, may establish his paternity and has the right to keep her there, since there is no way to prove he is not the father. You, however, are a citizen of England, and as such have a right to legal advice.

Contact me at the same address if I may be of further assistance.

Sincerely,
Christopher Wells, Attorney at Law

Sui looked up. The room tipped and began to spin uncertainly. She couldn't breathe. Her trembling fingers lost their grip on the sheet of paper she'd been grasping and floated silently to the floor. Sui followed.

Chapter 23

There was no gathering of Xhiang's relations, or even a few close friends, to say goodbye the night before Sui left. It almost felt as if she'd never been a part of Xhiang's life, as if she had no past. Sui silently left alone for the train station to make the lonely trip to the home of a man named Youn Kim.

At the last minute, she wanted to beg Xhiang to allow her to stay. But she couldn't. Xhiang would see her disappointment, witness the hurt he caused, and laugh. Without a backward glance, she left the house carrying one bag with a few personal belongings and her faith. No one could take that away.

As she stood on the landing to watch for the train, her heart began to shatter. But she refused to look back as the train pulled out. No one would care if she never came back.

She was reminded of the time Xhiang took her to school. He left her with a stern-faced instructor. Dark eyes nearly filled her small face as she looked down dark hallways. Strange noises sounded threatening. She felt almost as she did now. Alone. And she wanted to cry, but she was too terrified to make a noise.

Sui's hands lay clenched on her lap. She watched the changing countryside from the dusty window of the train, ignoring admiring glances of a man sitting across the aisle from her.

Business and industry gave way to open country. A fruit seller walked along the dirt road bearing shoulder poles with peaches, one basket at each end. Farther on, Sui saw bent backs of women between rows of dark green cabbage and plump red tomatoes. And farther still, water buffalo pulled wooden plows in muddy fields. It seemed almost as if she'd entered an entirely new culture, giving Sui the impression of leaving the familiar far behind.

The crowded train felt stuffy and smelled of smoke. Sui lifted dark hair from her slender neck and unbuttoned the collar of her sleeveless light yellow *cheungsam*, feeling overheated, tired, and very old.

When the train crossed the river, Sui leaned back against her seat and began to absently imagine what Youn Kim would be like. Xhiang had told her the name of the man who'd paid for her, but nothing else. She didn't know if he was old or young, married or single, if he had children, or what would be expected of her. But in her mind she pictured him as a peaceful, grandfatherly man with a motherly wife who enjoyed cooking and loved children. Then Sui realized she'd imagined them as an older version of Elliott and Effie Pepple. Very little chance of that. Her eyes strayed back to the window.

As the train wound its way across the landscape, it stopped at each small town along the way. Sui stayed on the train at each stop. But the closer they came to her final destination, the more tempted she became to get off and lose herself to the world. But she didn't.

Youn Kim waited impatiently outside the terminal, located on the outskirts of Shanghai. When the engine slowed to a halt, he stepped inside, pulling the weighty entrance door closed behind him.

A young woman in a yellow *cheungsam* stepped lightly off the train ramp. Youn sucked in his breath when he saw her. He resisted looking over the full length of her. Tall and slender, Suiteiko Wong possessed loveliness at its finest. Her clothing caressed creamy skin. The scarf he'd suggested she wear draped her open collar. The effect stopped him cold in his tracks.

His eyes narrowed. Perhaps he should have sent someone else to the train station for Suiteiko. Her kind of temptation he could do without. In little hurry to address her, Youn Kim waited for her to come through the door. Another few minutes would give him enough time to gain composure.

Taking a calming breath, Youn Kim closed his eyes briefly. When he opened them she reached the door, but he still made no move in her direction. He distanced himself from relationships by choice. Desiring a life with no sentimental entanglements, he considered senseless feelings a weakness in others.

Youn Kim dropped his eyes in an attempt to conquer unfamiliar stirrings. Forcing himself to concentrate on the purpose for which she had come, he examined what his chances were of pulling it off. Looking at her impersonally, Youn seriously doubted he could remain detached. He felt a moment of actual regret for expecting such natural beauty to submit to mundane housework.

She belonged in an English garden, surrounded by servants. Absently, he reflected on her aristocratic looks. They spoke of privilege and money. Why would Xhiang force a woman like Suiteiko to become a common servant? Only a woman, certainly, but she was also his daughter. Youn Kim certainly wouldn't have sold her, especially for so meager a cost.

He continued watching her from a distance and allowed her his grudging respect. She possessed dignity and an innate sense of distinction he appreciated. She held her shoulders back, despite the uncertainty she must be experiencing, and glanced around curiously.

Youn Kim gave her a final appraising look. If he was smart, it would be his last. He stepped back, seeing her jump when he said her name.

"Suiteiko Wong?"

"I am looking for Youn Kim." Her voice had a breathless quality. She lifted her face. A pair of soft, brown eyes peered at him from beneath long, sooty lashes. Instantly, he felt as if someone forced air from his lungs. An angry red scar marred her pale skin. He cleared his throat.

"At your service. I nearly gave up on you."

He wasn't at all what she expected. Tall and thin, hooded coppery eyes traveled over her face. Thick dark hair pulled back tightly from a clean-lined jaw and high cheekbones drew attention to his unwavering eyes. To some, the lean, hard-boned features would be considered admirable. His austerity and pride were to evident for Sui to consider him handsome. In some small way, he reminded her of Xhiang-unapproachable.

"Xhiang made a deal, Mr. Kim. Of course I would be here."

He nodded and she bowed, her skin the color of bleached rice. Up close, she looked as if she hung onto control by a thin thread. Sui fingered damp hair off her forehead. Humidity curled the ends.

Sui caught his intent expression and flushed, conscious of her unkempt appearance. She probably looked a mess, she thought uneasily. Something about the way he looked unsettled her.

Youn Kim lifted an eyebrow. "Is that the only bag you brought?"

Sui nodded.

"You won't be needing much. Follow me."

She must have done something wrong, Sui thought. She wasn't sure what. Youn's frowning expression became dark as she settled in the passenger seat of his *jinrikisha*.

Youn directed the vehicle out of the lot and onto the dirt road. As he drove, she could see thin muscles running close to the bone. Unlike Drew's, with a mahogany sprinkling of hair trailing along corded muscles, Youn's forearms lacked hair.

Sui watched the center of town roll past. It wasn't large, a central park, a rooming house, and a foodmarket with a drugstore. To Sui, it meant other people. She glimpsed Youn Kim and remembered what brought her here.

Youn brought the *jinrikisha* to a stop outside a curving, lofty house. Sui looked past the pink stuccoed building and the ornate balconies to the well-kept garden centered around a centuries-old banyan tree. The atmosphere struck her as very different from the back streets where homes were built of wood, bamboo, broken mats, and scraps of iron on waste ground.

"Well, this is it. I'll take you inside. You have no need to look so alarmed. You will soon become acquainted with your responsibilities. After that, you're on your own."

"It's very kind to allow me to work for you," Sui told him politely.

"Tell me, Suiteiko, have you ever worked before?"

"Of course I have."

"Of course. Do you have any idea what's really ahead for you? You will be expected to work, and you will work hard for as long as you are here."

"I may not be muscle-bound, but I am able to handle a job. If you find I do not work to your expectation, let me know. I will try harder."

Youn Kim glimpsed her perfectly done nails and suppressed a frustrated sigh. She would never make it in his household. Not now, not ever. But he'd paid for her, so what difference would it make?

"You're bound to lose sleep, working a twelve hour day."

"Twelve hours?" Sui had to smile. Compared with her old life, a twelve hour day would add four hours of leisure time.

Youn still didn't understand why Xhiang would let a daughter such as Sui out of his sight. Wasn't Xhiang afraid someone would take advantage of his daughter? Youn thought about other places she might have been sent and felt sick. Images that came to mind were not comforting by any stretch of imagination. Someone would take one look at those soft eyes and...

He took an unsteady breath, aware of the results. For some absurd reason, he couldn't walk away from Sui.

She raised her eyes to Youn. "Are you having second thoughts? Because if you are—"

"No." Youn felt his jaw clench in a hard line. "I made a deal with your father. Do you have the papers?"

"Right here." She searched in her bag.

"Forget it. You can give them to me later."

Sui pushed the heavy bag back in the seat.

"Ever done any housecleaning?"

"At home, and at Xhiang's."

"You didn't live with your father?"

"I meant to say, I cleaned at Xhiang's Emporium." And she had done everything else there, but she didn't say that.

"How about record keeping?"

Sui nodded, fighting the strong impression she'd somehow pleased Youn Kim. That bothered her.

"How unusual."

"For a woman, you mean." The hint of a smile inclined the outline of her mouth. She could tell her remark upset him. "Sorry. Perhaps I spoke out of line."

Youn allowed his clenched jaw to relax. "I will let it go this time. Don't let it happen again."

"I will try to remember."

"I'm going to be gone for a couple of days. By the time I get back, you should be familiar enough to get along on your own."

Two days would give him a chance to put his position concerning Suiteiko into proper perspective. Perhaps by then he would have this attraction for her under some sort of control.

"Okay then, let's go inside."

Sui found Youn's home surprisingly comfortable. Shade from the banyan outside offered relief form wind and sun.

The following morning Youn Kim called her into his office. Seated at his imposing desk with steepled fingers hiding his mouth, he watched her through narrow eyes. He wore a navy tailor-made suit of western origin, a fashionably pressed cream-colored shirt, and a thin string tie. His long black hair was pulled straight back in a pigtail again.

Youn Kim stopped himself short. He'd hoped that seeing Suiteiko in the light of day would vanquish his feelings for her.

Sui sensed his inner struggle, but she depicted it as something totally different. "Did you want to see me?"

"I do." Youn sat back. "How did you sleep last night?"

"You called me here to ask how I slept?"

"Among other things."

"What other things?"

"Look, Suiteiko, I own this place."

"It's very nice."

"Yes, I think so. And I own you."

Sui gasped.

"Now is a good time to set something straight."

Sui didn't respond.

Youn continued. "I was informed that you are a foreign devil."

"By whom? Who told you that?"

"That same source also informed me that you ran off with a foreigner. I'm surprised. You are not what I expected."

Sui caught her breath. "I am sorry."

"Yes. So am I."

Sui blushed and looked away.

"You will forget the foreigner. Do I make myself clear?"

"I understand."

"Xhiang assured me that you are very amenable, although a foreigner."

"My previous employer...Xhiang? He is no authority where I am concerned."

Youn raised a brow. Sui didn't know him well enough to tell if she'd upset him.

119

"Xhiang never really knew me. I was born and raised in Shanghai. I do not consider myself a foreigner. And it is true, my biological parents were both English. But I am not a devil." Sui's fingers dug into cold palms. "I lived with Xhiang Wong for a long time. I will try to overcome his...influence, to please you with my effort."

If work is what Youn Kim expected, then she would work. But no one could erase Drew from her heart.

"I will keep that in mind. Meanwhile, Kei will instruct you as to your duties and provide you with uniforms. Basically, you will be expected to keep the house clean and in good running order. You may begin work immediately."

Sui bowed. "I thank you."

"Come. I will take you to meet the other amahs." Youn Kim turned to leave, then stopped. "Have you eaten this morning?"

"I am not hungry." That was true. She couldn't remember the last time she'd felt hungry. The very thought of food made her queasy.

Sui learned Youn Kim owned four women besides herself. He introduced each of them. Sui made a little bow, listening carefully to each name-Makischuk, Kei, Murinko, and WuMa.

Middle-aged Kei and Makischuk worked in the kitchen. Murinka and Sui shared the same birthday, December 1. They cared for linens and gardening. Relatively older than the rest, WuMa boasted sixty-two years. Her eyes remained clear and intelligent.

"It is very kind of you to include me. I am sure we will get along fine."

"Are you from China?" WuMa asked.

"Shanghai," Sui answered softly.

"Shanghai," WuMa repeated, as though she left there the day before, when in fact she'd been gone from Shanghai for twenty-three years. "It is certainly a lovely city."

Murinka asked, "Are you married, Sui? Did your husband come with you?"

Sui flinched. Pain pierced. Take one day at a time, she reminded herself. Nothing can bring back the past. Make the most of the future.

But the future looked bleak. Sui ran a hand down the side of her face, tracing the scar as a reminder of hard times. Things would get better. They had to.

"She is not married," Youn Kim filled in for her.

"Yes, I am married," Sui whispered. "Until I know for sure my husband is not alive, I will carry on as if married."

Youn's eyes widened. A horrible sinking feeling dropped to his stomach. "Come with me."

"Admirable girl," WuMa said. "She reminds me of my sister's niece in Chang Jiang. Very polite."

"Aiee-ya," Makischuk clucked her tongue. "Bad scar on face. I can't help wondering who owned her before Youn Kim."

In the days that followed, Sui found the house well-maintained. And though friendship was not forbidden, neither was it encouraged. Hers wasn't a happy existence, but her gentle ways and kind hand were readily accepted, that and her experience at cleaning and gardening.

The rest of the week became routine. Sui spent her days polishing dust-less furniture, scrubbing shining floors, shaking clean rugs, and laundering outside in the sunshine.

Loneliness compelled her to work especially hard. Five o'clock began her day. She spent endless hours in silence, quick flows of conversation, numerous chores, incessant scrubbing. Lonely hours filled with unnecessary tasks, well after the others went to bed at night became a way of life. Sui rarely ate, hardly slept, pressed her body beyond its endurance. She looked extremely gaunt when Youn Kim summoned her to his office once again three weeks later.

Sui couldn't imagine what he expected this time. But she refused to be frightened. In the struggle to get through each day, her mind had become numb. Besides, Youn Kim certainly couldn't complain she wasn't putting forth enough effort. Maybe he would, and Effie People came to mind. But she wasn't foolish enough or blind enough to overlook the power China held over a foreigner. And she wouldn't cause trouble for her dear friends, even to gain freedom.

Sui stood before the massive door of Youn's room and carefully smoothed the skirt she wore. Her knock was immediately answered. "Come in."

Youn Kim watched her as though he couldn't quite figure out something about her. The contemplative look in his eyes made her very nervous. She waited for him to say something. When he didn't, she spoke. "You wanted to see me?"

"How are you doing, Sui?" Sui was startled to hear him call her by her first name. She felt her heart begin to pound heavily, ignoring his attempt at a wan smile. "There's no need to be scared of me, you know. I simply want-ed to assure myself of your well being."

"I am fine," she said in a clipped tone.

"Would you speak a little louder please, so I can hear you."

"I feel fine."

Youn Kim frowned. He looked her up and down as a shopper would look over a select piece of meat. In the past few weeks, he'd intentionally observed her work habits, and he wasn't surprised to see her looking tired. But he was-n't prepared to see her looking so pale. "You do not look fine. You seem thin-ner than when you arrived three weeks ago. Your skin is ashen. Perhaps if you spent a little more time out of doors?"

"I don't seem to find the time."

He looked her straight in the eye. "Make me understand. Do you feel I expect too much of you?"

"Not at all. In case you have forgotten, I promised to please you with my efforts."

"So you did, and you have." Youn turned away, hiding an amused smile. "Tell me, Sui, do you always keep your promises?"

"I try to. It makes things more pleasant for everyone concerned. Don't you agree?"

Youn Kim raised an eyebrow. "Absolutely." Her eyes met his. Something in her forlorn depths provoked an unfamiliar desire to protect her. He fought the urge and made light of the subject. In doing so, he hit a nerve without intending to and felt troubled when he realized her distress. "So, describe for me one of the most recent promises you've made."

Sui wasn't certain how much to admit. But Youn seemed so kind that Sui faced him with a silent plea for understanding. She grew even more pale. "I promised my husband I would love him and be faithful for the rest of our lives. And I will."

Frosty ice glazed Youn's stoic expression. He sat straight up, fast. His chair struck the hard, wooden floor. "Tell me, Sui, did Xhiang have knowledge of this...husband...when I paid for you?"

"Xhiang would not acknowledge Drew."

Youn seemed to draw inward. "Don't even whisper his name in this house. Do you understand?"

Sui refused to allow the tears that filled her eyes to flow. She nodded and blinked them away.

"Answer me!"

"Yes."

"Yes, what?"

"I understand." Sui watched Youn closely as he moved from window to window.

"Good. I am glad of that. I wouldn't want you to be out of your head with worry about some guy you will never see again anyway. Isn't that right?"

Sui nodded.

"Where is he now?" Youn forced her chin between his thumb and forefinger and lifted her face.

"I've been told he died. I'm not certain."

"Go to him then." Youn released her face swiftly. At that precise moment he meant it. Sui seemed bent on torturing herself. She must settle her own mind, to eventually forget the man. He would offer her a home, happiness, and even freedom. He would not offer a shoulder to cry on when the tears were brought on by another man.

"If you leave these premises, I promise these doors will not open to you again. Think about what could happen out there before you make your choice."

"You would allow me to leave?" Sui couldn't believe what she was hearing.

"I said you could. But if you choose to leave, you will be making the wrong decision. I promise you."

With a long moment of silence between them, Sui knew she had no choice. She chose her words carefully. "I still love him."

"We've all loved someone at one time. The secret is to leave bad times behind you and not look back. Forget him."

This time Sui gave in to something she promised herself she wouldn't do for a long time. She spoke out. "You give the order and memories vanish? Is it as easy as that?"

"Time will heal."

"You're right. Time does heal, but sometimes scars are left behind."

"Why are you doing this, Sui?"

"Doing what?"

"Fighting me."

"I'm not fighting you. I simply want you to know where I stand."

"Presently you stand in my house. While you are here you will not mention...whatever his name is. Understood?"

"Clearly. Sometimes it is impossible not to look back," Sui whispered.

"Life is a decision."

Sui nodded. "I will stay here, at least for the time being." She didn't see the satisfied look cross Youn Kim's face, or the tightening of his lips.

Chapter 24

Youn remained silent for perhaps two minutes, lost in his own thoughts, planning his own strategies. While he considered his next move, he slowly rolled his head on his neck and lifted his shoulders, loosening cramped muscles.

"It's only a game. Make your move," Sui told him cheerfully.

"What is you hurry?"

"What's my hurry? We've been playing fan tan for nearly three hours. I have to be up in a few hours and I haven't even been to bed yet."

"So take the day off."

She gave Youn a ready smile. "What, so you can find an excuse to criticize me?"

"Do I criticize you, Sui?"

"I've never given you reason to." Her voice sounded triumphant. "So let's call it a night. We can pick it up tomorrow. I've got to warn you though, I may not allow you to win next time."

"Allow me? You're saying you allow me to win?"

"We have been playing fan tan now for what, five weeks?"

Youn nodded. "That's about the time you arrived."

"That's long enough. Tomorrow you're on your own." Sui gave him a teasing, sideways look.

"But of course." Youn offered his hand and Sui extended hers. When he'd pulled her to her feet, Youn bowed at the waist. "Until tomorrow."

"Tomorrow it is."

"I accept the challenge," Youn Kim said, with mock forewarning.

"I have all night to plan my strategy." Sui heard him chuckle an instant before the room began to spin and just before she slumped to the floor.

Sui opened her eyes, then quickly closed them again. Youn Kim stood above her, looking down intently. "You have been ill?" His tone seemed almost accusing.

"It's nothing. Really, I am okay." If her eyes opened, she would vomit. Her stomach recoiled with movement. But the wavering in her head became so intense that she retched anyway. Sui lowered her head and waited for the dreadful nausea to pass.

"I will not have it!" Youn Kim locked eyes with her. "You have been working too hard."

"I won't die of work," Sui managed. But suddenly she wasn't so sure. Something felt terribly wrong. She'd fainted for the second time in a week. And dizziness became worse and more often.

"I am calling a doctor."

In spite of feeling dreadfully green, she whispered. "No, please don't. I promise I'll slow down. I just didn't want to disappoint you."

In truth, Sui was not a disappointment to Youn Kim. She gave all she had and more. Youn felt ashamed. In an attempt to hide his desire for her affection, he'd come across as harsh in the beginning. Considering how hard she worked to please him, he'd relaxed his attitude. Her pleasant nature and gentle smile began working its way into his heart. No amount of money could buy something capable of filling his senses as Suiteiko did. He no longer felt concerned about satisfying her debt to him.

"I feel you should see a doctor." He said it more gently this time.

"Please, Youn Kim. I'm better now."

So Youn Kim insisted she eat more and rest often. He even took Sui for long walks and followed her with anxious eyes for the next few weeks. Sui would have been humiliated if she knew he'd heard her getting sick on several occasions. And when Sui nearly fainted at the table one morning, Youn Kim rushed to her side immediately. His eyes fell from her face and traveled downward to her waist. With a sinking heart, he called the doctor. By now he was quite certain of her diagnosis.

The doctor listened to her heart, her lungs, her pulse. Then he asked questions. With a gentle hand, he touched the small protrusion on her lower abdomen. Sui was almost certainly three months pregnant.

"What is it?" Sui whispered. "You can tell me. It's not that I hate dying. I just don't want to feel so sick, or so exhausted."

"Mrs. Kim, you have baby."

Sui smiled weakly and gently pushed a stray hair from her forehead. "I'm not Mrs. Kim. I-" Then her eyes widened. "What did you say?"

"Mrs. Kim or no Mrs. Kim, you have baby." Suddenly Sui knew with certainty that the doctor was correct. She'd wondered a couple of times, but then dismissed the idea because she wanted Drew's child so badly. Everything she'd ever loved seemed to vanish. But now this.

125

"Baby arrive in late December." Sui calculated the date in her mind and decided that the doctor must be correct.

"Relax now," Youn Kim said, wiping away a stray tear with his fingertip. "We will talk about it later."

For the first time in weeks, she became plagued with nightmares. Drew lay crushed among rocks while she watched helplessly. In the next instant, she stood on shore, begging Drew to come to her, screaming desperately that she needed him. He smiled calmly, waving her goodbye from the deck of his ship. Tall and strong, the one man she knew she would love forever disappeared.

Sui awoke alone and crying. She longed desperately for Drew and remained very quiet during the day. But at night she sobbed silently because she missed him. Finally she admitted she might never hold Drew again.

Weeks went by without event. As she went through the motions of living, her mind became drawn to the life growing inside her. Each morning, just before she crawled out of bed, Sui rested a hand on her growing tummy and whispered a greeting.

Time passed. As Sui grew rounder and slower, Youn Kim put her in charge of filing books in the library. Sui insisted she was pregnant, not ill.

Chapter 25

Not a speck of dust remained in the library. Every weed in the garden suffered at her hand. Now Sui rested beside the bubbling pool. It seemed a good place to ponder Youn Kim's influence in her life.

"How are you feeling?" The sun shone in her eyes when she looked up. When Youn Kim dropped to the ground beside her, she felt quite surprised. He wasn't in the habit of dawdling beside the pool. He seemed somber, but he looked happy to see her.

"I'm feeling huge. Do you suppose every mother gets this tired and feels this immense?"

Talking about the baby with such tender affection didn't make him happy, but Sui persisted. "Possibly. I wouldn't know. My mother died of food poisoning when I was a boy, about ten." He said it very calmly, but she could see the anguish in his eyes.

"I am sorry." There was nothing she could say to ease his pain. Everyone lost someone. And the loss felt awful, even worse if you really loved them.

"Her death seemed difficult, but it's especially hard at that age."

"What was your father like?"

Youn Kim shrugged. "Big, tough. He sent me away to school so I could follow in his footsteps."

"I've wondered about that. Just what exactly do you do while you're gone all day?"

"I'm an accountant. Sometimes I teach at night, too."

"An accountant." Sui sat back to study him. Everything about Youn was done with deliberation and careful planning. Rather good looking, he rarely made mistakes or permitted himself to be influenced by emotions. But something slightly forbidding made him seem unapproachable. His personality matched his vocation. He even looked like a business man.

"I'm afraid I got stuck with this particular career."

"It's an admirable profession. Don't you enjoy it?"

"I don't know. I've never been given a chance to try my hand at anything else."

"There are worse vocations." She smiled warmly.

"I suppose." His thoughts seemed a thousand miles away as he stared at her hand. "I've noticed the ring you always wear. You're not wearing it today."

Her smile faded. Drew's absence form her life caused the aching, gnawing void inside. "No, I'm not. My fingers are swollen. Part of expecting, I guess." Sui wasn't sure why she mentioned her pregnancy, except it would seem rude not to. Youn seemed increasingly interested in her and she wasn't prepared for that.

He glanced to one side. "Is that the only reason?"

"Yes," she admitted. "Why else would I take it off?"

"I'd hoped you were over him."

She knew he referred to Drew and it saddened her. To stop loving Drew would be like to stop breathing.

Youn Kim was being awfully good to her. Maybe she owed him more attention. "I'm sorry if I've seemed detached lately." She grinned. "I don't get much sleep these days, tossing and turning. I just can't seem to find a comfortable position."

Youn Kim knew her time was nearing and he worried. She looked tired. He dreaded the birth, fearful of what might happen to Sui. So many women died. He knew almost nothing about childbirth. He'd never given it much thought until now. It certainly wasn't an issue he could discuss with anyone.

Youn Kim showed passing interest in the baby because it pleased Sui. "Have you considered the welfare of your baby?"

"The baby and the father are all I consider," Sui whispered, staring at the water intently. These were curious things to discuss with a man.

"I know what it's like to grow up with one parent. Your baby will need a father."

He looked troubled and she laughed lightly. "Are you volunteering?"

"I would, you know."

"I don't know what to say."

"Then say you will marry me." Taking her hand in his, he placed a small box wrapped in lavender paper and tied with a gold ribbon.

Sui stared at him for endless seconds.

"Open it. I had it made especially for you."

"You had it made for me?" Sui peeled back the paper and opened the lid. There was a sharp intake of her breath. "It's a necklace, a cross." It was exactly the sort of thing she would have bought herself. "You shouldn't have."

He was pleased that she liked it. It sparkled beautifully against her slender neck. "It's gold. I've watched you reading from that black book, the one with the cross on the front. I know how much that sort of thing means to you."

"Do you know anything about that book?"

"It must be good. You seem to enjoy it."

"What exactly does it mean to you-the book, I mean?"

"If you marry me, it will mean the world."

The world. All his hopes and dreams centered around this world. She could tell by the tone of his voice that he wasn't excited by the Bible. But she could hardly expect him to live by what he didn't understand. Two little frown lines appeared between her delicately arched eyebrows.

"So you like it?" He sounded like a little boy seeking approval.

Sui glimpsed at her image in the pool. The sun reflected shimmering glitter off the gold. "I like it very much. But you shouldn't have spent all that money. I'm sorry, I can't keep it, Youn Kim."

"I see." Youn suspected the reason she couldn't accept his gift, and he hated the idea of her loving someone else. He started to rise, then thought better of it. Sooner or later, Sui would realize the man she considered herself in love with was never coming back. And he would still be here when that happened. "Keep it."

"But I-"

"Forget it. You say it best when you say nothing at all." Youn Kim sprang easily to his feet, hesitating for just a moment, as if he meant to say something. He silently left her alone at the bubbling pool.

Sui spent the evening alone. And for several days Youn Kim avoided her. It was just as well, she thought. But hers became a lonely existence, filled with thoughts of Drew. She talked to the baby as if he or she could respond by talking back, convinced the baby knew her every thought and felt her every mood. So she made a habit of reading aloud from a small New Testament.

She knew the baby enjoyed the Gospel of John most of all, because the baby seemed to do handsprings while she read from that particular book. Sui read, the baby played, and they communicated for hours.

The house seemed unusually quiet when Youn Kim let himself in. He'd given everyone the day off. Today, silence suited his mood. Almost a month since he'd spoken to Suiteiko, he hoped to catch her before she fell asleep. Quietly he made his way to her room and tapped lightly on her door.

After a slight hesitation, Sui opened the door just a crack. Everything looked tidy, except the bed. The coverlet was wrinkled in the center where she had been laying on it. And the black book she was so fond of reading was flipped open and turned over to mark her place.

"I'd hoped you weren't asleep." He held out his hand, offering the book he held. She didn't respond.

He cleared his throat. "I thought you might enjoy this."

Sui looked uncertain and tried to hide a smile. "Thank you."

Youn Kim looked as if he was going to say something. Instead he wheeled around and walked away.

The book of poetry looked very old. Sui sank to the edge of the bed. She began to read and it brought tears to her eyes. One poem in particular could have been written for Drew and herself. Of course, lately everything made her emotional.

At seven o'clock, Youn Kim found her dusting shelves in the library. They discussed the book over tea. Sui realized how much she'd missed talking to another adult. In a very short time, their prior easy relationship became reestablished.

For Youn Kim, their lively conversations were a special experience. His relationship with females were limited to childhood, with other children. He'd become too deeply involved with business to seek out women.

But Sui proved different. He enjoyed taking time for her. They talked, shared his books, and though he didn't always agree, she shared her convictions with him. There became so much he loved about her.

He knew she felt comfortable with him. But it frustrated him that she hesitated to allow their feelings to grow. And he suspected the child she carried was at least partly to blame.

On a lovely evening in November, she and Youn Kim walked a path through his two-acre garden. Sui watched her breath make miniature clouds and felt chilly air tickle her face.

"Are you cold?" Youn Kim asked.

Sui smiled into the darkness as she stepped along the path they followed. Glowing lanterns were spaced every few feet.

"Yes, I am. But just cold enough to feel really good."

"You don't want to get sick." Youn Kim halted a few steps from her and slipped his jacket over her shoulders.

"You would think I am made of porcelain, the way you hover over me lately. I am not the first woman in the world to carry a baby. I will not break, and I certainly will not get sick. Tonight is just lovely."

"You shouldn't take unnecessary chances."

Sui laughed softly, her cheeks glowing a peachy pink in the path lights, her eyes lustrous. "I don't."

They wandered and talked as they headed back to the house. Just before they reached the door, Youn Kim caught her arm and turned her toward him. Sui looked into his eyes and saw desperate hope there. And she guessed what he was thinking.

"How long have we known one another now?" His voice grew very serious as he tried to read her thoughts.

"Five months?"

"Five months," he repeated. "Suiteiko, you can not begin to know how much I have grown to love you."

Sui stiffened. Youn Kim gathered her to him. He stroked her hair until he felt her begin to relax. But Sui didn't respond, not even when Youn pulled her against him and gently kissed her. She wished with all her heart she could feel about Youn Kim the way she felt about Drew.

When she stepped back, Youn Kim reached out to her. "Sui, stay with me. Be my wife. I'm so alone without you."

Sui shook her head to clear it, all the time wondering if she had heard him correctly. How could he have forgotten their previous conversation?

"I have allowed you time to reconsider." Sui saw the desperate hope in Youn's eyes. But she knew she owed him complete honesty.

"I can't." It cost her a great deal to admit it. She valued his friendship. "I don't want to give you less than you deserve. You've been nothing but kind to me, Youn."

Without saying a word, his eyes continued beseeching her to become his wife.

"I can only guess what he meant to you, Suiteiko. I wouldn't expect to replace him. Under the circumstances, I think I understand why you do not want to give him up."

Sui's hand found her enlarged belly and patted it. The baby delivered a hefty kick in her ribs. She took a deep breath and let it out slowly. "It is only partly the baby that forces me to resist your generous offer."

Youn Kim looked down as if he wanted to kiss her again. Sui turned her head and his mouth touched her chastely on the cheek. For a moment he looked worried. Then he lowered his mouth to hers again. Feeling his arms go around her, Sui sensed his need. She began to push him away, then stopped.

"Don't answer me right now. Think about it for a while. Just know that if you should change your mind, I will be here for you," he whispered against her hair. "I need you desperately."

She tried to be amiable. It wasn't easy. What could she say without risking his feelings? She stood very quietly, surprised to hear herself say, "Okay, Youn Kim. I'll think about it."

Youn Kim felt certain he would eventually wear her resistance down. So while Sui thought, Youn Kim put his scheme into motion. And for the first time all day, the baby didn't move.

Chapter 26

Sui took a deep breath just outside of Youn Kim's library and ignored the tightening in her abdomen. When it passed she stepped inside, looked the room over slowly, and smiled. She found pleasure in the various wonderful paintings and books, some over one hundred years old. The volume she came for still lay on the center of the desk where she'd left it.

With a concerted effort, she made a quick inspection of the room. Her eyes paused at the top of the bookshelf. She wouldn't be climbing up there now. Today didn't even warrant considering dust. She was overheated from exertion and she pushed her hair back. She felt hot and exhausted, and her back ached.

So many of Youn Kim's books were in dire need of rebinding. At times, however, it seemed like a senseless waste of time. Most of the books would spend their entire life on a shelf. Maybe, just maybe, once a month Youn Kim took one off the shelf to impress a colleague. In other words, Youn Kim invented the job to keep Sui occupied. But it became a pastime she enjoyed.

Perhaps it was fitting that the pen she held would smudge an unsightly blot of ink across the first order blank at that particular moment. In any event, Sui opened the drawer for a blank copy. And she was dealt the blow of her life.

Her own name, written in bold print, leaped out at her. She swayed on her feet and grasped the edge of the desk. Frowning, the song she hummed came to a halt between verses. Sui lifted a very legal-looking document from the drawer. A duplicate contract lay beneath the first, written on a separate page, part of a list of three that ran along the bound edge of a receipt pad and peeked out from beneath a stack of envelopes. Sui nudged the envelopes aside and lifted the pad from its hidden confines into clear view.

She stared at the lined white pad, the type preferred by professionals. The top page held legal descriptions, the bottom three names, her own listed first.

132

Sui didn't recognize the other two. The first column registered addresses, the second a monetary amount. The last listed terms to the contract.

Unexpectedly, a shadow darkened her shoulders. With a start, Sui realized someone now stood just behind her. The shadow might mean anything, but she could only hope it didn't belong to Youn Kim. She swayed on her feet and settled back on her heel. Pasting a smile on her face, she eased the receipt beneath the envelopes on the desk. The cover closed with a snap. Forcing back sudden burning around her heart and behind her eyes, Sui turned quickly, too quickly. She paused to catch her breath. Her face looked lined, exhausted, and very frightened.

"You did not hear me, Suiteiko?" Something seemed terribly wrong, WuMa decided. She could see it in Sui's eyes, in the rigid way she stood. But the older woman decided not to ask questions. If Sui wanted to talk, she would.

"Oh, WuMa, it's you." Sui's voice sounded strained and shaky. "Why didn't someone tell me you would be working in here today?"

WuMa laughed softly. "Why Sui, you know I do not work down here. We are all aware Youn Kim assigned this room to you alone. I simply wanted to surprise you. I have finished the mending early. We can go for a walk, if you would like." Everyone took turns walking with Sui. Youn Kim insisted she not go alone.

Sui licked dry lips. Her throat seemed to fill with cotton in just about the same spot her heart thudded so heavily. She gathered the dustrag from off the desk and held it in shaky hands. "You would be surprised how much dust collects in this place. Well, maybe you wouldn't be surprised, but I was. If it weren't for this room, you would find me beside the bubbling pool every day."

"Maybe fresh air is exactly what you need."

Sui waved nervously across the room. "Thanks just the same. But with so much to finish today, I think I'll pass."

"Maybe is good idea. Bad weather may be on the way." WuMa seemed to sense something not quite right. But she gave Sui a little smile and left her alone. Pregnant women sometimes act strange. They can become very emotional.

Sui was alone again. She rolled the desktop back, scattering papers in her frantic search for the receipt. There it lay, neatly in the corner. She flipped back the first sheet and began reading the next series of notations. Inside she found a bill of sale for an astronomical amount.

As she considered what she saw, the reality of Youn Kim's intent sunk into her stunned mind. It couldn't be true. It just couldn't! He'd lied to her, deceived her. He'd never intended to become a father to her baby. What sort of man sold an infant! And why her infant?

Tears blurred the words as she read them again, slower this time.

...to be received by Youn Kim Bao-Zhi upon delivery of a foreign infant no later than the first month of the new year. It is agreed by both parties that this matter is to be kept silent and never referred to upon such delivery of said infant.

Below, the seal of Cheng Shen Hui appeared, with Youn Kim's bold signature just beneath.

With so much loss, so much unhappiness in her life, Sui's throat tightened until it became a struggle to breathe. Losing Drew had been painful, was still painful. But his death was the result of a rare accident, not a premeditated abduction.

Youn Kim attempted to replace him. He made her accept himself as a companion, so understanding, so endearingly patient. It seemed almost unimaginable that Youn Kim was capable of such duplicity. But even as she thought it, she stared at the evidence in her hand. And Sui realized he was. He'd seemed a very trusted, very valued companion.

Xhiang had seemed harsh at times. But in comparison, Youn Kim had no ethics. He had deceived her into believing he cared for her, cared for the child. Now she wondered how many other things he'd lied about. Without a plan in mind, Sui settled back in a chair. Her mind raced, her body trembled.

Youn Kim would always be smooth and proficient. He'd been born to deceive. He must be valuable to his company. He could move money around and become wealthy at their expense. And he did it all with such ease. Beneath black hair and conservative clothes lingered an evil, calculating mind.

If she hoped to remove herself from his latest scheme, she had to go, and go quickly. No legislature would stop Youn Kim. She belonged to him. As such, her baby did also.

So Sui left the house quietly, still stunned by the startling discovery five miles later. It was getting dark and the temperature fell fast. Her small amount of cash wouldn't even buy a train ticket.

Chapter 27

Wind off the sea had an edge to it, the weather going from mild late fall to the first day of December, raw and cold. Dark, sodden clouds hung dankly to the earth's surface, impregnated by moisture that threatened to burst and spill over in the form of snow, and did little to warm the chill inside Sui.

Even the open-air market at the end of Yichuan Park closed shop to those who came to buy cattle-gut fish, shellfish, eel, poultry, rice, bread, bean curds, hot wrapped dumplings, dried seaweed, herbs, and spices.

Sui was deep in thought. She walked through Yichuan Park, the district's most popular place to shop. It had its problems, of course. Wandering scam artists gave birth to an unsavory undercurrent in the overwhelming stream of humanity flowing around it.

Sui passed by people seeking shelter in nearby alleyways or running from the narrow street to the entrance of buildings. She longed for a place to live peacefully among them.

It wasn't only the weather Sui was concerned about. She clutched her coat tightly beneath her chin against rawness in the air. All day she'd used her plan of escape to keep apprehension about Youn Kim's reaction to her escape at bay by concentrating on the reason she'd fled. Now, alone on the street, uneasiness grew. In her mind, she visualized in vivid detail what Youn might be capable of, until her heart nearly pounded out of her chest. Edging slowly toward a hole in the crowd, she stepped into the only vacant spot visible along Yi Ping Street.

Evening frost crunched beneath her feet. The noise grew unsettling. She fought an impulse to check behind. In a world of male dominance, it seemed hard to imagine Youn Kim allowing her to leave without a fight.

Dodging an oncoming ricksha, she walked two blocks down then three blocks over. Quiet streets housed government living quarters. Along

Xiapoing Alley she passed companies that did contract work for large foreign clothing manufacturers. Xiapoing Alley stopped. Footpaths wound several blocks uphill from the market place.

The office she sought sat tucked between an herbal shop and a little grocery store. The herbal shop was considered a pharmacy, in that the products they sold were thought to cure ailments. Sui made a wide path outside the grocery store to avoid items strung out to dry: a string of raw garlic, cloudy-eyed fish, a stiff plucked goose, and a variety of vegetables.

When at last she reached her destination, it looked dark and deserted. Doctor Zhong's name had been erased. A sign now advertised Asian art work. The new shop displayed small pieces of inlaid furniture.

Sui felt a wave of disappointment. Doctor Zhong had voiced his concern over the ever-increasing rent the last time she'd seen him. Perhaps he'd been unable to make payments. She would miss all of his humorous stories. The man remained compassionate to a fault, compelling poor and homeless through his doors. His eviction removed any possibility of Elliott or Effie Pepple's return.

Sui allowed herself two minutes for the uncomfortable tightness in her back to ease and another minute to consider her situation. On impulse she bought a cup of hot tea, kimchi, and cooked rice from the grocer. Then she looked for a comfortable place outside to eat. A bench next door gave an accessible view of the neighborhood. Sui opened her heavy diary and settled in. The book opened to a passage Effie had written such a short time ago. Sui took a quiet breath and began to read.

Dearest Sui,

Recently I have noticed that the tangle and pressure of the world and the obligations of your commitment have left you weary and sometimes troubled. I just want to remind you that God is always there. Permit Him to give you peace within where the world can never reach. Make Him a part of you, and He will calm your mind and heart.

His love will not dissolve like love the world gives. So don't let your heart be discouraged, and never be anxious. Just learn to trust Him.

With Love, Effie

Sui reached in her pocket and found one of Drew's handkerchiefs. She wiped away a stray tear and sniffed. It smelled just like him-wood and spice. Just holding it near brought him close and made her miss him desperately.

Passersby looked at her skeptically. Two ladies stopped talking and turned to stare. She'd become used to the familiar reaction. To the Chinese, she looked out of place on the street, too foreign to be one of them. So when a man turned to look back, she pretended not to notice. He was short and so thin that he all but disappeared when he turned to the side. His wiry hair stood awry. He had buckteeth and no chin. His squinting expression made it clear his vision was very poor. And it became quite obvious he was not having a good time. The scar on his right cheek caught and held Sui's attention. Bright red and deep, not unlike her own, it looked as if someone had intentionally scraped it with a sanding stone. Sui raised a hand to her face. That's when an idea struck. She didn't know why she hadn't thought of it before. It seemed a long shot, but the notion had possibilities.

There remained no one to protect her now, no one to help until she was able to provide for her baby. Since early that afternoon she'd acted on leaving with little idea of where to go. But what about Marissa? She would talk to her. She had to respect the fact that Marissa might not want to share what little she had. So she wouldn't get her hopes up.

Sui began to relax against the back of the bench. A lot had happened since she'd visited the city with Drew. But she had, and now she was especially glad.

Before Sui began her long trek, she looked up at the sky and touched the scar. "Thanks," she whispered.

Sui deliberated on the muddy little path that reached to the valley and headed slowly east. In a couple of hours it would be dark.

A few miles back she had passed the last house of the residential area. Now every bit of her concentration went to work deciding which path would get her there quickest. Suddenly a short burning pain in her middle made her gasp. She stopped until it let up. Her muscles tightened with more intensity. The baby wasn't due for almost two weeks. That particular reality didn't offer much comfort at the moment.

Thirty feet up, the path proved steep. Covering ground was difficult with the combined weight of mother and baby. As awkward steps took her upward, the wet snow that fell induced agony. Moisture soaked her thin coat and seeped through. Wind picked up, tugging damp hair and slapping it against red cheeks.

Evening turned to night, bringing with it darkness. Sui crept along through prestorm gloom, following a route she outlined in her head. When the trail vanished, Sui felt a moment of panic. She took a deep, calming breath while playing a mind game. She imagined the hottest, muggiest day of the year, one of those miserable days when simple breathing became an effort, a day you longed to step into a snowstorm. It brought a little comfort, very little.

When the next contraction passed, she examined her circumstances uncertainly. By now snow covered the wet ground and kept falling with increasing haste. Her own pain and uncertainty increased as well, until even life with Xhiang sounded wonderful in comparison. It all seemed so far away. Her warm bed lay empty now. Her clothes hung unused in a lone closet.

Sui lost track of time and wasn't even aware of her next step. She knew by now she'd become desperately lost and laughed at a dot of light in the far distance, thinking how cruel of your mind to play such heartless jokes. But when she closed her eyes and opened them again, that same light continued to glow in the distance. With light to guide her, she began to stagger toward it.

Strong gusts of wind intensified the cold, slicing through her coat as if it were thin lace. Spurred on by agony, Sui stumbled when a contraction racked her tormented body. This one felt different, beginning in the center of her back and making a full circle to the front of her abdomen.

Each breath stabbed like an icy knife. Her heart drummed painfully as breath came in gasping pants. When another pain started, followed by warm, sticky wetness, she knew labor was progressing in earnest.

Sui could have cried when she topped the hill. Lights shone warmly from the interior of the closest house. Beyond glowed others, promising people, warmth, and help.

Sui squinted against brutal wind and driving snow. It numbed her face and stung her cheeks. She stopped at the front door, amazed when she looked back. Her tracks had all but disappeared. Snow covered the ground as if she'd never set foot there.

She blew softly into the darkness as another piercing pain stilled her. When she knocked timidly against the door it opened, and she felt heat from the front hall rush out at her.

For what seemed like eternity, she stared at a man framed against the inside glow. Tall and dark, he stood silent and motionless in a flowing scarlet robe. His slicked-back hair gleamed in the light of the doorway. With a soft chin and hard eyes, Sui's mind flashed to Youn Kim and set off memories better forgotten. She shivered, looking past him and into a room that didn't look all that homey, but it felt warm.

"You lost?" He looked rigid and very stern.

"Yes, sir, I am." Sui swayed unsteadily.

"Who are you? What do you want?" His expression suggested Sui was his worst nightmare come true.

"My name is Sui Bach."

"It's awfully dark and wet to be walking around out there this time of night."

A wave of heated air struck Sui's face. "Yes, sir."

"It's suicide, that's what it is."

As if on cue, a woman's voice called out. "Deng!"

Deng glanced across his shoulder and back at Sui impatiently.

"I'm sorry to have bothered you." Sui stood silent and still, pressure building with intensity.

"Then why did you-bother me, I mean?"

Sui swallowed hard. The need to cry made her throat ache terribly. Snow and rain dripped off ends of icicles hanging from her hair. She looked so pathetic and defenseless, Deng winced. "I need help."

Deng flinched and looked away.

"I don't have anywhere to go. I am willing to work, but first..."

Deng wanted to laugh. The woman could barely stand. "Put you to work?"

She tried to smile but she couldn't. "I'm not seeking charity."

Deng raised his eyebrows ominously, ran a hand through his hair and looked over his shoulder. "Look, I'm rather busy at the moment." He met with soft, pleading eyes filled with desperation. Relenting, he drew a couple of bills from his wallet and held them out to her. "I am not in the habit of supporting beggars, but under the circumstances..." He shrugged.

He began to close the door. "I don't want your money. I need a warm place to have my baby." Another pain ripped through her. Sui could barely talk she was crying so hard. When it eased, her eyes begged him for assistance. "Please." Panic crept into her voice.

"I-" Deng began, but he didn't finish. AnWon would be angry if he allowed her to spend the night.

"Just let me stay one night. I will leave in the morning, I promise."

"I can't." Deng looked away.

She was pushing and she knew it, but she just had to try. "An hour then, just an hour to warm myself by your fire?"

"Look, we all have problems to contend with."

Oh God, she thought, what will I do?

"Town is that direction," Deng said, pointing out the obvious. "A woman shouldn't be out on a night like tonight. You really should find a place to stay." Deng didn't soften at all as he closed the door.

"I just did," Sui whispered, sweeping sodden bangs off her forehead with a numb hand. Pain gave way to anger, which became grief that led to desperation, then returned to pain. With each step, Sui fought to maintain her balance as the cold, sopping dress wrapped itself around unsteady legs. She nearly tripped over a sign hidden by snow and darkness. Sui vaguely made out worn letters: ZHONGHUA.

"Zonghua? That means I'm as far from Fusuma as I can get and still be in the county limit." It occurred to her that she wasn't too far from Hudong, the town the Pepple's lived in. That was something.

Darkness intensified until almost complete. She came to an abandoned industrial square. A row of deserted warehouses lined the street, their inanimate shapes illuminated by a single oil-burning street lamp. The empty building nearest the lamppost stood out in gloomy dimness. Faded black lettering above the door identified it as having once been a fish packaging plant. The prospect to the left looked no less depressing. Windows were broken. Snow-covered crates leaned against a bowed door.

Sui settled against one of the crates and stared into blackness. From somewhere came strains of Asian music. So she crossed the alley to a food market. She was positioned between two buildings when a pain hit so hard and for so long she dropped to a snow-laden bin. Smothered groans were lost in the storm as she pushed against the increasing pressure of the next contraction. One wrenching pang hardly passed when another came on with tremendous force. With accelerated viselike agony, the baby was coming with urgent speed.

For the first time since her ordeal began, hopelessness sliced through her like a shaft of pain. Her cries were smothered by wind. The snow beneath her grew crimson. Eight minutes later the world became hazy and out of focus. In spite of frigid air, large beads of perspiration stood out on her heated face.

A tiny baby girl was born that night in a flood of liquid, perfectly formed in every way. She made a small cry, squirmed weakly a few times...and then nothing.

With infinite tenderness, Sui lifted her little daughter, placing her gently beneath her coat. A quick tug removed a chain from around her neck, a token of Drew and of their love together. Sui wound it gently around her baby's wrist, fingering the attached gold ring.

Giving in to the peace that surrounded her, a soft kitten-like whimper brought her back. Sui tried to signal help, to lift a hand, to comfort the small bundle. But her arm lay limp, her last conscious thought of warm sunshine. Even the deadly cold became forgotten as she closed her eyes. In a haze, she prayed for her precious baby one last time before she slept. That is how they found her.

Jian Chu stepped out the door whistling a tune through his teeth. Carting a brown shopping bag under each arm, he stumbled and would have fallen if he hadn't caught himself on a protruding window ledge. Groceries were flung to the ground and tumbled out. Clambering about on his knees, he attempted to gather items, to shove them back in the bag. He reached for a packaged duck and saw Sui.

Standing slowly to his feet, he carefully examined the situation. Upon closer inspection he grew uneasy. Then he took a really good look, shocked to find a dead woman with a sheen of blood gathering about her in the crimson snow. Still stunned for having the wind knocked out of him, Jian stood immobilized, staring at the corpse, not certain whether to call for help or run. Too frightened to think rationally, he decided to do the latter. He was scrambling on his knees when he heard a soft mewing sound. Maybe he'd misjudged the situation. Maybe the woman wasn't dead after all.

That's when a door to the store opened. From where he stood hidden between two incinerators, Jian recognized the figure in the darkness as the younger son of Zhiu Chou.

Jian stepped into the shadows and stiffened. But it was too late. The boy spotted Sui and called for help.

Chapter 28

A combination of darkness and record snowfall made it nearly impossible to find the sign identifying the town as Zhonghua. Elliott Pepple decided the world could keep the record. He simply wanted to share a roaring fire with Effie.

A long day with a succession of obligatory meetings left Elliott Pepple unbelievably tired, very hungry, and restless. His triumphant effort to plea on behalf of the school proved his only bright spot. Added to the frigid night he'd walked out into, the roadblock had made necessary an alternate route, thus an additional mile. He figured he'd earned the pounding headache that kept him company on the lonely trek home.

Icy rain penetrated his heavy coat and hat. Gusty wind whistled through the alley and blew against him, adding to his discomfort. Lifting a wool collar over his ears, Elliott trudged into the gale. The promise of Effie kept him from stopping to find lodging for the night.

All remained black, except for the faintest of lights shining from the other end of an alley. Who would be foolish enough to stay outside on such a frigid night? He drew closer. Elliott heard excited voices. Something wasn't right. He stood in darkness long enough to allow his eyes to adjust and saw three men with one small boy.

In the dim light, the boy looked to be about ten or eleven years old. An elderly man shouted to another across the crowded alley. Elliott had never seen so much stuff crammed into such a small space. Wooden shelves covered a wall loaded with bottles and boxes. Crates piled high with what appeared to be broken furniture lined the opposite building. Mounds of snow covered everything.

Then Elliott spotted the woman who lay in a pool of blood. Heat from her body melted snow that sought to cover her. That heat wouldn't last long in this weather.

Elliott would have walked on, but something compelled him to stay. Walking silently through the deep carpet of snow, he moved aside long enough to allow a cart to pass. When it came to a stop, Elliott took a deep breath, squared his shoulders, and stepped forward.

The boy tossed a blanket over the woman and he shouted loudly enough to attract the store keepers attention. Jian muttered something about the woman being a foreigner, and flung the blanket back. When Elliott would have turned away he looked back, shocked to see a baby. It became immediately apparent what had happened. But as Elliott looked into the newborn's face, his heart felt as if it had melted. She was so perfect and yet so still, as though she simply slept peacefully. Then he watched her tiny chest rise and fall.

As Elliott reached a work-roughened hand out and gently touched her eyes, her cheeks, her mouth, and each tiny finger, he experienced an overwhelming need to hold the newborn, to protect her, to replace the tinge of blue from her soft skin with healthy pink.

Jian stepped over Sui to help place her in the wagon. When he looked up, Elliott was no longer there. He'd lifted the baby carefully from her mother and tucked her inside his thick wool coat. Not a sign of life could be seen in the baby's face, no feeling, not much more than the quiet stillness of death. She lay silently pressed against Elliott's chest.

"It's too late," Jian bellowed at him. "Leave her to be buried with her mother."

Elliott shot the man a look that spoke volumes.

In spite of Jian's militant bearing, he backed down. He knew some men felt differently about death. He shrugged. The child wasn't his problem. "She can only bring you trouble."

"I'm not leaving her." Elliott's deep voice sounded composed, his eyes gentle as he patted the still bulk beneath his jacket.

Jian nodded slightly even as his eyes narrowed. "May the problem rest on your shoulders."

Jian's response was accurate and Elliott knew it. Taking the child may bring trouble. But Elliott had already settled in his mind that he would take the chance. The idea didn't seem rational even to himself, but he felt somehow convinced this baby needed him.

"I will report her to the proper authorities in the morning." His tone did not invite argument. Taller than most of his neighbors, Elliott proved a formidable sight in the dark of night as he walked away with purpose. Feeling the frail weight against his chest, he became desperate to reach home. If there was any chance of survival, he had to get the child warm and dry. And even that might not be enough, a still voice whispered. It concerned Elliott that she did not struggle while he gently stroked his hands against her. It tied his stomach in knots.

Elliott freed his hand of a glove and slid it into the opening of his jacket. The outer layer felt wet and cold, but the fabric inside remained dry and warm. A rapid heartbeat beneath his palm offered a trace of encouragement.

For just the one night he wasn't going to think of responsibilities, the unfortunate fate of the baby's mother, or regrets for having rescued the infant. He would forget everything and sit in front of a warm fire with the baby.

With eyes narrowed against the driving snow, Elliott reached home. His legs felt numb as he climbed the steps, one at a time. Heat from inside rushed out at him. He thought how generous Effie was with wood, sometimes overly generous. But in that instant Elliott promised himself he would never complain again.

Elliott shrugged his coat over the back of the kitchen chair. Sweaty palms and panic would not save the baby. Neither would the urge to go after Effie. A note on the table informed him she'd gone next door to settle in a new student.

The house seemed empty without her. It served to remind him he alone must take charge of the tiny human he held. He supposed he'd depended on his wife for too long to be comfortable with the predicament he now faced. However much he claimed he was unable to cope, he would do what he had to do.

Elliott imagined what Effie would have done in like circumstances and softly crooned to the baby. "Together we can handle this, little one."

So he unearthed a small basin, filled it half full of warm water, and sat it on the table. He was pushing a cupboard door aside in search of a towel when the baby stirred. Large capable hands steadied her. She felt cold to the touch. Her delicate skin was tinged blue as Elliott eased her into a reclining position and slipped her into warm water. With a trembling sigh, he brushed cold lips over the tiny forehead, experiencing a tenderness more overwhelming than any emotion he had ever known in his life. And suddenly he was rewarded with a whimper.

Tipping his head, Elliott looked down and began to laugh softly. The baby's tiny mouth was pursed and sucking. "So, you're hungry. That's good. You'll have to be patient with me though, little darling. I'm new at this sort of thing."

He wanted to stay forever within that moment, sensing the slow unfolding of love deep within his heart. For the first time in his life, he knew the captivating sweetness of a baby laying trustingly in his hands. No wonder Effie wanted a baby daughter so badly.

Nestling her against his chest, Elliott turned his eyes toward a commotion at the door. The knob turned. When it opened, a very amazed Effie walked in.

She saw Elliott first. He stood at the table with a towel over his left arm. But she was even more interested in the baby girl held against his shoulder. Dark hair stuck to her perfectly round head. The infant couldn't be more than a few hours old.

Effie's mouth fell open. She deliberately closed it. "Well, welcome home, dear." After the initial shock, she made a quick survey of the room. "I don't see her mother."

"She doesn't have one."

Effie moved toward her husband. With one hand on the baby, her eyes traveled over Elliott's face as possibilities raced through her mind.

"Do we have ourselves a little problem here, Elliott?"

"A very little one, I suppose."

Following the path of his gaze, Effie moved her hand from a small leg to a soft, red cheek. The baby's head jerked toward Effie's finger, her mouth open and ready to be fed. Urgent whimpers escaped drawn lips. When her mouth failed to encounter a nipple, resounding wails erupted from quivering lips. Elliott grinned.

Effie laughed and reached up to kiss her husband. "Do you care to explain?" Having been raised with three brothers and daily surrounded with precious little boys, viewing a baby girl felt almost like looking into a treasure chest. Little girls were no more special than little boys, but Effie certainly longed for a daughter.

"The woman, her mother," Elliott corrected, with a tired smile on his face, "met with tragic misfortune."

"Is she..."

Elliott nodded his head wearily.

"What do we plan to do with her child?" Even as she asked, Effie began warming milk on the stove.

Elliott looked deeply into his wife's eyes, searching them. "You've always wanted a daughter."

Effie stood very still for a long moment. Then she laughed through sudden tears. "She is beautiful...oh, so beautiful. A gift straight from God."

Elliott wrapped the baby in a thick white towel, and they continued to marvel while the baby enjoyed her first feeding. When her eyes grew heavy and she gave in to sleep, Effie kneeled beside her husband's chair and stroked the fuzzy head.

It had been a long, tiring day. Elliott was very grateful to be home. "I sat through some of the most tedious and incredibly boring cases in history," he said, nudging off his boots. "When the road closed, I was forced to take an alternate route. That's how I found the baby and her mother. It was awful, Effie. She froze to death just outside a market. If only I had been there an hour earlier."

"You can't blame yourself. You did what you could."

"I have to believe there was a reason." Elliott kissed them both. The baby sighed contentedly, grasping Effie's finger a little tighter. "She lost her mother, Effie."

"Yes, but she has us. Maybe we will just have to love her a little more."

Elliott held the little bundle against his chest and stared into her angelic face.

"You make a very good daddy."

Elliott smiled in answer.

"We stopped praying together for a daughter years ago, Elliott. I sort of figured that maybe it just wasn't meant to be. I tried to let go of the idea of having children. But I have to admit something. In my heart I still pray day and night."

"I know."

"Maybe this is God's way of giving us a daughter?" Her pleading expression almost undid Elliott. He looked at her with worried eyes.

"I hope you're right. Lord, how I hope you're right. But somewhere out there is a father. This is his baby, too. We can't lose sight of that."

"I wonder if we'll hear from him soon." She hoped so, in a way. The baby had a right to her father. And yet, Effie felt wonderfully drawn to the little pixie.

Elliott shrugged. "I don't want to live with false hope. That would be cruel. It does seem as if her father would have been with his wife."

"If he was able."

Elliott gazed out the window. Swirling snow filled their tracks to the door. How quickly life changed. His hair showed a little gray now, and age was robbing him of vigor. The only thing he could be certain of was trust in God. Closing his eyes. Elliott offered a silent prayer that everything would turn out as God saw fit. He looked up when Effie returned bearing two steaming mugs. She slid one in front of Elliott before reclaiming her place beside him.

"I have an idea," Effie declared. "For the moment, let's just care for her. Let's pretend, for just this one night, that she is ours, yours and mine."

This could change a lot of things for them. It made him think seriously about their future. But he had to admit, he didn't mind the idea of a baby. Suddenly he couldn't imagine life without her. Elliott didn't voice his concerns or his hope. But given the court's position, adoption shouldn't be difficult if no one claimed her.

A very eventful day, along with the warmth of the crackling fire, began having an effect of Elliott. When next Effie looked up at him, he lay dozing comfortably in his oversized chair.

With gentle care, Effie eased the baby from the warm tangle of Elliott's arms. While Effie gazed longingly into her beautiful face, the baby instinctively snuggled closer. Effie kissed a soft cheek and brushed warm fingers over her forehead. With equal care, she eased the sleeping baby into the temporary bed she concocted from a drawer.

For a long moment she watched her husband sleep, and thought how fortunate she was to have the privilege of marriage with such a wonderful man. After almost twenty years, she couldn't imagine living without him. Life hadn't always been easy, but it was all right. Sometimes, only the memory of how God had brought them through the last experience took them through the next.

Quietly, Effie straightened the house. Then she saw Elliott's jacket hanging over the chair and thought how they insisted the boys pick up after themselves.

She grinned good naturally. Elliott stayed her boy sometimes. She wouldn't trade him.

Effie was shaking water from his coat when the book fell out of his pocket and tumbled to the floor. So she picked it up and turned it over in her hand. The plain blue front cover wasn't titled. It flipped open to pages filled with writing. Something familiar about the lettering caused her to pause. She couldn't place where she'd seen it before.

"It belongs to the baby's mother. I decided to keep it for her."

Effie looked up quickly. Elliott was watching her.

"I thought you were sound asleep," Effie admonished him. "You startled me."

"Sorry." He nodded toward his jacket. "There's a chain in my pocket. I found it attached to the baby's wrist."

Effie dipped her hands into his pocket. The ring hanging from the chain had a craftsman's mark impressed on the band. Something about it jarred her memory. Effie turned it over and over, trying to remember where she had seen it.

"Lovely, isn't it?" Elliott asked her.

"I've seen this ring before. I'm just not certain where." Opening the book to the first page, everything suddenly fell into place. They were all part of Sui, the book, the ring, and the baby.

Effie clasped her hands, trying to massage warmth into suddenly cold fingers.

"Lord, oh Lord."

Then a strange calm settled over her. Having Sui's baby made it nearly perfect. They were touched by knowing that a very important part of Sui would live on in their lives. They would have part in nurturing Sui's baby. The baby became Gin Sui, according to Sui's wishes.

They went to bed that night and talked softly about the child and the dreams they shared for her. And the world never looked so sweet.

Days became weeks and weeks became months. The adoption went through without a hitch. Gin Sui Bach Pepple became theirs to love. And they couldn't have loved her more if she had been born of their flesh.

Joy coursed through Effie like a flood whenever she looked into Gin's sweet little face. How precious, how miraculous she seemed. She never tired of picking the infant up from wherever she was laying, playing, sleeping, crying, eating, or fussing. Sometimes she would even neglect her chores to hold the most precious answer to prayer against her heart. At least for as long as Gin would allow it.

Elliott wondered what they ever did before Gin filled their home with such vibrant life. He couldn't begin to describe the fulfillment welling up within him every time he walked through the door. Gin couldn't talk yet.

Her body language said it all. Chubby arms never failed to reach for him. Sparkling eyes followed him wherever he went. And those little legs, sometimes he feared she would kick her way right onto the floor when she saw him.

Elliott came home early one afternoon and found Effie crooning to the baby as they rocked back and forth in the chair he'd built especially for her. For a long moment he stood silently in the doorway watching them. He leaned against the door frame and realized for the first time that the look of rapt joy Gin brought to his wife's face was a permanent expression now.

He began to speak, then broke off as his throat swelled with thanksgiving. For some reason he did not fully understand, God answered their prayer in a way of which only He was capable. God had said "yes" when they asked for a baby girl.

Chapter 29

Lum Lee limped through a dim back room of the morgue a little after eight in the evening. He'd skipped eating dinner as he normally did. A painful right ankle made him eager to prepare the corpse, clean his equipment, and call it a night. With the last of four cases, Lum paused for a moment to catch his breath and glance up at the clock. He seemed to be making good progress.

Frozen rain pinged against the roof of the otherwise quiet chamber.

Lum Lee began to turn away from the counter, when a deep wracking cough from beneath a sheet unsettled him. He jumped, and his mouth went dry. His palms grew moist as he faltered suspiciously forward. Lum responded by reaching slowly behind him for a scalpel. Approaching the side of the slab, he pulled back the sheet with a snap. Sui's fever-burned eyes were closed. She lay pale and wasted, her hair matted against a flushed forehead, her garment soaked with dark blood.

Lum Lee stepped back, recoiling in disbelief and dread. His uncharacteristic loud cry brought Murinka to his side immediately. When she saw what was happening, his wife too drew back. Murinka clasped a hand to her face. She wanted to escape but she couldn't. Instead, she stood as if frozen in place. Neither one moved or spoke. Their eyes remained glued to the rapid rise and fall of Sui's chest.

Murinka felt her breath catch. Her eyes met those of her husband. "Well, this is a first! What happened?"

Lum Lee touched her shoulder without making a sound. "I don't know exactly. She supposedly died while giving birth tonight. The child is dead."

Murinka's hand went to her mouth. It seemed an eternity before she turned pain-filled eyes from Sui. "Her heart must be breaking."

"Of course." He stepped back to give Murinka room.

Murinka looked at Sui's pale face. "Who is she?"

Lum Lee shrugged. "The three men who dropped her off an hour ago didn't seem to know."

Murinka nodded silently. "Do you not find it strange that she is a foreigner?"

Lum Lee didn't answer, but rather ran a hand through his black hair.

Murinka smiled sadly and touched Sui's wrist. Raging heat issued form her like fire. "This woman needs a doctor."

"Do you really suppose a doctor would come out on a night like this?"

Murinka glanced out the window. Trees whipped back and forth in the howling wind, snapping branches beneath the weight of frozen rain. They heard a loud snap. In the background they listened to ice cracking and the beating of frozen pellets against the roof.

"We must find a doctor." Murinka sensed the young woman hung onto life by a thread.

A glowing candle caught a brilliant reflection at Sui's throat. A strange expression crossed Lum Lee's face. "Even if you were able to find a doctor, he would likely refuse to treat this woman."

"What are you talking about?"

"She wears the cross of Christ."

Murinka turned to her husband with a smile. He ran a tired hand through his tousled hair. They both knew it wasn't unusual for a professional to refuse his services to a Christian. The gospel of Jesus Christ was not preached openly. However, a couple came to their village recently, presenting the gospel in a way that touched them both deeply. Since then, their lives had changed miraculously.

"Well then, we will place her in His hands and ask for a miracle."

Lum Lee reversed his direction to his private office. Exhausted and unsettled, he blew out candles and covered instruments. "It looks as if we have a long night ahead of us."

They exchanged a smile, and Murinka felt very thankful for her husband. Lum Lee remained such a considerate man, and better looking than she would ever admit to him. He tended to let his hair grow beyond what most considered current fashion. But his deep set dark eyes and shaggy style added to his appeal.

"I shall make tea."

"I would enjoy a cup."

Murinka settled in to care for her patient. She pulled up a chair beside the young woman. Despondency turned to fever. For two terrible days and nights, sweat trickled off Sui's forehead one minute, to turn to chills the next.

A groan caught Murinka's attention, and she bent anxiously over the sleep mat. She heard Sui mumble something disjointed, then she went silent. Murinka dipped a clean cloth into a fresh bowl of water and pressed it to Sui's parched lips. "Lay still, my friend. You will be well shortly." She prayed it became truth.

Sui woke up at two o'clock in the morning. She raised her head and leveled large, worried eyes at Murinka. She lay in the dark, reliving the awful dream, and very thankful the contractions had stopped. Her last thought as she fell into a deep, restorative sleep was for the baby. For the first time in months, the child didn't move.

She awoke later to blazing pain in her cheek. Propping herself into a sitting position, the throbbing ache in her head clenched tightly. The room tilted crazily. She pushed herself forward and fell back.

Murinka heard a stirring. What she found at seven o'clock wasn't what she expected. Sui sat on the edge of the bed, her face flushed, her cheeks covered with tears.

"Tso sun." Murinka poured a glass of water and held it to Sui's lips.

"Good morning." Sui choked on the words. "I can't," she said in a strangled voice.

"Sip it slowly, a little more. That's better." Murinka set the glass on a table and met sad eyes. "I am Murinka. And you are?"

"Suiteiko. I am Sui."

"Welcome to our home, Sui. You look much better." Her voice was soft with emotion.

Sui asked what was foremost on her mind. "Where is my baby?"

Murinka sat down on a chair next to the bed and patted Sui's hand gently with her own. The look that passed between them said it all.

Tears spilled over Sui's face. Her entire body began to tremble as she tried to accept her loss. With the death of her child came the loss of expectancy, of life, of the future. Her abdomen felt flat when she touched it. Sui gulped down a cry and squeezed Murinka's hand. "Not my baby. Why not me?"

"I am so sorry." Murinka seemed genuine. Sui looked awfully young. But Murinka sensed an inner courage that would likely carry her through, given the proper support. She could do nothing to ease the pain. Murinka began to cry as a flood of tears poured down Sui's cheeks, not too embarrassed for Sui to see it. She was familiar with the tenderness, the agony, the grief, the blame a mother experienced at the loss of her child. Being alone made it worse.

"Sui, she is gone. But she is in a better place."

"Was she brought here too?"

"No."

"Then how do you know...?"

"The men who brought you here told my husband."

"I want her here, with me."

"I know it is hard on you, Sui," Murinka said softly. "I wish there was something I could do." She hated the fact that she couldn't. Sui needed time alone now so Murinka left quietly.

Sui rolled into a ball and sobbed until she gasped for air. She remembered holding her baby. She thought for a long time of the tiny face, the wet dark curls she'd stroked a few days before. She would never again see little round cheeks begging for feathery kisses, or watch eyes light up when she discovered butterflies or bunny rabbits. And she would never again hold her protectively.

After days of pouring her heart out, Sui lifted her face to the winter sun, considering giving up. And for a while she did. For two hours she lay still and silent, falling asleep, loving her, thinking of her, remembering that a short while ago her baby had been alive.

For two days, Sui lay somewhere between sleeping and waking. On the morning of the third day, she awoke to find Murinka sleeping in the chair. Dark circles underlined the woman's eyes. Her head was tipped back while she softly snored.

Sui silently raised herself into a sitting position at the edge of the mat, watching the older woman. She looked tired. Sui realized she herself was the reason for Murinka's pale skin, and she suddenly felt ashamed. Rising slowly, Sui silently slipped a blanket over Murinka.

Murinka stirred. Sleep still clouding her face, Murinka cracked her eyes open. She was pleased when Sui hesitantly smiled at her.

"It seems I owe you a debt of gratitude." A look of genuine distress crossed Sui's face. Murinka felt compelled to reassure her.

"That's all right. When you lose someone so suddenly, you feel sad and alone."

Sui nodded, focusing on her clenched hands. "I'm okay now. Thank you."

But Murinka knew she wasn't okay. Sui was finding her way through a tough time right now. She herself had been there-the hiding, the nice things to say in order to obtain seclusion in silence, a place to mourn in peace away from intrusive eyes and condolences, a polite way of driving people away without saying how bad it really hurt.

"You are not okay, Suiteiko. But you are not alone."

Sui's eyes misted. She felt wide awake. And sleep only provided a brief escape before pain returned. She could do nothing to change her situation, and that hurt the worst. Closing her eyes, she fought back a swell of fresh emotions. Her greatest desire was to die quietly.

When Sui looked up at Murinka, she felt sobered by the tender expression. She rarely talked about something as personal as losing two people who meant everything to her. Yet something about Murinka's quiet manner encouraged her to open up, silently assuring Sui that she just might understand all the complex feelings she held inside. All the same, pouring out her personal life did nothing to bring her husband and baby back.

"You can't know what it's like to lose everything," she told Murinka, sounding uncommonly firm.

"We're not talking about me. I want to know about you. Tell me how you feel."

Sui began to sob. A moment later she felt Murinka press a handkerchief in her hand. Through healing tears, Sui managed to pour out all her hurts-the loss of her mother, Xhiang's position and his indifference, her love for Drew and his untimely death, her escape from Youn Kim and the reason behind it, and now the loss of her precious baby girl. Events and circumstances were all muddled and nearly unintelligible, but Murinka managed to figure out the essence of what Sui was trying to share.

When Murinka suggested they take a walk, Sui thought of pleasant walks she and Drew shared together, and she cried harder. A half hour later, when Sui couldn't cry another tear, she stood on weak legs. They walked through the garden with slow, wobbly steps.

"You're doing all right now."

"I can't believe I fell apart so badly. I am sorry."

"Don't be. I know how it is." Murinka focused on a blade of grass at her feet. "Did I tell you I lost three babies?" Murinka spoke so softly that Sui almost didn't hear. "Not one of them became easier than the last."

"How did you get through it?"

"I'm not. And I'm not certain I ever will be, not completely."

Sui blew her nose and wiped away a fresh tear. "Do you ever feel as if your little one depended on you totally, that you failed her miserably?"

Murinka nodded and wiped away a stray tear from her own cheek. "Yes. That and a lot of other things."

"I long to hold Gin against my heart, to feel her breathe, to whisper that I love her, to watch her grow." Closing her eyes, Sui swallowed the fresh lump in her throat. "I'll never be able to do that."

"You're right, but someone is," Murinka whispered softly. "I believe your little Gin knows how you feel. She would want you to go on living."

"Do you really think so?"

"I'm counting on it." Murinka smiled sadly. "At one time I felt like you do now. Then one day I faced reality. I could die, or I could live and make my life count."

"I'm glad you're here."

"So am I." Murinka lightly patted the back of Sui's hand.

They stopped beside a small, quiet pond. With tossed hair, swollen eyes, and a red nose, Sui looked up at the towering branches of a nearby shade tree. "Drew and I walked through the Yu Garden in southern Shanghai."

Murinka nodded. "I have been there."

"We were standing before the ancient ginkgo when he said something I thought was strange at the time. He told me there is something very special about an old tree reaching for heaven, that it silently whispers praise and worship to eternal God."

"Your Drew sounds like a very wise man."

"He is, or he was. Drew died almost a year ago. We had an accident."

"Oh Sui, I'm so sorry."

"Me too."

"And you were happy."

Sui nodded. "We were very happy."

"We all live way up high in our own mountain from time to time. Life is wonderful there. It's very rare that we walk above life's struggles. But then something nearly always comes along that brings us back down."

"What are you saying?" Sui asked quietly.

"Is your God of the mountain also God of the valley?"

Murinka shifted the knife to her other hand, dropping sliced chicken into a clay bowl. She peeked at Suiteiko from the kitchen window. They had come to love one another as sisters. And before she walked back to the drawer, she looked again to make sure Sui was all right sitting alone in the gazebo.

Sui's time of restoration came to an end. Threat of discovery by Youn Kim or Xhiang filled her with urgency to leave China for the country from which Drew came. She would miss Murinka and Lum Lee sorely after a three month friendship. Considering all the little things the couple did, Sui felt touched deeply with affection. Their generosity stirred her heart. She knew God had brought them together. He felt closer than ever before. Throughout sadness, joy, laughter, and tears, He remained a prayer-answering God who really did care.

When she looked back over the past year, she thought of all her prayers, all the favors she ever asked of Him, and she smiled. He'd heard them all. Sometimes He answered "no," but He listened.

Only God knew why He chose to say no to Pepple's cry for a little girl. And it would erase so much pain from Murinka's lonely heart to hold a baby to her breast. She must keep in mind that God loved them even more than she was capable.

She wasn't sorry Drew came into her life. And even if she could erase the memory of their baby, she never would. Every recollection of her husband and child would be cherished each day of her life, despite the regret those thoughts may bring.

Now she had to leave. But how? Seeking transport became increasingly discouraging. For a week and a half she'd plagued the dock, volunteering to work aboard various ships in exchange for passage to America. One particular officer did thank her for the offer, promising that he would keep her in mind for a return trip.

Sui became worn out by her uncertain future. Murinka suggested she remain home today, away from the wharf. Tomorrow she would try again. It seemed all she could do at the moment. Alone and puzzled, Sui turned to God with pleading eyes.

"Father God, I choose to rejoice in You. I trust that everything will work together for good....because I love You...and I am called according to Your purpose. I look forward to talking to You face to face someday. I have so many questions, and You have all the answers.

"Search my heart, Lord. If there is anything unclean, anything that would make Your stay there unpleasant, please reveal it to me, and wash it away through the blood of Your Son, Jesus."

Sui paused a moment, drawing strength form His Spirit.

"A real urgency to leave seems to be pressing on my heart and nearly squeezing it in half. I tried everything imaginable, but each door just seems to close. Did I mention I'm willing to work?"

In her mind, Sui considered various jobs. Work didn't bother her. She simply needed an opportunity.

"Now it's Your turn, Father. I will just close my eyes and listen. If You have anything to say, please speak to my heart."

Chapter 30

Gulls plunged into the water, rising to complain about the size of their catch. The sun was rising very gradually as Drew guided the *Marybeth* through gloom. A maze of buildings became hazy shapes against the morning sky. By the time he approached the mouth of Soochow Creek, a beacon became clearly visible. While his ship slipped down the channel and around the coast toward the Port of Shanghai, Drew flicked off the running lights and cast the lever into reverse. Slowly, he backed into the dock, just starboard of a loaded freighter from Japan.

The taste, the smell, the very experience seemed so familiar. It invoked images of simple things, past, but hopefully not over. Sui remained alive in his mind. He closed his eyes, regret tearing at him. She was the kind of woman a man cherished. She made all the wrongs of this world fall into proper perspective with her breathless laughter and gentle kindness. He groaned, hefting the cable starboard. He would look and continue looking until he found her.

Drew stepped aside at a tap on his shoulder. "Captain?"

"Hey, Jeff."

"Want me to take over at the helm?"

"I'm comfortable out here," Drew mumbled into his coffee cup. He tightened his grip on the wheel with one hand and inched forward, his mouth tight, and a deep line between his eyes.

"You look beat." With crossed arms, Jeff leaned against a crate and stared straight ahead, watching the ship's steady progression. He knew how troubled the captain was over his wife. Drew hadn't allowed himself to relax since the accident. The effect was wearing on him. They all prayed Drew found her, and soon.

"If your Sui is half the woman you say she is, she'll understand when you explain. You wouldn't have been much good on the sea with your eyes hidden behind gauze for months."

"Don't remind me."

"I don't suppose I have to. You were a mess."

They exchanged a smile. Jeff was a good friend. He made the trip more enjoyable by joking with the rest of the crew. Behind all that fooling around hid a very ambitious young man who handled life with concern and curiosity.

"How is the head?"

"Head's fine," Drew replied dully.

"Fine. You would say your head is fine if someone split it wide open."

"Someone did."

"Did that fancy surgeon indicate how long your vision would be blurred?"

Drew shrugged. "The technique is still in experimental stages. He couldn't say for sure."

"I'll bet you're thankful you made it through this whole ordeal. I don't know if I would have gone under a knife." To Jeff's way of thinking, going through a surgery that had never before been performed on a human remained a gamble. He was fascinated by people who risked life and dared to face uncertainty with such assurance.

Being blind proved more dreadful than Drew ever imagined. Through it all, he'd tried to think positively. Pain alone took its toll. But the anxious months of recovery, of not knowing if his vision would ever return, had been frightening. He'd broken down and cried like a baby when he looked into Doctor Kanter's face for the first time. He would be eternally thankful for the knowledge and skill of the doctor and his staff. But Drew hoped never again to breathe in the antiseptic smell of a hospital or see molded bandages lying heaped on the floor beside his chair. If he'd ever taken his sight for granted, he never would again.

"You would do the same if something pinched your optic nerve closed. It's not much fun being shut away from the world in darkness. Some risks are worth taking."

"If you say so." Jeff looked at the back of Drew's head for a long time. New hair growth hid the worst. It hit him again, what a terrible loss they would have experienced if Drew hadn't made it. As a boss, he couldn't be replaced for fairness or sound judgment.

"This would be a good time to get things together, before we disembark."

"Holler if you want help, Captain."

"I will."

Hazy reflections of dim light led him through a maze. Due to foggy conditions, the trail reminded him of the inside of a cave, with dim light and tangy air scented with decay. Sort of like hell, Drew thought. No escape, just death and grief. No need for importing and exporting, buying and selling, no invigorating salty air. A fiery, inescapable prison. A crushed heart filled with remorse for what had been and what could no longer be.

Drew dropped onto a chair, leaned against the cushioned headrest, and closed his eyes.

Silence intensified the sea's gentle swells. From deep within, his senses clamored loudly, demanding answers to questions. Sui was out there somewhere. Perhaps she was alive, or maybe they were physically separated by death. Their bond remained indestructible, coming from somewhere deeper than flesh. They shared the same spirit.

Drew lifted his eyes to upward. "Thy kingdom come, thy will be done." And without another word, Drew stepped onto Shanghai soil.

Two long sets of stairs separated the waterfront from the market place, where the neighborhood began opening for the day. The Tian Yuan suburb lay ahead, spreading north form Cheng Hong to Cannes, a crowded quarter of small shops, two banks, a book store, a police station, a bakery, and neighborhood pubs. Cannes Street consisted of a complex tangle of narrow back streets, cramped with cheap housing. For the first time, Drew noticed how dingy and worn the area had become.

He made his way around an early morning street vender who dragged out crates and display bins. A thin, dark man with a long, lank ponytail and weathered face glanced up as Drew approached, looked away, then turned to face Drew fully.

"Andrew? Andrew Bach." Before Drew could respond, the man bowed at the waist with much more respect than was usual for a foreigner. Drew's reputation as honest and just was becoming the subject of many discussions on the streets of China. This man had heard about Drew Bach, how he fed the hungry, and especially how he benefited the people. Youdh Kang had good reason to know. His nephew lived in Fusuma. To his way of thinking, Drew brought luck to his people.

"My name Youdh Kang. You not know me. I know of you." He smiled, exhibiting gaps where teeth once grew.

Youdh Kang might have been thirty-five. He might have been fifty-five. His face was brown, deeply sun-tanned, his bony frame suggesting either illness or a very active lifestyle. Drew took a slow breath, accepting the gesture with hesitation.

"You know me? I'm sorry..."

Youdh began to rub the tips of his fingers over the double stream of scrawny beard hanging form his chin. "Everyone know you help at Fusuma. Not so many speak of it."

When Drew remained silent, Youdh Kang offered, "I am uncle of Li-Tou."

"Li-Tou, but of course." Though Drew half smiled, Youdh Kang thought he looked troubled. "If you're as qualified selling all this as your nephew at picking pockets, you should do very well."

"I do all right. Do better if I get export license. Then I sail ship like you."

"A trustworthy ship doesn't come cheap."

"*Aie*. I lose everything. You can see my ship there, Andrew Bach?" Youdh Kang pointed to an admirable vessel bobbing about in a small clearing on the east side of the wharf. "If you walk to Shanghai bank, I show you through."

"Maybe another time."

Youdh Kang folded his arms and rolled back on his heels. His laugh sounded hollow. "You want to know why I work out here."

"That's your business."

"I have no choice." He glanced up and down the street. "British work in Hong Kong Trade Department now. English official refuse to issue export license unless I pay him bribe." He shrugged. "The amount he demands will force me into bankruptcy."

"Turn him in to the authorities."

"My problem. No one concerned. They laugh at me." The little man kept smiling but his pink-rimmed eyes focused on Drew with bitterness.

"Did you go to the police?"

"Police not take Youdh Kang seriously."

"Now you have no way to export that linen."

"That right. Linen very good."

"I can see that." Drew felt himself smile. The sense of duty which forbade him to interfere in government affairs was squashed by Youdh Kang's silent plea for help. "Deliver all the fabric you can get your hands on to the *Marybeth* this morning. Ask for Noah." Drew jotted down a quick note. "This authorizes him to pay the going rate. I'll see to it you receive an additional 2 percent of the profit when it sells."

Youdh Kang closed his mouth and bowed deeply. "I work honestly. I bring only the best."

A strange noise alerted them to a human moving in the shadows between buildings. The tall man neatly blended with the solid walls. Slit-eyed, Youdh Kang motioned Drew to silence.

"Follow me, we talk." They cut across the driveway and a narrow stretch of turf between the drive and the linen factory. Youdh Kang glanced sideways at Drew's profile and stopped at the angry red scar that rose form his eye and disappeared beneath his hairline. Youdh Kang looked away and gave their present position an uneasy glance. They stepped into a dark alley between two factories.

"I think we should stay where we are."

Youdh Kang stared at Drew wide-eyed. "Do not take chance. Just this morning China issued warning against what it terms 'foreign provocation.'"

Drew looked around them. "I see no one else here."

"Good." Youdh Kang opened his hand to show Drew three coins he held there. "I help Fusuma." He grinned happily. "Well?"

"I'm impressed." Drew could only guess how many hours it took to earn the meager change. He accepted the money, not because it would make an impact on Fusuma, but because the man's action held some real meaning.

"You good man. Help people. I help, too."

"I'll see that Li-Tou gets this, if that's all right with you."

"Is okey-dokey. I there when Li-Tou born. Big celebration. Li-Tou father wait long time for son. When he born with one arm missing, father sad. He say his gods very angry. We all go home. Give son away."

"Perhaps Li-Tou's father should find the living God."

Youdh Kang stepped back. He seemed to draw inward, his dark, hooded eyes wide. "Gods will destroy you."

"Why? They don't care about me. They don't care about you either, not if they turn their backs to those less than perfect. My God doesn't hold it against me because of the scar on my face. He's more concerned for my soul. My God tells me not to fear that which kills my body but is not able to kill my soul. He tells me to fear him which is able to destroy both soul and body in hell."

Youdh Kang knuckled his stringy beard thoughtfully for a moment. "Yeah?"

"Yeah."

"When your god say that?"

Drew sensed more fear than anger in the man's response. He reached into his jacket and pulled out the New Testament. "Here. This is translated to Shanghainese. It's all in there. Every word of it's true. I think you'll like it. LI-Tou does."

"Li-Tou? Li-Tou gone. Not in Fusuma."

Drew nodded. "Li-Tou is with friends."

Youdh Kang crossed his arms and grasped his elbows with each hand. "Ahh. Is good. I worry. Is good boy. Learn bad things."

"Yes, and he learned them very well."

For the first time Youdh Kang's face hinted at a smile.

"Are you willing to keep in touch with your nephew?"

Youdh Kang stared at his feet. "Li-Tou not know nephew."

"Why not? The boy may be pleased to discover he has an uncle."

"Father be angry."

"Maybe it's time you and his father show Li-Tou you care."

"His father lose face."

"And it's better to lose a son." Drew let him think about that a minute. "Somehow, it doesn't make sense, does it?"

"Is too late."

"Think about it. Are you willing to throw away something so good for something so ridiculous?" Drew thought about telling him where Li-Tou lived. After considering it for a minute, he did. He could tell the man cared about Li-Tou.

Drew jotted down Pepple's address. "These people can answer questions about the boy and that book I just gave you. I'm not planning a lengthy stay or I'd explain myself."

"You come for Suiteiko?"

The question came as a blow. A muscle leaped along Drew's clenched jaw. He lowered a hand to Youdh Kang's shoulder. "Do you know Suiteiko?"

Youdh Kang shook his head back and forth rapidly. "Not know. Only hear."

"What? Tell me what you heard."

"You good man. Take care of people."

"About Suiteiko. What have you heard about Sui?"

"You marry Suiteiko."

"Have you seen her?"

"Not see. Rumor on street, Xhiang sell to Youn Kim."

"Her father sold her?" Drew's voice was husky with emotion. He forced himself to keep his tone mild. "Then she must be alive."

"Maybe only rumor."

"What other rumors did you hear?"

"It is rumored you are dead."

"We both know that's not true."

"Maybe Suiteiko dead. Xhiang look. He not find."

"Why? What does he want with her?"

Youdh Kang shrugged a bony shoulder. "At one time Xhiang most feared man in Shanghai. Overnight he change."

"I don't understand."

"No one understand."

"I'll go to Xhiang if I must."

"He go crazy, sell everything, give to poor. Xhiang not tell you."

"Won't, or can't?"

"Xhiang gone."

"Rumors again?"

"This not rumor. I see with own eyes. Xhiang leave town."

"Where? Do you know where he went?" Emotion swarmed him, stirring up a fresh need to find Sui.

"No one know."

That left one source open to him. Drew pulled a watch from his pocket, amazed it was getting so late.

"Goodbye, Youdh Kang."

Youdh Kang bowed his head. Drew offered his hand. Slow to recognize Drew's gesture, they stood there a long moment while his thoughts gained sufficient strength to propel him into action. The instant he took a penny from his pocket, Drew realized his mistake and bowed very low, a sign of honor.

"Read that," Drew said, tapping his finger against the Bible.

"I try." Youdh Kang bowed. "*Xi'e Xi'e.*"

"You're absolutely welcome."

Walking south, Drew passed a warehouse alive with hawking peddlers, fortune tellers, magicians, and crackling geese. Loud music from inside a neighborhood pub accompanied his sharp steps.

Thick as flies, people flocked around portable kitchens where tantalizing aromas spewed forth. A group of seagulls soared on stationary wings, riding currents of wind, waiting for tidbits, and screaming as if tortured.

Drew worked his way through the mass and around clutter. Soon town gave way to less busy streets. Gradually, sounds faded and the hush of humanity closed around him. Drew pushed on. The walk seemed much longer than it had last time. And he began to worry that he'd somehow taken a wrong turn. He stopped to look ahead, expecting at any moment to see Elliott's familiar picket fence.

But what he saw jolted him like a flash of lightning. A blue cotton *cheungsam* hung loosely from Sui's thin frame. And she came straight toward him.

Chapter 31

"**May** I ask where you're going with that package?" Sui felt some-one tug at the bag beneath her arm. She turned with a trou-bled frown on her face, prepared to defend the small bundle, to protect her-self against a thief. No one wanted to be robbed, and she was no different. But today she felt more determined than ever to overcome any obstacles standing in her way.

She couldn't afford to lose anything, she thought to herself as she swung around with imposing words on her lips. Then she gasped. As if in slow motion, her package fell to the sidewalk and she was being drawn against Drew's solid length.

Fresh tears sprang to her eyes as she melted into his arms. He was alive...oh dear God...Drew was alive. And in the middle of a very busy crowd, it seemed as if they were the only two people alive. Clinging desperately to one another, many brows were raised and knowing looks exchanged. But they were only aware of one another and interested in keeping the other in their grasp, as if they would disappear or fade away if they relinquished their hold.

Drew's rough hands carefully traced the contours of her thin, pale face and stopped on the rough scar. He drew Sui close and whispered her name over and over, while stroking his mouth against her earlobe. "Oh my love."

Sui stepped back within the circle of his arms, drinking in the sight of him until their lips met in silent, desperate longing. She whispered his name yearningly, the softest of anguished moans. And his solid arms held her all the tighter against his broad chest.

"I can't believe you're actually here." She was laughing and crying all at once, as he rocked her back and forth in his arms. "What happened, Drew? Where have you been? Are you really all right?"

"I am now." He looked down at her from his vast height as if memoriz-ing every feature, and Sui looked back just as urgently. His clothes were clean but wrinkled, his face rough from beard stubble. He explained that he had just arrived and hadn't taken time to shave in his anxiety to find her. The past didn't matter now. He was alive, she was safe, and he silently thanked God.

Caught up in the glory of the moment, Sui closed her eyes and rested in his rugged strength. After all the months she'd believed him dead, to have him hold her possessively now was bliss. And then suddenly a notion shattered the urgency that engulfed her. Drew hadn't been dead. And for another entire year they had been separated!

Her eyes sprung open. And without warning, she pushed against his solid chest. A teardrop splashed on his upraised hand, followed by another. "You aren't dead," she choked out, struggling to gauge his appalled expression.

"Is that why you're crying, because I'm not dead?" he asked, sounding calmer than he felt. As he strived to understand her, his heart pounded erratically, terrified he might somehow lose Sui again. Perhaps circumstances he was unaware of had driven her from him forever. That possibility filled him with alarm. "Tell me. What is it? What's wrong? Did I do something, Sui?" He almost strangled on the words.

It was a considerably long moment before Sui could trust herself to answer. "You stand here staring at me as if you left yesterday, as if nothing happened. If you were in prison or...or...unable to be with me, I could understand why we have been apart all this time."

His hands were on her waist and turning her to face him before she was aware he had moved. Cupping her chin in his hand, Drew forced her to meet his intense gaze. "Do you think for a minute that I would have left you of my own free will? Why do you suppose I promised myself to you if not to spend the rest of our lives together? You are my life, Sui. I don't know what happened while I was gone, but I do intend to get to the bottom of this."

Her breath caught in her throat and she stared at him for a long time, unable to hold back the bitter laugh. "So, where have you been?" she asked almost harshly. She had survived tragedy before, certainly nothing that came close to the magnitude of losing their child. But she would survive again, maybe. Sui shook her head as tears streamed down her face, and looked bleakly at Drew. If he intentionally stayed away, deliberately failed her, they didn't stand a chance together.

Gently his thumb brushed tears away. "Let's go somewhere quiet, somewhere we can talk."

"First of all, why don't you tell me where you've been. Where were you when your daughter died.... when I had your baby all alone in a frozen alley?"

Drew stared back, speechless.

"Well, fine then, don't tell me. I don't know where you were, Andrew John Bach. But I can tell you where you weren't! With me!" Sui was sobbing uncontrollably now. When Drew would have reached out to her, she stepped back and blew her nose. "I waited, Drew. I waited for you to come for me. I could hardly face life when I thought I would never see you again. I loved you!"

Sui hiccoughed then, which upset her more than she already was. "I thought you were so different. Are all men so cruel that they would simply come and go as they please, with no regard to their wife and child?"

Drew opened his mouth but nothing useful came out.

"Remember me, Drew? I am the woman you promised to cherish, your wife!"

There was no doubt of the impact her words made on him. His white, stricken face stared at her while she accused him of desertion. She took a step back and gasped when Drew physically lifted her from her feet, planting her in the shadows of an alley between two tall buildings.

Then he looked at her, really looked at her. Drew had trouble speaking, but he had to ask. "We had a baby, you and I?" His voice rasped painfully.

"Don't act so distraught. If you hadn't left you'd have known. I thought you were dead. Just where *have* you been, Andrew?"

Drew caught her arm and drew her back to bring her face into focus. He gazed into it earnestly.

Sui saw his eyes fill with curious moisture and she cried all the harder. He looked as defeated as she felt.

"Sui, I never left of my own volition, I promise. My crew found me the same night as our...encounter." He tried to smile, but it was not an inspiring success. "I wasn't sure what happened to you. I was told you died. That was about the same time I discovered I was blind."

Sui's anger faded as Drew's eyes burned into hers. The muscle in his jaw tightened. "After all you've been through, I'll understand if you don't want me. I may not like it, but I'll understand."

Recognizing the hurt in Drew's words, Sui stood unmoving. Fight went out of her as she acknowledged all the disappointment and pride she'd bottled up and spilled over onto Drew. He'd suffered as sorely as she, and she'd just added to his pain. A familiar sort of helplessness overtook her. She turned away to hide tears spilling down her face and folded her arms snugly. A quiver shook her voice as she whispered, "It was awful not knowing where you were taken, if you were dead or alive, if by some slim chance you would one day show up. I felt helpless waiting and wondering." She tossed her hair back from her face and stared at a particularly dark spot on a wall.

"I know."

"Do you?" Sui looked Drew in the eyes." "Yes, I suppose you do."

"That's right."

"How did you find me?"

Drew lifted her chin with his thumb. "Does that really matter? We're together now." Sui wilted against Drew's chest. His chin nuzzled her hair. "Oh babe, let's not ruin our lives because of something neither of us caused."

"I needed you so badly." Her voice squeaked.

"I know." Drew smoothed the hair from her face, and right there in the alley he placed feather-light kisses on her brow, nose, and cheek. "Give me the rest of my life to make up for everything."

Sui flattened hands against his back and felt his heart beat against her own. For a space of several heartbeats they didn't say a word. Then Sui stepped back far enough to look into Drew's eyes. "None of it matters now. Take me home."

Drew and Sui passed Lundh Kang, and he smiled. It was pleasant to see a happy couple. Life is so easy when you're in love, he thought.

Chapter 32

Music and muffled laughter floated up softly. The voyage to America would live in her memory forever. From where Sui stood on the open deck, the atmosphere in the warm, salty air seemed so peaceful. Tomorrow they would sail into the Port of San Pedro, California. She searched for a glimpse of land, another ship, or anything that spoke of dry land, but darkness made it impossible to see.

Their crew was anxious to return to their homes, their friends, and family. Three months proved a long time to spend aboard a ship, even for honeymooners.

Night remained clear. Stars shone brightly as Drew looked over the dark water. The gentle breeze felt good after the hot, stuffy air below. He breathed deeply and paused momentarily to study the stars' positions. Yes, the *Marybeth* held her course. Silently, he leaned against the rail and watched Sui for a long, quiet moment. When he coughed, she turned her head to discover him watching her.

"How long have you been standing there, darling?"

Drew stepped out of the shadow. He touched her shoulder and rested his hand on it. "For a while. I've been enjoying the quiet, and watching you."

"Mm. This is our last night together, here I mean. Tomorrow we'll be busy moving into your house."

"Our house."

"I have to admit, it sounds pretty good. I'll enjoy feeling solid earth beneath my feet again, even if the waves do lull me to sleep at night."

"As I remember, those same waves made you sick on several occasions."

She didn't look up. "You're not going below right away, are you?"

"Not if you don't want to. I like being close to you, wherever you are."

Sui buried her face in his chest. "What did we ever do before we found one another?"

Easing away, Drew studied Sui for a moment. "I never want to find out again."

"Thank you."

"For what?"

"For loving me, for coming back to find me." Sui leaned against the boat's railing, enjoying the breeze caressing her hair. Closing her eyes, she allowed herself a pleasant moment to enjoy the soothing sensation. When she opened her eyes again, Drew was watching her intently.

Reaching out, he touched her cheek. "For a time I wondered if I would ever see you again," he said so softly she wondered if she imagined it.

"I know," she whispered. "But we're together now."

"Forever."

"Forever. It will be sad, really, to leave all this. But I am anxious to start a home. Will you be going back out to sea soon? I'll miss you, but I'll understand if you do."

Drew shook his head, "It's been good. And sailing served its purpose. But it's over for me now. Living on the sea isn't the life for a man who is married and plans to start a family. Noah is anxious to take up where I left off."

"Will you miss it?"

"Maybe, at times." Drew clasped the boat's rail then, one hand on each side of her. "But not as much as I would miss you if we were apart from one another." Gently, very gently, he pressed his mouth softly against her neck. "You have that dreamy look, Mrs. Bach. Care to tell me what you're thinking about?"

"The breeze, the sea, and you."

"Not in that order, I hope?" Drew lifted her hair and pulled it up to rest on the top of her head. His lips traveled behind her ear.

"I save the best for last." And with a slow, happy smile, Sui decided now was the perfect moment to tell Drew what she strongly suspected. "You mentioned starting a family." She touched his shoulders with both hands, distancing them just enough so she could look into his face. "Have you given any thought to having another baby?"

His eyebrows shot up. "That's it, you want to have a baby?"

"We're going to...around late November."

He smoothed away a dark strand of hair from her face, searched her eyes, and didn't find what he looked for. And it worried him. "You're not overwhelmed by the prospect, are you?"

"Overwhelmed? That doesn't begin to describe how I feel about having a baby with you, Drew. I am thrilled beyond words." She took his hand in hers and squeezed. "It's just that...our first child is never far from my mind." Sui took a step away from him. "How long will it take to stop hurting, to forget?"

Drew shook his head, his voice soft. "Never. You don't really want to forget her, do you? We will see our daughter again someday, Sui, we will. Maybe not on this earth, but someday."

167

Sui groaned. Images of her nightmarish experience swam before her eyes. Then she realized she couldn't carry a burden so heavy. It wasn't humanly possible. So with heart-wrenching grief, she took one last look. Then she stepped into Drew's open arms and hid her face against his chest, breathing in his male fragrance.

"I will always be here for you, Sui. I promise." Drew grinned, and suddenly life wasn't so bad again. "No one has ever reached so deep inside me with her smile, with her touch, ever."

Sui snuggled closer. "That's good. That's real nice."

THE END